ARES

L. Neil Smith

CAEZIK
SF & FANTASY
ARC MANOR
ROCKVILLE, MARYLAND

*

SHAHID MAHMUD
PUBLISHER

www.CaezikSF.com

This is a work of fiction.

Cover art by Christina P. Myrvold; artstation.com/christinapm

ISBN: 978-1-64710-078-0

First Edition. First Printing. December 2023.
1 2 3 4 5 6 7 8 9 10

An imprint of Arc Manor LLC

www.CaezikSF.com

This book could never have been for anyone except my Cathy,
the soulmate I searched half my life to find.

CONTENTS

PROLOGUE:
DESERT FREIGHT

Conchita said, "Apparently what these Wimpersnits
are so afraid of, Desmondo, are the dangerous side-
effects of too much freedom—too much prosperity,
too much happiness, and too much health."

— *Conchita y Desmondo
in the Land of Wimpersnits and Oogies*

"Lock that down, Jerry! Lock it down hard, or we're gonna
lose it!"

Blasting across the terraformed Martian desert at
more than 700 miles an hour, Big Mike Malone, longtime long-
haul truckdriver and Martian "pioneer," shouted against the wind
into his headset microphone.

Even in the relatively sheltered spaces between cargo
containers—sixteen of them, this trip—winds of hurricane force
prevailed. They could suck a man or a huge cargo container right off
the truck, scattering its contents, or his insides, all over the bright-
yellow prairie.

It wasn't so much, on this occasion, that an EVA outside the cab,
enduring the shrieking wind of their passage, was absolutely neces-

sary. Big Mike was "showing the ropes" to his new assistant, rookie Jerry Austin.

"We're gonna lose you, too, if you don't transfer your tether properly!"

In 23rd century Solar System-wide civilization, Martian container freighters had become something of a symbol of the rough-and-ready new society that had created them. Their drivers were interplanetary folk heroes. The enormous tractors that pulled four "quadcars" today, each holding four containers, were driven by six huge ramjet engines, two per side, and two more on top. A catalytic fusion reactor turned the machine's gigantic wheels until it reached about 200 miles per hour, at which point, the ramjets cut in and took it to just below the local speed of sound.

Behind the powerful tractor, four many-wheeled frames carried two more-or-less conventional containers each, side by side, with two more atop them. Narrow alleyways, left for inspection and maintenance, separated each of the containers. That was where Big Mike and Jerry were at the moment, securing a corner the computer had said might come loose. This was a short run in more ways than one: six to ten quadcars made up the typical truck-train. On each individually braked quadcar, adjustable spoilers on the sides and top protected it from the tractor's engines and provided streamlining needed even in the relatively thin Martian atmosphere.

Once it was fully up to speed, the tractor burned a synthetic fuel generated by a "Biomass-to-Petroleum" process capable of converting almost any organic waste—the Martian desert was covered with it—into "light sweet crude." There were no laws to govern it—there were no laws of any kind on Mars—but a trucker's failure to burn "B2P" was considered antisocial by many, because it put much-needed carbon dioxide into the air and, even more importantly, water vapor, helping to maintain the red planet's more-or-less recently acquired atmosphere.

A tiny minority felt differently; few of them were "native" Martians.

When they returned to the apartment-like control cabin and shed their outdoor gear, Big Mike started coffee and lunch for the pair. Jerry turned on an editorial 'cast from a 3DTV station in Coprates City.

"… an offshoot of the Mother Planet's latest gang of anti-tech nutcases.

"Making their presence known on our world, they have proclaimed that Mars now has a 'Mass Movement' of its own. On Earth, if you pay attention to such nonsense, the group's professed concern is about how importing material from the Solar System, mostly the asteroids, may cause Earth's crust to slow and buckle, resulting in super earthquakes that will wipe out all life. On Mars, their expressed fear is much the same, although our giant truck-trains are blamed for Marsquakes, as well.

"A violently militant wing of the Mass Movement, which calls itself 'Null Delta Em,' for 'No Change in Mass,' will be holding a rally—"

"For which read, 'riot,'" Big Mike interjected.

"—at Virginia Dale," the beamcast went on, "a popular truck-train eating and refueling stop between Bradbury and Coprates City."

"Our next stop." He drew his pistol, thumbed a lever to let the barrel pivot upward, and checked the weapon's chamber to make sure it held a cartridge ready. "Looks like we got us a truck and cargo to protect."

On this leg of the trip, the terrain was flat, the highway ruler straight. To take their minds off their worries, Big Mike turned off the beamcast, programmed the autopilot, and brought their lunch to the table.

"You know if you look out any of the port-side windows—better yet, I'll put it on the monitor and magnify it ten or twenty times—you can catch a glimpse of one of the most important buildings on Mars."

"How vat?" Jerry asked through a mouthful of macaroni plant. He was new on the planet. Big Mike was always filling him in on the local history. Just now the man was pointing at the image of a house, half castle, half Victorian gingerbread, all of it built from the local ochre-colored stone.

Big Mike answered, "It's 'The house Conchita and Desmondo built,' Jerry."

"I know those books," said Jerry. "I grew up reading them."

Mike nodded. "More likely had 'em read to you. If Mars had a real queen that's where she'd hang her crown, partner. She's a living reminder of what being on Mars—being one of the first Martians—was like before the planet had enough atmosphere to breathe, back when simply staying alive was an everyday struggle, and all the politicians and generals of every nation on Earth wanted everyone who lived on Mars to die. You know the story?"

CHAPTER ONE:
JULIE SEGOVIA

"One thing you can always be sure of, Desmondo,"
said Conchita to her little cousin, "people will rise—
or fall—to meet your expectations of them."
—Conchita y Desmondo
in the Land of Wimpersnits and Oogies

J ulie waited in the dark at the top of the stairs, surprised her heart
wasn't pounding harder. In minutes, she was going to do something that couldn't be undone—something that badly needed
doing, nonetheless. She'd always avoided doing what couldn't be
undone whenever it was possible.

It hadn't been easy, breaking the hallway plasma bulb inside its
titanium cage and bulletproof polymer cylinder, but Julie had lived
in spaces just like this all of her life, little more than storage units
for the faceless masses whose only function in society was to keep
voting the same morons, lunatics, and criminals—and their vile
offspring—into office, while breeding even more faceless masses
to vote for the next generation of morons, lunatics, and criminals.
This was Julie's turf, and she had been determined. Half the plasma
bulbs in this structure were already broken in the same way, almost
certainly for similar reasons.

No part of this would be easy. The individual she waited for was fifty-five years old, knew every dirty trick there was, weighed two and a half times what she did, was a foot taller, and had a longer reach. Julie was seventeen, five feet four standing on her toes, and only weighed a hundred pounds. In this undertaking, she needed to have every advantage she could muster. It had to be done right the first time.

Julie considered herself fortunate that the elevators in this part of the building—grandly called an "arcology" by politicians, but in reality a hundred-story concrete tenement—hadn't worked, almost from the first day its inmates had been swept off the streets and forced to move in. The President of East America and his hundred-car entourage were paying an official visit to Newark, and it wouldn't do at all for him—or for the 3DTV cameras of six networks—to be forced to look at the hordes of ragged, hungry, desperate people who normally occupied the streets as his highly photographed convoy drove through.

She looked at the long row of battered steel doors she had just passed by, hearing the muffled sound of 3DTV from some of them. A popular song, "Melinda Sue Sweetie Pie Iron Maiden Bitch" was playing. She heard the nonsense words, "Schmorgly dorgly!"—a comic's catchphrase. People made their own worlds behind these doors, inside these apartments. They had to. Outside, the corridors smelled of urine, feces, and vomit, with an unmistakable overtone of alcohol and marijuana. It smelled of rats as well—an aroma that seemed downright homely and wholesome compared to the acrid tang that cockroaches left in the air.

There had been a loudly trumpeted government program, shortly before Julie was born. Microscopic machines, designed to reproduce themselves and kill rats and cockroaches, had been created by scientists and engineers employed by the state and funded by the federal government. When the first batch—meant for rats—was released, given what government projects are, they left the rats alone, and killed every cat in the city.

The cockroach half of the program had been shut down immediately, and everybody associated with it shipped off to the South

Jersey labor farms. Nobody ever asked what had happened to the people in the rat program.

Julie took a deep, calming breath. Four flights of steep concrete steps ought to slow him down a little, even if he weren't a massively overweight, beer-gutted, middle-aged former *Mafiya* enforcer, enjoying his retirement by running a string of girls he'd been given as a gift—like a gold watch—for his many years of ruthless, brutal service to the local dons.

Millicente had been one of those girls.

Julie tried to remain focused on the task at hand. But her mind kept drifting back to the sight of her big sister lying like a smashed doll in the crowded, noisy, indigent ward at Garden State Memorial. She was smiling up, still trying to be the wise, calm, brave, older sibling. However, she couldn't speak above a whisper and there wasn't a long bone in her body Kalmakov hadn't broken—along with half a dozen ribs, her sternum, jaw, skull, even her pelvis where he'd stomped her as she lay helpless and unconscious on the floor of the flat now at Julie's back.

Millicente wasn't even certain what she'd done to anger him. She told Julie that it might have something to do with the fact that, at the advanced age of twenty-six, she was more than a little past her prime, and therefore expected to perform services—and to service individuals—in ways that hadn't been required of her when she was younger and prettier. Her internal injuries might kill her yet, they'd said. At least that kept her safe from harvesters operating here under the noses—and possibly with the permission—of the Garden State administration.

Julie heard the man well before she saw him. She'd met him twice, at the place she shared with Millicente, and he'd tried to recruit her into his business. The first time had been two years ago, when she was fifteen. She could picture him now, huffing up the stairs, pausing now and again to let his heart slow. He was a huge man, with dark hair in oily curls and an enormous moustache, born of Balkan refugees who'd pushed the Italians and Haitians and everybody else out of the market and taken over in the first few months they were here. He'd been big before he'd grown fat, and had gigantic hands, each the size of both of hers.

Every now and again he'd used Millicente himself, when she was younger, and he never finished with her until she was sobbing and bloodied. Julie wondered how she'd stood it all these years, then she realized all over again that it had been for her—Julie's—sake, so that her younger sister wouldn't have to do the same things to survive. So that she could spend a few hours at the library every week, learning what she could about the world beyond Newark, New Jersey.

Beyond the borders of East America.

And here he was at last, pausing on the landing below, exactly as she'd expected, breathing raggedly. It was pretty funny, she thought, that even the *musor* couldn't get the elevators running in these places. It served too many interests to have people forced to use the stairs or stay penned up and out of the way in what had become their kennels.

She stepped back into the shadows she'd created so arduously, and waited for her prey to come to her, slowly climbing one treacherous step at a time. The steel strips originally used to line the edges of the steps had long since been torn away and ground into crude knives, pry bars, and other useful implements. For the arkies' weary tenants, it made coming home each night a lot like climbing a mountain path. She'd always thought Millicente lucky only to live on the ninth floor.

The instant he put a foot on the crumbling landing, she stepped out in front of him. Without wasting a word, she pushed his wall of a chest as hard as she could with the heels of both hands. He reeked of garlic, vodka, and tobacco smoke. Making an animal noise, he began to pitch over backward, snatching at her wrists. She squirmed free and somehow her right hand ended up on the grip of a large pistol he carried in a shoulder holster under his left armpit. For an adrenaline-attenuated moment they were frozen in space and time, his weight and momentum temporarily checked by the shoulder harness. Then the weapon slipped free of its holster, and he tumbled backward, over and over, down the stairs.

Julie ran down after him. He'd settled on his back in a corner with his head propped against the wall at an odd angle, as if he were sitting up in bed, reading. He looked up at her as she stood over

8

him, tried to grab at her ankle, but he was slow now and feeble. She stepped back.

She'd expected him to be dead or paralyzed.

Glancing at the weapon in her hand—it was a heavy CZ plasma burner, chrome plated like a mirror, with checkered, reddish grips of some exotic hardwood—she raised it and centered the sights on his chest.

"I sincerely hope that you can hear me, you son of a bitch. This is for my sister, Millicente." Meeting the man's eyes, which had suddenly widened with a realization that he was about to die at the hands of this little girl standing over him, she pressed the trigger. A fireball seemed to leap from the weapon. In an instant, she could see through a fist-sized hole in his chest to the scorched concrete floor beneath him—which was quite a feat, considering how broad that chest had once been, how obese.

She knelt, wiped the burner on the tail of his expensive silk jacket, and, using the coattail, laid it in his right hand. His coat had swept back, and she could see his billfold in an inside pocket. Using the same care that she had with the burner, she examined its contents.

Somewhere, from the floor above, she could hear somebody's 3DTV in their apartment, wailing out a commercial for Spoonies— "Aw, just gimme a little Spoonie!"—Millicente's childhood favorite. At this particular moment, it sounded completely insane. "Spoonie! Oonie! Oonie! Oonie!"

He had over eighteen thousand dollars in illegal West American currency.

She decided to keep the money, if only for Millicente's sake, for the decent care that it could buy her in that snakepit of a hospital. There was no East American currency, as such—the government wanted an electronic record of every transaction—so people who desired privacy, or anonymity, used West American money. One of her best-paying jobs was to mule the stuff all over Newark to consumers from distributors. It was unlawful, in theory, but worked all the same. You could even pay fines and taxes with it—you were encouraged to—and it traded one lone West American gold certificate to over a thousand East American bucks.

The next person who came along would take the money if she didn't. She should probably take the plasma burner, too, but that was carrying social responsibility a bit too far for Julie just now. She'd never killed anyone before. She pulled out the thick roll and threw the billfold back.

She'd be long gone by morning, anyway.

CHAPTER TWO:
LAFCADIO GUZMAN

"The police are not your friends, Desmondo, no matter what the 3DTV says about them. They are always
and only the friends of the highest bidder."
                                        —*Conchita y Desmondo*
                           in the Land of Wimpersnits and Oogies

T he question, however, was where to go.
         As she left the building, Julie was alert by lifelong reflex.
         There was no steaming, fetid, predator-haunted jungle on
Earth; no bandit-ridden mountain fastness, that was as dangerous
as the spaces between the Project arkies in the failing light of day.
Making her cautious way toward the center of the old city, she
began counting her options.

She could simply stay put, try living her life unchanged. That
would certainly make keeping an eye on Millicente a whole lot easier,
but the "mobski" would be after her, once they managed to figure it
out. The cops never would, and they wouldn't give a damn—unless
her sister's dead pimp had been a reliable source of extracurricular
income. Then the *Mafiya* would tell them, and they'd come after her,
too.

She could head for Canada, she supposed. But for all intents and purposes, the border between the two countries had rotated ninety degrees generations before she was born. Eastern Canada was every bit as bad as East America. If she were going that way, it would have to be western Canada. If she went that far, it might as well be to West America.

Not once did she consider her father's native land, Puerto Rico. Julie had never known her father. Once a splendid tropical paradise, it was now an island covered, from one coast to another, with the corrugated sheet-steel roofing of shacks one notch above the cardboard box cities of Brazil and Argentina. As far as Julie knew, it was the only place in the Western Hemisphere, possibly excepting Haiti, worse than Newark. Her *papi* had survived PR and come here to live the dream—he'd had a sidewalk hotdog cart—only to be knifed to death because he wouldn't pay for "protection." The pushcart being an unlicensed business, the police considered her father's murder an act of volunteer street cleaning and wouldn't investigate.

Nor did she give a thought to Ireland, her mother's place of birth. Julie had always heard it was lovely, but she didn't belong there.

Even given her long-legged strides, it was dark by the time she reached the middle of town. Newark was often compared—mostly on West American 3DTV—to East Berlin after World War II, or to Beirut, repeated victim of the Two Hundred Years' War between the Israeli Empire and practically everybody else on the planet, or to Miami after it became the site of the first (and, so far, the only) example of nuclear terrorism in history. Unless, of course, you counted Hiroshima and Nagasaki. The West Americans referred to it the "Glass Parking Lot."

The streets were all but deserted. Anyone caught outside at this time of night (it was 8:45) was assumed, by cops and citizens alike, to be up to no good, and therefore fair game in a free-fire zone for guns, knives, clubs, Mace, Tasers, and those telemetered Glocks the cops had taken to carrying, which could be turned off from a console down at police headquarters. "Up to no good" included Julie, now, she realized with a start. In the need to concentrate on keeping her eyes on the dark corners all around her, she had almost forgotten: she had killed a man today.

Well, hardly a man, but certainly others wouldn't see it that way.

That process—forgetting, then remembering with something akin to shock—would repeat itself for a long while, she guessed. She kept seeing his eyes in the instant he'd realized he was going to fall; in the instant he'd realized he was going to die. But the bastard had deserved it, and she'd have done it all over again, in exactly the same way. Finally, in the middle of a crumbling city block, she found the dead-end alley that was her destination. Wishing now that she had kept the pimp's burner—although it was a big weapon, heavy, and expensive to feed—she turned into the alley and buried herself in shadows.

She felt her way along the wall until her left hand found a screen door. As usual, it was hooked from the inside. He was home. Standing to one side, protected by the brick wall the door was set into, from whoever was inside—and his sawed-off shotgun—she knocked, very gently.

"Go 'way!" hissed a voice.

"You look different somehow, Lafcadio Guzman," she said to the face in the narrow space that had appeared between the door and the frame. The eyes were at about the level of her belt. "You do something with your hair?"

He laughed, genuine and friendly. "No, is my new wheels—see?" He opened the door the rest of the way. She saw a young, bearded man of about twenty-five, normal from the hips up, but who had been cursed with the shriveled legs of a crippled child. They were folded atop the kind of low wooden cart mechanics use to slide under cars—only the wheels were twice the normal size and swiveled. As she'd expected, a shortened 12-gauge double-barreled shotgun lay across his withered thighs.

Julie laughed. "So Safeway's got another quadruple amputee."

"Beats the roller-skate wheels I had. Now I'm an inch and a half taller!" The man pushed himself backward, out of her way. "Come in, come in, *mi bonita*. I was about to make myself a big pot of hot coffee!"

She had never been inside before but had only done business at the door. "Got something alcoholic to put in it? I just killed my sister's pimp."

"Never regret it, *mi bonita*. It was the right thing to do. Even the rest of the Russian Mafiya were afraid of him. He was a very bad man."

Lafcadio poured out the last of the coffee he'd made, sharing it between them, adding a shot of dark rum to her cup. He was surprised but not alarmed when Julie told him the details of what she'd done.

The dirty, dingy entryway to Lafcadio's home concealed a neat and tidy dwelling, warm, welcoming, and full of modern conveniences. Julie had never been entirely sure what her friend did for a living, but it obviously paid well. He certainly produced—and consumed—a lot of West American currency. In what served as his living room and office, she saw half a dozen computer screens, a couple of monitors showing the alley outside and the street beyond—he'd known she was on his doorstep all along—and a television set for each of the six major networks.

On one screen she saw Richfield Chen, the closest East America had to a robber baron, denouncing the infamous Curringer Corporation which had successfully terraformed and settled the asteroid Pallas, and now planned similar feats elsewhere in the Solar System. Like most people in her stratum of East American society, Julie was unimpressed with Chen's expensive suit and haircut. To the extent she ever thought about him at all, it was as a billionaire crybaby, always whining about the way this country had been outdone by private, international, non-governmental organizations.

Maybe it was time, she thought, for Chen to pick another country—or at least another government—to invest in. This one was running on fumes. No state west of the Mississippi recognized its authority, obeyed its laws, or even bothered to send elected representatives to Washington anymore. "Every dime we've ever spent on government," she could remember her mother saying, "every moment of time, every bit of effort, has been *worse* than wasted. It has been turned against us to destroy us."

Lafcadio had lifted himself from his cart when they'd first come in, and turned now in what he called his "high chair" (it did resemble an outsized version of kids' dining room furniture) so he could see her better.

"Can I get you anything else, *mi bonita*?"

She protested, "Please don't call me that, Lafcadio. I'm not pretty—"

"You don't know what you say, *mi bonita*. Looking at you is like staring directly into a great searchlight, so dazzling a creature are you!" He was not exaggerating. Julie was a pale brunette with flawless skin, a cute, upturned nose, and a full-lipped, generous mouth.

"And I'm not yours. We're friends, as we have been almost since the day we were born—and as we will be for as long as both of us are still alive. But I belong to no man, Lafcadio. No, nor to any woman. And I never, ever will. And just so you'll know, my one and only regret is that I didn't kill the *pendejo* a long time before he hurt my Millicente."

Lafcadio's face wrinkled up into what she was fairly certain was a grin. "Ah, *mi bonita*, but then it would have been the wrong thing to do."

"How's that?" She shook her head. "He would have been the same man, doing the same things. He had deserved to die for years. For decades!"

"But he had not done them to you—" He held a hand up. "I know what you're going to say, *mi bonita*. But the awful truth is that Millicente did what she did of her own free will. Even when he abused her, she didn't try to get away. I offered to get both of you over the border into West America, but she believed the state propaganda about it and was afraid."

"So what made this time different?" Julie didn't like to admit it, especially to herself, but all of Lafcadio's talk regarding the minute differences between right and wrong never failed to fascinate her. It was a vice. Where she came from, such distinctions were a dangerous luxury.

15

"Because she said it was—the difference between sex and rape, after all, is it not? Consent. You said she told you that, for the first time, she begged him to stop, begged him to let her go, and he did not. He crossed a line and you, quite properly, punished him for it, *mi bonita.*"

"I asked you not to call me that, Lafcadio."

"I will try, *mi* bonita. If only you could see yourself as I do. Alas, I know better than to hope. What will you do now?"

She mentioned some of the ideas she'd had about that on the way here.

"It's extremely hard to know what's best to do." Lafcadio agreed with her. "The cops may just decide that somebody has done society a favor. On the other hand, they may be watching every bus and train station in the city, every taxi. The seaports are already under constant surveillance. Also, every airport and heliport, considering what you took from his wallet."

She blinked. "How the hell do you know what I took from his wallet?"

"Because I've never known you to be wasteful, *mi bonita.* My advice: use it to get out of town, out of the state, out of the country. If you could get off the planet, I would advise that, as well."

"I had other plans for it, Lafcadio. I was going to give it to you—to watch after my Millicente for me and see she gets all that she needs and isn't harmed by that place. Oh, and while you're at it, please pick up a couple of Spoonies—'Aw, just gimme a little Spoonie! Spoonie! Oonie! Oonie! Oonie!'—they're my sister's favorite candy bar." She pulled the enormous wad of West American currency from her pocket and watched his eyes grow big. "Eighteen grand and change. Could I ask you to do that for me, my friend?"

CHAPTER THREE:
RICHFIELD CHEN

"You can be good by yourself," Conchita told Desmondo. "But somehow it's easier to be bad in bunches."

—*Conchita y Desmondo*
in the Land of Wimpersnits and Oogies

"Ambassador," he said, shaking the hand of the man wearing "soup and fish." "It's very good to see you here. I sincerely hope you enjoy yourself."

The new Nicaraguan ambassador responded enthusiastically, his host being one of the wealthiest, most famous, and powerful men in the world. Overtly political guests, the host reflected, especially foreigners, were a rarity at this particular event, but this one was married to a DuMore, one of the Rhode Island DuMores, and so it appeared unavoidable.

Dismissing the fellow, Richfield Chen gazed down with a satisfied feeling from the head table on the dais, at the enormous room below him, filled, so it seemed, with white linen, glittering crystal and tableware, mostly middle-aged men in tuxedos, and mostly younger women in high heels and expensive, revealing dresses. Occasionally it was the other way around, middle-aged women in dresses that were far too revealing, accompanied by tuxedoed younger men with expensive, silly haircuts.

An enormous security staff, very heavily but unobtrusively armed, and dressed in the same attire (albeit especially tailored) as the guests, guarded every entrance and watched every window, making certain that the public—and in this case that particularly included the round-heeled mass media—knew absolutely nothing of what went on at this annual affair. The guests, here by invitation only, were the individuals who actually ran the country, who owned it and everything (and everybody) in it. It was the single night of the year in which they could revel in it fairly openly—at least among their peers—and freely.

The dinner was served by convicts—nobody guilty of anything violent, of course: former businessmen serving time for excessive competitiveness; others for having been too innovative, taking unfair advantage over their less-gifted colleagues in whatever avenue they pursued, and coldly, calculatedly seeking a profit at the expense of human values. Instead of the usual waiter garb, they wore comically striped prison clothes of a kind that had been abandoned for more than three centuries.

Add to their number, a smattering of the usual convicted traffickers in West American currency, importers of a myriad of illegal objects and materials from there, from other countries, or from the so-called "Settled Worlds." (The list of contraband was secret so that criminals could be taken by surprise.) Antisocial miscreants of every kind imaginable in East America—a phrase nobody here would ever utter. Officially this was still the United States of America, whether those states west of the "Webb Line" chose to participate.

Or not.

The stubborn non-participation of those western states, in fact, offered certain benefits to anybody who knew how to make the best use of it. Chen considered himself a high-minded socially responsible industrialist and had never held or sought political office of any kind. Nor, in fact, had he ever actually manufactured anything, greatly preferring to buy up companies he found teetering on the brink, build them up or break them down, then resell the parts or the whole before he became bored with them.

Chen had also bought and sold American Presidents for most of his adult life. And owing to a precedent first established during the Civil War, Chen's Presidents had the power to appoint individuals to occupy those seats, in Congress and the Senate, left vacant by the West's insane but adamant refusal to send elected representatives to Washington.

Under his patient, thoughtful direction, Chen's people provided lists of suitable candidates—aspiring politicians who would support the appropriate policies—to the White House. His own son-in-law, an extremely ambitious young fellow by the serendipitous name of Maxwell Promise, had been identified as one of those suitable candidates. He would now receive a Presidential appointment—Chen would make the announcement tonight; it was to be a birthday surprise for his daughter—as the United States Senator from Nebraska, a place to which, he was willing to wager, young Maxwell had never been and couldn't point out on a map.

To his left sat his daughter and her new husband. Gwendolyn Chen Promise was one of those rare Asian females who managed somehow to be unattractive. Chen admitted it to himself: all of the cosmetic surgery on the planet hadn't been able to make her look a bit better. Chen blamed it on her mother, a non-Asian he'd disposed of something like a decade and a half ago. His current mistress, a spectacular redhead (one of the big advantages to not being directly involved in politics), sat beside him on his right. Another pair of beauties, a stunning blonde and a sultry brunette, whom he also liked to keep handy, sat across from him, seemingly escorted by two of his junior executives whom he knew to be safely homosexual. In fact, they were a couple themselves.

Although this dinner was an annual event, Chen always tried to make sure there was a theme, some current occasion to be celebrated, or, failing that, an historical milestone to be commemorated. As luck— and a little artful management—would have it, there was just such an occasion available tonight. Chen rose and, before he could clear his throat, an expectant hush fell over the vast, high-ceilinged room.

One of the best things money buys, he thought, is silence.

"Good evening, ladies and gentlemen," Chen began, "and welcome to the annual 'Dinner With No Name,' an event so exclusive that the Bilderbergers, the French Masonic lodges, even the Bavarian Illuminati, can't get in." There was a ripple of polite laughter. He told the same joke every year.

"As you are all no doubt aware," he went on, warming to his topic, "the first of these magnificent banquets was held over a guttering candle, wedged in a souvenir wine bottle, in one corner of a basement lunchroom that was all that remained of the Bank of America's San Francisco headquarters after the 'Big One' of 2023. It is said that the menu that evening consisted of a can of Spam split twenty-three ways, and the contents of every vending machine that was left in the building."

This time the laughter and applause were genuine. It *was* a great story, Chen reflected, not for the first time, for all that it was a total fiction, created for him out of whole cloth decades ago by a highly talented 3DTV situation comedy writer who had possessed the courtesy and aplomb to expire shortly afterward. Nobody in that Bank of America building had survived the Big One of 2023. It had practically been at the epicenter.

"Since then, we have come a considerable distance," Chen finished the thought. The applause rose until it sounded like angry surf on a storm-lashed beach, rattling the room's huge and complicated crystal chandeliers.

"A *considerable* distance. We celebrate that tonight, as always. But, as we should, we look ahead to the future as well—in this case, the immediate future, as we recognize the launch, tomorrow morning, of a joint United States/United Nations expedition to the red planet, Mars."

The applause became ambiguous, a trifle tentative. He'd taken some care not to evoke the previous six expeditions to Mars, each of which had ended tragically—gruesomely—but everybody here would have them in mind. The high-resolution photographs taken from orbit had burned themselves into the souls of three generations, as had the space shuttle disasters of the late 20th century. The subject couldn't be avoided, Chen knew. It just had to be gotten through before he could continue.

As consolation he took a quick look at his son-in-law's face. The boy was a laugh riot, although he didn't know it. Promise detested the concept of space exploration and settlement—it was one of the few issues that he and his father-in-law disagreed on—believing that it ultimately threatened to deprive their class of subjects it could control, whose labors it could tax at the present rate of 85 percent. Basically, the younger man saw astronauts and would-be colonists as runaway slaves.

Expressed in those terms—although he would never admit it publicly, of course, even here—Chen himself viewed space exploration and settlement as a way to expand the plantation. If anything, he felt stung by the way East America had been outdone at every turn in space exploration (among other things) by certain private, international, non-governmental entities. Organizations like the infamous Curringer Corporation had successfully terraformed and settled the asteroid Pallas and were now performing similar feats elsewhere in the Solar System.

"I don't have to tell you," Chen continued, "this mission to Mars is vitally important to us for many reasons." In fact, he did have to tell them. There was hardly an individual in this room—below the dais—with the brains of a sea urchin. None of them could remember events that had happened more than a year ago. They were inclined to agree with whatever the last individual they'd spoken to had told them. If the lights in this ballroom were to go out suddenly, he believed, they'd probably eat one another before it occurred to any of them to feel for the doors.

"Aside from the scientific knowledge it has to offer us, as well as the advanced technology it promises to help us develop, we have a serious moral responsibility to assure that the planets—the stars, the *universe*—remain in politically, environmentally responsible hands."

Thunderous applause. He could have said "notary *environmental sojac*" and they would have reacted the same way, just like trained seals. It was a spinal reflex that the government and certain organizations had been grinding into them all since the mid-20th century.

"We all remember vividly," he lied, "how we lost lovely green Pallas, second largest of the asteroids—which should have remained the common heritage of all mankind—to a criminal band of selfish, greedy, exploitative, polluting *capitalists*, rampant, unapologetic individualists like the notorious William Wilde Curringer whose heirs still cling obscenely to the world they stole from the rest of us today."

21

Never mind that when the notorious plastics billionaire Curringer found Pallas, it had been a naked, airless rock six or seven hundred miles in diameter. The truth, this evening, would do nothing to advance the cause.

Chen took his time, refusing to hurry his speech. When dinner was finally served, he knew, it would consist of tofu, carefully molded into the shape of a lobster and dyed fire engine red, accompanied by a warmed yellow liquid—he could swear it was a petroleum byproduct—to dip it in. He and his three talented young women would enjoy the real thing later on tonight, or perhaps something just as politically incorrect, possibly Japanese sirloin—before getting on with the evening's real entertainment.

"We dodged a bullet in the early 21st century, when fluctuations on the surface of the sun mitigated atmospheric warming on Earth, saving us from a threat we were all unable or unwilling to do anything about. An angry Mother Planet got revenge, however, with the Big One of 2023, an earthquake that destroyed California and with it, a quarter of the nation's economy.

"Today humanity stands on the precipice, the crumbling brink of losing even more. The sociopaths of Pallas openly look forward to destroying Ceres—'terraforming' it, they say, just like they 'terraformed' Pallas, as if it were something to be proud of—the largest, most majestic of the 'flying mountains.'"

Perfunctory applause. He waited it out.

"We may be too late to save Ceres," he told them. "Time will tell. We are doing everything we can, things you'd really rather not know about. Extreme circumstances often call for extreme measures. But I tell you it is still within our power to save a major planet from these evil plunderers, and in this unusual instance I don't mean the Earth."

The audience reaction this time was mixed, uncertain.

"We have gambled very heavily, invested much on Mars." Including, he thought, the lives of almost three hundred people. "Because there is so much to win or lose. Mars has the same surface area as all the land on Earth put together. Think of it: all of Asia, all of Europe, all of Africa, all of Australia, all of North and South America combined."

With an environment less hospitable than that of Antarctica, he thought. Anyone who wanted to go and live in such a place had to be stark, raving mad, but there were uses to which such madmen could be put.

He took a deep breath. Here goes, he thought. "Just as important—no, perhaps even *more* important in the long run—is that absolutely sacred principle, attested and agreed to in dozens of treaties, signed in good faith by many among this government's predecessors more than a century ago, that ownership of Mars—and of every other body in the Solar System—is 'the common heritage of all mankind.' It is not that of the spoiled, grasping, evil Pallatian settlers squatting on their fancied-up, country-club rock. They are what President Theodore Roosevelt once called 'malefactors of great wealth.' They must therefore be warned, in the strongest possible terms, that the planet Mars falls legally, and beyond debate, under United Nations protection and control."

Tumultuous applause followed this bold assertion. "United Nations" was yet another expression, like the word "environmental," that never failed to set the trained seals off, even though its actual track record made the Third Reich look like the Ladies' Gardening Society. Still, "under United Nations protection" actually meant "under East American control," he thought. And for all practical purposes, that means under *my* control.

Time now to wave the "bloody shirt."

"My friends, unless we want to see the planet Mars turned into … private property"—he spat the words—"owned and controlled by ruthless profiteers, converted into a replica of America's Wild West, we cannot stop trying to attain a permanent foothold there before they do."

He paused for breath and to let the words sink in.

"If we were to stop trying now, then all two hundred eighty-eight members of the six previous U.S./U.N. expeditions will have sacrificed themselves for nothing. Today we still possess the means, and for a long time, we have had the method—Dr. Robert Zubrin's ingenious and groundbreaking 'Mars Direct' plan, first enunciated in the late 20th century.

"The question before us is, do we have the *will?*"

CHAPTER FOUR:
THE NGUS OF CURRINGER

Conchita read aloud from the book. " 'All that is necessary for the triumph of evil is for good men to do
nothing.' I suppose that's true, as far as it goes, but
once they've done nothing, and evil has triumphed,
can you still say they were good?"

—*Conchita y Desmondo*
in the Land of Wimpersnits and Oogies

"*Billy!*"
Stirring the fire within a little circle of blackened stones,
the young man experienced an old, familiar thought. It
never failed to strike him, doing this, what an enormous miracle
this small campfire—and practically everything else he could see
and feel around and above him—represented.

An enormous, entirely man-made miracle.

As long as the young man could remember, he had felt an emptiness inside him, a dull ache, a certain yearning he could never
quite define or explain. Moments like this one helped him a little.

A light breeze carried a hint of autumn chill across the leaf-
littered ground. It was as much a smell as anything else. The great
trees, vastly taller than they would have grown on Earth, marched

in their stately manner down the gentle slope toward Lake Selous. Then there was the lake itself, formerly a gigantic impact crater, now filled with water wrenched virtually molecule by molecule from the grudging carbonaceous-chondrite soil. Far away, out on the lake, a dozen pretty sailboats were still making wakes, their colorful balloon sails glowing like holiday ornaments, lit from within by the setting sun.

And of course, there was the great house behind him. His father's house, the Ngu family house. Ngu House, as it was known by half the Solar System. Less than a century ago, every bit of this, everything within sight of the Ngu property, had been the dead, airless surface—

as cold as space itself—of the second largest asteroid in the Asteroid Belt. His dad had been among the first to come here from Earth and make it a human place. He felt a need to do something like that himself, to have some achievement of his own.

"*Billy!*" A young female voice was calling to him. "*Billy!*"

"That's my name," he shouted back, grinning without looking up. "Don't wear it out!"

He turned where he was hunkered down stirring the fire, to see his little sister Teal. At sixteen, she was a woman grown, by a frontier world's reckoning, yet he always thought of her as his baby sister, which he almost certainly would still do when she turned sixty. She'd come running down from the house a hundred yards away. In one hand she held a clear plastic package with white puffy contents, in the other, half a dozen long, stainless steel skewers. Would that be more or less dangerous, he thought, than running with scissors?

Billy laughed. Teal had that effect on him and everyone else. There were two big, fancy firepits with fine, steel-mesh covers up on the verandah (or on the patio, or on the lanai: his brothers and sisters all took perverse pride in calling that flagged surface something different every time they mentioned it). It was where they'd partly grown up, wide as the house itself and sixty-feet deep, with a knee-high wraparound stone wall. Truth was, the Ngu kids, all eight of them, had always preferred making their own small fires down here by the lakeshore. Billy secretly believed that it had something to do with his having been the first Eagle Scout on Pallas.

25

Or not.

Behind young Teal, her twin brother Brody, and their older sister Mirella, nineteen, followed at a somewhat more sedate pace. Teal had so much energy that other young people—even her twin—often marveled at her. She was a skinny thing, and fragile looking. Yet she was as solid and strong as titanium steel rebar and could easily eat her older brother Billy—at twenty-three, the oldest of the eight—under the table. She'd already endured a lifetime's worth of jokes about hollow legs.

"You got enough fire left for marshmallows?" Teal asked him, holding out her cargo for him to see. Of all the Ngu kids, Teal showed the Asian in her genes the most. Dad, Emerson, was half Vietnamese and half Cambodian. Mom—the famous xenoarchae-ologist Rosalie Frasier—was English, Irish, German, and Polish, an ordinary American mixture. From her father, Teal got her little round face and huge almond eyes that were set diagonally above her prominent cheekbones, flushed pink now with exercise. Her pixie-cut hair was shiny black and ruler straight, and she had freckles scattered across her cheeks and the bridge of her nose.

They had discovered early: dress her up in a shiny, embroidered, brocade Chinese jacket, she would tear your heart right out of your chest.

Mirella and Teal were such physical opposites that strangers would never guess they were sisters. For all that, Teal, at sixteen, was a gifted graduate student in biochemistry, and still mostly a little girl, happiest in denim bib overalls, colorful T-shirts, and soft shoes. At nineteen, Mirella—with the same golden blonde hair Billy kept closely cropped; nobody knew where it came from—lectured on applied genetics to millions of paid viewers all across the System-wide Solarnet. "Little" Teal—she'd grown up in Pallatian gravity and was the tallest of the children—was all angularity and high-speed motion. Mirella was long lines and languid curves, a lab coat thrown over a sheer, clinging summer dress.

Teal's young mind was uncommonly quick, magically bright, a perpetual, noisy fireworks display of thoughts and feelings, attitudes and ideas. But the old adage "Still waters run deep" might have been written to describe Mirella, who, aside from her Solar System-wide lectures, tended to be extremely soft-spoken—when she spoke at all. However, when Mirella did speak, everybody listened, and remarkable things usually began to happen.

As far as Billy knew, Teal had yet to kiss a boy (or a girl, for that matter, although he didn't think that likely). Frankly, he was happier not knowing. He loved all of his sisters with an unreasoning, overwhelming passion that helped to fill his inner emptiness. But somehow Teal—and everybody knew it—was something special.

The older of his two brothers, Drake—who had remained inside, no doubt on the Solarnet with his girlfriend, Amy, was a graduate student in astrophysics, presently work-studying at the newly constructed Culver Observatory on their home world's tiny moon, Pallas B—could take care of himself. Billy's five sisters, Henrietta Rose, Gretchen, Mirella, Teal, and little Cherry, were all younger than he was, and, therefore, his responsibility.

To a certain extent, he envied his brother Drake. Miranda Trilby, Billy's only real girlfriend—born, like him, on Pallas—had gone with her parents at age sixteen, when they had returned to Earth. It had been a terrible mistake. A year afterward, unable to withstand the acceleration that could otherwise have carried her back to partial weightlessness, she had died of circulatory problems and bone failure in the Mother Planet's crushing gravity, twenty times that of Pallas. Seven years had gone, and he wasn't sure he was ever going to get over it. Sometimes he wondered if that was why he felt the way he did, with some kind of hole in his being.

Billy was pretty sure that he had loved Miranda Trilby, the prettiest girl he had ever known, with the prettiest name he had ever heard.

"For you, Tealy-wealy, I'll make more fire." Billy had originally excused himself and strolled down here after dinner, saying that he was going to rake up and burn some leaves before it got too dark, although the family usually left the land between the house and the lake pretty much to nature. He had scraped up something like a bushel and a half of red and yellow and orange and purple leaves from the flagged pathway between his mother's amazing black rose garden and the boathouse.

Although you could get almost any place on Pallas using one of the flying belts that their father had invented, starting with an office fan (the boats in the shed were purely for fun), lately, Dad had recently acquired a floatplane—a high-winged catalytic fusion-powered electric Cessna—for longer trips together in greater comfort. Their worldlet was covered, from one pole to the other, with thousands of small—and not-so-small—round lakes that had begun as impact craters, so finding some handy place to land and take off seldom presented a problem. Planning to become an asteroid hunter himself, Billy had begun what he considered his space pilot training by taking flying lessons.

But as he watched the little Cessna bobbing at its moorings, he recalled that he had actually come out here to do some serious thinking.

Alone.

"Alone" had always been kind of a problem with seven brothers and sisters, even in a house as grand as the one they'd all been born and grew up in. Designed by Emerson, the place was constructed almost completely of native materials—mostly huge sheets of rock quarried from almost straight across Lake Selous and brought here on pontoons, to create sweeping horizontals and at least eight levels of various sizes within the house.

Here and there, recycling water cascaded over the edges of various levels in miniature waterfalls. The Ngu kids had all wanted bedrooms with windows behind these sheets of falling water. Their father had obliged them, slightly altering the design of the house to make it possible.

Even the structural stainless steel and other metals, glass, and fiberglass that were used in the construction of Ngu House had been mined or manufactured among the lesser asteroids, smelted by factory ships in orbit—there were limits to what the artificial atmosphere could absorb—and landed at the airless polar spaceports. Aside from items like his father's floatplane, the Settled worlds were remarkably self-sufficient, requiring little from Earth and nothing at all from countries like East America.

The entirety of their small world was covered with a tautly inflated "plastic bag"—if that was the term for billions of square feet of air-transparent, thumb-thick, selectively permeable, self-healing "smart" material—held in place by hundreds of the longest steel cables, stretching pole to pole, that humankind had ever manufactured. When the sun was right, you could see it glinting off the cables two miles overhead. When the sun set (or rose) there was a display of saturated rainbow coloring that science had not yet been able to explain.

Once the whole bag of marshmallows was gone, there was a comfortable silence among the siblings for a little while. Of the eight Ngu children, this oddly assorted four, Billy, Mirella, Brody, and Teal, seemed to share something unique that even they didn't understand. Then Brody spoke at last, finally giving voice to what was on the minds of all of them this evening, including the rest of the family whom they'd left back up at the house.

And everybody else on Pallas.

"So it's true," he said, gazing downward, into the ashes. "It must be true. The great and powerful Chen has spoken, after all, to a somewhat wider audience than he intended to."

All four of them laughed briefly.

The powerful billionaire's supposedly secret address to his supposedly secret banquet had been captured by commercial hackers on Earth, transmitted here, and shared all over Pallas by KCUF, the asteroid's original radio—and later, 3DTV—station. Richfield Chen wouldn't be very happy. He had paid a great deal of money for security, and heads would roll. But the people of Pallas had no qualms at all about spying on East Americans this way, not when its various governments, for nearly a century, had continually denounced and threatened them. Someday it might come to blows— at the moment, Earth had a limited number of spaceships—but Pallas, or rather, the Pallatians—were prepared.

Brody stirred the fire. Pallas' spectacular technicolor sunset had begun. It was one of those divides in life, a moment they would realize later, following which absolutely nothing would ever be quite the same.

Like his twin sister, Brody Ngu was relatively slightly built, compared to both his older brothers, who had the broad shoulders and natural build of athletes. (Brody compensated for this by spending hours in the weight—more accurately, the machine—room that his father had built into the house.) But that wasn't what people first noticed about him. Unlike his twin sister Teal, his personal energy was directed inward. Even in repose, the young man carried himself with an intensity often misinterpreted as anger. Their youngest sister, Cherry, had called him "Broody," and Henrietta Rose and Gretchen had taken to imitating their baby sister.

Brody invariably protested that when he looked most out-of-sorts with the world, he was at his happiest, or at least his most content, contemplating some novel thought or observation that had captured his imagination. They all believed him because their father showed similar tendencies.

"Mars." Brody's youthful face was wrinkled up in an old man's bitter pucker. While the youngest of the three Ngu brothers invariably struck other individuals as more serious than was supposed to be usual for his age, most Pallatians felt exactly the way he did about this particular turn of events—a tragedy, a travesty they'd been watching unfold for years. Brody exhaled wearily and stirred the embers again with one of the skewers until the sugar-coated end acquired its own small blue flame. "Those rotten rat-bastards are going to do it all over again."

"Do what?" Asked a soft, female voice, only slightly mocking.

Brody said, "You know perfectly well what I meant, Mirella. We all watched the same bootleg 3DTV signal together, didn't we? A seventh goddamn East American/United Nations colonial expedition to Mars. Anybody want to bet it won't end exactly like the first six did?"

Teal and Mirella shook their heads. Billy answered his brother. "With another three or four dozen quick-frozen corpses on the ground, struggles we can all witness with our own orbiters over the last breath of oxygen, the horrible evidence of cannibalism, and a lot of gassy excuse-making and ass-covering back home in the land of the fee and the home of the slave? No, Brother Brody, I won't take that bet. These poor so-called 'pioneers' were dead meat the picosecond they were recruited for the mission. They were just too stupid to realize it."

"Public education," Teal mouthed the words, as if they were obscenities.

Mirella said something none of the others quite heard.

"What was that?" her older brothers asked simultaneously.

"What I said was, it doesn't have to happen that way this time." Mirella gave her head a toss to get her long, silky hair out of her eyes, a completely unselfconscious gesture that had distracted more than one young man within sight of her. "Things have changed a lot here on Pallas since the last Martian expedition. We're a lot better off than we were. And we have better ships. Somebody could do something this time."

"She's right!" Teal clasped her hands together in her lap, new hope beginning to dawn deep within her. "You're right!" she said to her sister. She took Mirella's hand. "She's right!" she repeated to the others unnecessarily.

Billy put a hand over his mouth, stifling a laugh.

"She means *we* could do something." Brody pretended to glare at Mirella.

Billy grinned. "I'll bet she does, at that."

CHAPTER FIVE:
HORTON WILLOUGHBY III

Conchita sighed. "Somebody said, once, 'The higher, the fewer'. I don't know exactly what they meant, Desmondo, but if it was about folks who are good, smart, and not crazy, they knew what they were talking about."

—Conchita y Desmondo
in the Land of Wimpersnits and Oogies

The President complained, "Helen, have you seen this ... this ... outrage?" He pointed at the upper middle 3DTV screen in the double bank of screens that occupied a portion of one wall in the Oval Office.

"Be quiet, Horton." Bent over, the telephone in her hand, his wife, Helen McClellan Willoughby, didn't bother to look up. She was sitting in his Presidential chair, behind his Presidential desk. He was seated on one of the sofas intended for guests. "Can't you see that I'm busy? Anyway, I thought you were going to go see Dr. Kraczinski this afternoon."

Willoughby protested, "But this is absolutely out—!"

"Horton, didn't you hear me?" To the phone: "Yes, he wants it yesterday—or tomorrow you're likely to find yourself posted to Kazakhstan!"

Helen was always rude to people she perceived as being beneath her, less powerful or wealthy than she—or her husband—was. Willoughby thought it the very height of foolishness, especially with waitresses and nurses who, one way or another, held your life—or simply your comfort—in their hands. He had never agreed to see that Kraczinski quack of Helen's, and he never would. That had been her idea entirely, and she couldn't imagine anyone not doing whatever she told them to. Kraczinski was a glorified cosmetician, and nothing more.

Helen wanted the man to darken her husband's skin a tone or two and give him an extreme permanent hair treatment, to emphasize his African-American ancestry, just as she had had her own skin lightened and her hair bleached, to emphasize the contrast between them, so that voters and the media would understand how very progressive she was, to be married to a black man, only the second black President in the history of the United States of America. Unfortunately for her, more than half of Willoughby's immediate ancestors were white. And, despite a massive effort to maintain the illusion, the United States of America, as such, no longer existed.

Willoughby sighed deeply. He would never have guessed in an entire lifetime that the editorial cartoonists would take to depicting the President of the (East) United States as one of those inflatable clown dummies, the kind that, punched on its big red nose, rocks back and then forward so it can be punched again. Every time he was snubbed or insulted by some foreign government—it seemed to happen with increasing frequency as America's once-great fortunes declined—or he was harshly criticized by some domestic politician with too high a profile to be disappeared (had Willoughby had that inclination, which he mostly did not), the 3DTV would be filled the next morning with punching clowns all wearing his face.

Punctuated by a big red nose.

"Yes, of course the President wants to see the whole damn thing right from the beginning!" Helen again, on the phone. "No, I don't give a shit who else gets to see it, the President wants the jamming shut off *now!*"

This occasion it had been the new king's "people"—France had suffered recent, radical changes to whatever Constitution it had possessed; a big golden crown now stood atop the Eiffel Tower—informing the President's "people" that he didn't have time for a visit, one head of state to another. No time. The next morning, His Majesty had been holographed by the cybertabloids, surfing with the pretty anchorwoman for "News in the Nude."

Helen: "Yes, yes, he's watching. What the hell are you waiting for?"

This was all Helen's doing, he thought. Perhaps she deserved that chair and desk more than he did. She certainly had the "commander" part of "commander-in-chief" down pat. He sometimes wondered why he'd married her. He couldn't actually remember consciously making the decision to ask her. She wasn't pretty like that anchorwoman. Or even pleasant. She wasn't particularly smart. She wore too much perfume. It exuded from her pores and hung on her like a malignant cloud. Her metabolism made it smell like insecticide. They hadn't had sex—well, together—for over fifteen years.

The truth was that, before his nomination, Willoughby had been more than content in his relatively modest position as a professor at a small but prestigious New England college, specializing in the origin and history of International Law. He had spoken to no more than a couple of upper-level classes every week. He had written—or at least attached his signature to—half a dozen scholarly publications every year.

He'd enjoyed tenure, a suitable residence, a reserved parking space (although even in the winter, he mostly walked to work, in quiet solitude, across the postcard-beautiful campus), his own private table in the faculty club dining room, and an attractive, gratifyingly compliant secretary. He'd loved his membership in the faculty health spa where he enjoyed the sauna and swam laps every morning and evening just like a citizen of Ancient Rome, on whose Twelve Tables of the Law he happened to be one of the world's foremost authorities.

He hadn't much enjoyed being President of the United States so far. Outside the groves of academe, he hadn't encountered a single individual who knew who Hugo Grotius was.

"Helen, look at this!"

There it was again, that blasted punching bag cartoon, crudely animated. This time it was on PNN, the "Progressive News Network," which had originally endorsed him as a candidate. However, times and circumstances tend to change. The new king of France, Chlodio II, stood high overhead on some kind of medieval castle rampart, threatening in an extremely silly voice and mock French accent to open his nostrils in the President's general direction. It sounded like a quotation. He wondered where it had come from.

The sudden *POP!* was more seen than heard. There was a flash, and suddenly, all six screens showed the same image, that of Richfield Chen, the dynamic mercantilist who had more or less hired Willoughby to become President of the United States, much as he had decided (or so it had been rumored) who would be the Prime Ministers of Canada and the United Kingdom, the President of Mexico, and Secretary General of the United Nations.

But not, Willoughby thought with an inward grin, the King of France.

"I don't have to tell you," Chen had been speaking to a big banquet audience, "that this mission to Mars is vitally important to us for several reasons. Aside from the scientific knowledge it has to offer us, as well as the advanced technology it promises to help us develop, we have a serious moral responsibility to assure that the planets—the stars, the *universe*—remain in politically, environmentally responsible hands."

There was a roar of applause. As the camera panned across the audience, Willoughby saw that they were wearing fancy evening clothes, tuxedos both black and white, and dresses cut down to there, even when there wasn't any there there. Some faces he recognized from the news; even more he'd never seen before. This was the famous and mysterious "Dinner with No Name," the former college professor realized, the most exclusive, secretive annual event in Western Civilization. Even he, the President, was not invited—which annoyed him beyond words—and no cameras or recording devices were ever permitted within the hall.

So where was this live feed coming from? The NSA? the CIA?—West American Fox?

Old Anonymous?

He turned where he was seated on the sofa, to look at his wife. She was paying rapt attention to the image on the six big screens. "Helen?"

"Yes, yes, Horton, what is it?" Her tone was impatient. She didn't look away from Chen's face.

"This is your doing." He didn't make a question of it.

"Yes, Horton, it is." Still, she didn't look at him.

"How did you manage it? Who helped you? Why—"

Finally, she looked him in the eye. "Believe me, Horton, you'll be far happier not knowing. Now be quiet, please. I'm trying to listen to this."

Willoughby was grimly aware that, sooner or later, he would have to do something about Helen. True, she had her own capital connections, which he had found useful. And money. Her father had been a highly respected (and greatly feared) seven-term Senator from Maine. However, Helen had never wielded anything but borrowed power. She had been almost tolerable as a faculty wife (the politics involved in that were complicated and vicious), but here in Washington the media had started calling her the "Fist Lady" and that simply wouldn't do, not given the long-term image he wished to project on history.

The President was more than comfortable permitting others to judge him by his affable, almost passive exterior. Who was it that had coined the phrase, "harmless, lovable little fuzzball"? Somebody else had told him that his patron saint should be Perry Como. He'd had to look the fellow up, but he was not displeased by the comparison. It had allowed him to rise effortlessly among those of his colleagues who seemed eternally to be at one another's throats, who perceived him as a noncombatant, and who would far rather see him advance than any of their enemies. He was quite happy being the eternal, reliable "anybody but" candidate.

Very few—his wife least of all—understood that, underneath it all, he was made of equal measures of granite and fire. Barring the occasional accident like Andrew Johnson or Gerald Ford, no man had ever been President of the United States who wasn't. He had allowed Helen to push him into running for the Presidency, just as he had earlier allowed her to nag him into becoming head of the department, and later on, president of the college-wide faculty council. If he had wanted anything else, he would have let her push him into that, as well.

An armchair psychologist might have called him passive-aggressive. He greatly preferred to think of himself as being quite the other way around. True, Richfield Chen's sudden invitation to run for the Presidency had come as something of a surprise—he'd have said it was as likely as being elected Pope—but it had not intimidated him in the slightest. If he could simply avoid making too many mistakes, he had reasoned, he would write his own ticket afterward: president of any goddamn university that suited him.

Maybe he could even rid himself of Helen somehow. He was aware that his predecessor Barack Obama had claimed a right—an Executive Privilege—to have anybody killed—including any American on American soil—for any reason he cared to. Now Willoughby wondered if he'd had Michelle in mind. He wondered, too, whether the Special Forces would do it for him. He'd always been nice to them. Then he could find himself another attractive, compliant secretary. Compliance was a highly underrated quality, he thought—in secretaries, at least. Not one of them had ever called him passive-aggressive afterward.

He didn't have to observe Richfield Chen as intently as Helen seemed to be doing right now to understand the man's actual motives in employing the United Nations as a screen to send a series of would-be colonial missions to Mars. The fellow obviously thought of himself as Emperor—of precisely what, was something to be negotiated later—standing above politics, which he willingly left to underlings like Willoughby and others like him.

Chen's first purpose was to deflect the attention of the media and the public away from the government's—for all practical purposes, *his* government's—continuing domestic economic and foreign policy shortcomings, which, as always, were the direct consequence of pursuing contradictory objectives.

War had once been a practical distraction from domestic failure. But engaging in one ginned-up and ridiculous war after another overseas—mostly against poverty-stricken, under-developed Third World nations unable to defend themselves—didn't seem to work that well anymore. Too often those poor, backward Third Worlders discovered effective ways to fight back after all, utterly humiliating those who later claimed merely to be trying to "uplift" them. September 11, 2001, came to mind.

In West America, by law, total government expenditures could not exceed a tenth of one percent of GNP—if it did, *everything* was reduced automatically to restore the balance, and *all* terms in office ended. But what fun was that for anyone who reveled in political power?

Secret polling told Willoughby and the party he pretended to be the head of that they were losing popular ground at a rate too rapid to be measured. Various observers in West America had been saying for a long time that the 10,000-year-old Age of Authority was over, and that East America, the tail of a dying dinosaur, was just too stupid to realize it.

Thrashing tails could be deadly, of course. Not for the first time, Willoughby considered that it might be best to retire somewhere west of the Mississippi. Helen could always remain in the east, if she preferred.

He started thinking about warm, compliant secretaries again, and had to shake his head to get his mind back on track. It was an effort—and a gesture—highly characteristic of him, so much so that comic impersonators did it without knowing why. And he certainly wasn't going to tell them.

One by one, each of the first six East American/United Nations interplanetary missions had been disastrous, demoralizing failures. Usually, it was owing to some irrational change that politicians or bureaucrats had made to Dr. Robert Zubrin's original "Mars Direct" plan, purely for ideological reasons. One unfortunate expedition had been required to waste too much of its precious space and weight allowance—that might otherwise have been used to carry more food or medicine—by taking trees to be planted in the soil of Mars.

The frozen, desiccated, airless soil of airless Mars.

Before they died, the colonists had burned those trees in a cave for their warmth, using the last of their air supply, bitterly recording the event for their posterity. Those recordings remained a deeply archived state secret.

Willoughby didn't relish the idea of another of these dismaying, idiotic failures occurring during his own administration: doomed expeditionaries from a seventh mission to Mars, stranded hopelessly on that red planet, dying slowly—and all too publicly—for lack of food, water, or air, simply because some pathetically ignorant senator or representative (or worse, some unelected, overzealous, environmental regulator) thought that they should have to take a load of St. Christopher's medals, or yo-yos, or recyclable diapers with them.

There was already serious talk in Congress of banning powered vehicles—electric cars like they'd taken to the Moon—on the upcoming expedition because, "We wouldn't want to be polluting what little air Mars has left, now, would we?" Even Willoughby understood (he gave himself that much credit) that trying to survive and explore Mars without powered transportation would be like trying to survive and explore 19th century Wyoming without horses.

Beyond that, for all that Chen was currently leaning heavily on the ancient "common heritage of all mankind" argument, Willoughby understood perfectly well (as everyone else in Washington would) that the man's loyal underlings inside various Beltway think tanks would eventually "discover" legal pretexts under which Congress could lay claim to the planet exclusively, as the property of the East American government.

Which belonged, in fee simple, to Richfield Chen.

The same area as all the dry land on Earth, Chen had said. Lacking air and liquid water, it was a bit of a fixer-upper, but it was still the biggest real estate grab since the Pope divided the New World between Portugal and Spain.

And it would all belong to one man.

CHAPTER SIX:
EMERSON NGU

Conchita mused. "It's amazing, Desmondo, how angry some people will get with you when you won't let them *help* you. Do you suppose it's because they had something else in mind?

—Conchita y Desmondo
in the Land of Wimpersnits and Oogies

"**D**ad," complained a familiar voice, "the bastards are doing it again."

Emerson Ngu looked up from the screens, on which he'd been talking to three of his factory-ship operators. Although each rated the title "Captain," it was customary in the industrial fleet for them to refer to themselves as "Manager." Vessels like theirs (smaller and less sophisticated in the early days) had searched for, found, extracted, and processed all of the materials that had made terraforming Pallas possible.

Now Emerson and his competitors employed that technology, somewhat improved, to bestow shirtsleeve environments on smaller asteroids, where commercial activities were pursued—farming of various kinds, mining, ranching, fish and shellfish culture, that helped make life among the asteroids more enjoyable than many an Earth observer might have expected. Mostly it was done by families and small companies. Under the Stein Covenant, no provision allowed a group of individuals to gain special powers and immunities by declaring themselves a corporation.

As a result, companies out here tended to be much smaller.

Emerson's conference today wasn't critical, or he'd have shut his office door, a sign his family had always recognized and respected. He was helping his managers rewrite vessel assignments so that most of his ship-side employees could attend the annual company picnic here on Pallas. It had practically become a planetary holiday. He left a few minor issues to be settled later, signed off, and picked up his coffee mug.

"Now ..."

The man stood, addressing his eldest son as he replenished his cup from a coffee-making machine on a small table near his desk. Behind it an east-facing window admitted morning sunlight filtered through a shimmering wall of falling water. It wasn't like Billy, named for billionaire Pallas colony founder William Wilde Curringer, to sound whiny.

Emerson was not a large man like his two eldest sons, Billy and Drake, but he spoke and moved with enough dignity and grace that his relative size was not what people noticed about him first. He had a mostly gentle authority that they tended to respond to. His graying hair was of moderate length, combed straight back from his forehead. The mustache that he sported was a remarkable effort for an individual of his particular ethnic background.

One of Emerson's eyes was artificial, and slanted across his hips he wore an old military canvas pistol belt, a bit frayed at the edges and stained, bearing a somewhat antiquated .45 Winchester Magnum semiautomatic pistol, called a Grizzly, that he'd carried since he was a young refugee from a United Nations agricultural commune first established here on Pallas through a loophole in the Stein Covenant. In his personal view, it was the little world's only blighted spot. But it wasn't doing very well, and someday it would be gone.

As time passed, Emerson had grown wealthy supplying his fellow Pallatians with personal weapons of his own design and manufacture: the famous "Ngu Departure" 10mm automatic; a sort of three-wheeled automobile he'd created for the low gravity and unfinished roads of a rough frontier planetoid; and yet another unique form of personal transportation, the iconic Pallatian Flying Belt. He'd also used much of his wealth defending Pallatian independence and the absolute freedom of its inhabitants.

He took a sip of his coffee. "Who's doing what?"

"And with which, and to whom! Ha-ha!" On the slickly finished hallway floor of highly polished asteroidal stone, young Teal slid past her big brother on stockinged feet, where he stood just inside Emerson's office door, grabbing him around the waist to stop and turn herself.

"You're far too young to know that limerick, my dear," Billy told her.

"Ha!" she repeated. "You taught it to me."

"Ahem." Emerson actually said it as a word.

"Sorry, Dad. As we all learned last night, East America and their Yoonie-puppets are getting ready to send a seventh expedition to Mars."

Emerson nodded, understanding. "So I have heard. What exactly is on your mind, son?"

"We think we may have figured out how to do something about it this time." Billy held up a small space pilot's computer, a birthday gift from his father. "It says here that once they torch off, we have 270 days."

Emerson chuckled. "Who's 'we'—as if I didn't know already."

"You probably do know: Mirella, Brody, 'Trouble' here, and me."

"We're going to rescue them!" Teal blurted.

"And you're coming to me because ..."

"Brody believes your name will 'strike fear into the hearts of the enemy.' Mirella thinks that you could help us with Fritz Marshall. I don't disagree with them, I just figured you'd want to be in on the fun. We need a ship, and Fritz Marshall—who has been known to back the cause of liberty—has ships. It has to be a special ship in some ways, and I think I can manage that. But Mirella is holding the real ace."

"Where is Mirella?" her father asked.

"Oh, she went to her laboratory to get something," said Teal, pretending to an innocence she didn't presently possess. "She'll be back."

Fritz Marshall was an exceptionally large man, very tall and rotund, and he *boomed* when he talked. But like an iceberg, Billy thought, you were inclined to suspect, even so, that at least nine tenths of him was in another dimension, somewhere, doing something else. Much like Emerson, he seemed to have an iron in many different fires.

"Yes," he told his visitors—Billy, his father Emerson, and his mother Rosalie—as they were being served coffee, tea, and soda in his office, "I made my way out here to the asteroids like a lot of other individuals, absolutely certain that I was going to strike it rich."

"And here you are, today," Emerson replied, grinning at him. "Rich."

"Here I am today, my friend, only because I discovered early what not quite so many individuals ever did, that instead of looking for wealth or digging it up yourself, simply sell the prospectors and miners whatever they need or want—which you can easily find in catalogues and online—and they'll eagerly bring whatever they've found straight to you!"

"Like the notorious one-hundred-dollar eggs?" asked Emerson, eyebrow raised.

Marshall laughed. "Those goddamned eggs—do kindly pardon my French, Rosalie, my dear—cost me about ninety-eight dollars apiece getting them up here from Dirt." It was what many of the older miners called Earth. "And in the end, I lost money badly on the proposition. Next time around, the very next supply ship, I imported two dozen laying hens and kept them in this cave. You can still smell it back in there. I became Pallas's first underground chicken farmer. At one silver ounce per egg, I made out like a bandit."

"Which is what a lot of people called you, back then," Rosalie observed. She was a smallish, trim woman of middle age, light complexioned, with lots of black, curly hair and freckles. Having carried and given birth to eight children, nobody knew how hard she worked to keep her figure, except her husband.

For this business trip, she was taking time away from her research. She and two of her daughters, Mirella and Teal, had visited the cold, airless surface of undeveloped asteroid Ceres last month, and each had made some interesting findings in her own field. Rosalie's was xenoarchaeology, specifically, the study of "Drake-Tealy Objects" that she had made her reputation proving were alien artifacts billions of years old. Mirella and Teal had come home excited about a kind of fungus they'd discovered, living in hard vacuum and nearly Absolute Zero.

"*You* certainly never did, Rosalie. Nor Emerson, here. Nor either of his esteemed fosters, Horatio and Henrietta Singh—but that's right, poor Horatio had been dead for some time before Emerson met Henrietta."

"That's because one of my degrees is in economics," Rosalie replied.

"And hey," said Emerson. "I had eggs!" The U.N. commune had been vegetarian.

Marshall laughed, shaking the very windows around him. "My point, egg-zactly!"

The "cave" they presently occupied was now the stylish and very comfortable offices of Fritz Marshall Enterprises. The landscape that they looked out over, through enormous heavy windows, was the floor of a crater ten miles wide, featuring hard vacuum, broiling temperatures in the sun, and approaching Absolute Zero in the blackest shadows that any of the Ngus had ever seen. This was Port Admundsen, at the South Pole of Pallas. There was another port, Port Peary, very similar to it, at the North Pole. They were the little world's spaceports. The ring wall of the crater was tunneled through with multiple-airlocked roads that led out onto the airless, hostile crater floor at one end, and into the lush, life-filled world at the other.

Here and there, other commercial establishments, like Marshall's, had windows looking out onto the spaceport. Billy could see them glitter across the airless plain. There were scattered examples of every spaceship he knew—he had known each one of them since the age of six.

He saw asteroid-hunters sitting on their landing gear out there, and despite their ugly, snubbed-off utilitarian lines, they sang to his heart about a life of adventure in deep space. There was also construction—and destruction—vessels of several different kinds within view, diggers, borers, manipulators, although none of the giant factory ships that could reduce a two-hundred-yard rock to ingots in just a couple of days or chew up a carbonaceous chondrite and manufacture a roll of plastic two hundred yards wide. Those great ships never landed, since the stress of even a twentieth of a gee would be enough to break them.

Spaceships built for everyday use among the asteroids—something much like the family pickup in West America or the buckboard of the Golden West—were far more numerous than any other vehicle type here. Farmers come to market; cowboys (and buffalo boys, ostrich boys, emu boys, and jackelope boys) enjoying the bright lights of Curringer. These had been designed to be as uncomplicated, trouble free, and idiot proof as they could be manufactured. They all consisted of a simple cylinder, containing engines, a control area, and cargo space. Where they varied, were in the number of levels or decks they contained.

The single-deck model had all of its facilities and features on one deck, with everything wrapped around the engine or tacked on outside. Such vessels were noisy to ride in and hot to run, but they were relatively cheap to obtain and operate. They were often referred to as "jeeps" or "mules" or "beetles." They couldn't carry very much cargo, however, and the plans that Billy and his siblings were making required considerably greater capacity.

The vessel nearest to the Marshall office windows looked decades old, battered and dirty. The proprietor was just explaining that, among the many things a young fellow could get rich by supplying to prospectors and miners, transportation from one rock to another was foremost. "They can't walk or swim." Marshall laughed. The little ship that Billy was looking down at was named *Zelda Gilroy* for some reason. She was the first vessel, Marshall explained, that he had offered rides on—for a price comparable to what he charged for eggs.

In a ship like this one, "up" was also "forward," with fusion-powered constant acceleration gluing one's feet gently to the floor, probably at no more than one-tenth gee. Standing on her frail-looking landing legs, *Zelda Gilroy* was a blunt, unlovely cylinder some three decks tall, her engine and utility room lay below, her fairly ample cargo deck amidships, and her pilot house, galley, and the crew's sleeping quarters on the uppermost deck under a transparent plastic dome with antennae of various kinds planted all around it like garden flowers. Somewhere, Billy suspected, there had once been weapons. Hammocks could be slung on the cargo deck, if passengers paid better than bulk freight.

Marshall regarded Billy, who was gazing out the window with utter fascination. He could tell a young man in love when he saw one. He had once felt the same way about her himself. He could see that the boy itched to get aboard and look her over. She would be his first ship, and that, he knew, was something very special. "I had old *Zelda* brought around because I thought that she might be just what you're looking for, son. She's tough as nails, but very forgiving to a new pilot. She's got plenty of cargo room if she's properly loaded, and three fusion engines that will do all the lifting you could wish for."

"Almost all," observed Billy, absently.

Marshall took in a breath and let it out. "That's right, son, almost all." They both knew that, where Billy and his siblings were planning to take *Zelda Gilroy*, she was not coming back.

"So what is she going to cost us?" asked Billy's mother, determinedly clearing her throat. She and her husband were prepared to part with a considerable number of gold or silver coins.

The big man turned to the anthropologist. "Not a feather's weight, dear Rosalie. She will need a massive overhaul, which I assume Billy and the others can attend to. There certainly isn't a better way to learn a ship. They may use my hangar and dockyard facilities. She's got to be reinforced for landing in the gravity of Mars. I expect that she'll remain there as a monument of one kind or other. If, as seems likely, I never see the old girl again, there's the insurance. And one more thing—"

"What's that?" Billy and his father said it at the same time.

"If I want any form of payment, it's a list of everybody down there in the Angry Red Sandbox and an estimate of their knowledge and capabilities. It occurred to me a very long time ago that the 'best and brightest' East America's always bragging about sending to the stars are almost certainly among the worst of their chronic troublemakers; malcontents who detest conditions in East America so badly they're willing to stand in line and risk their lives to be sent to an airless desert a hundred times worse than Siberia. I suppose the government figures that if some—or all—of these 'heroes' die in the attempt to adapt to the inhuman environment of Mars, so much the better."

Emerson nodded, agreeing. Competence and courage were the rarest commodities in any culture.

"And ...?" Billy was curious. Rosalie already knew what Marshall intended.

"That's exactly the kind of people I want working for me, son. I'm backing you up because for me, this is a kind of treasure hunt. Gold, platinum, iridium, silver, and diamonds are nothing by comparison. You're seeking out the rarest values that exist: talent, intelligence, competence, discontent with the damned status quo. If you can't bring 'em back alive just now, you can at least identify them for later retrieval."

And suddenly, there it was, thought Emerson. The topic that they'd all been carefully avoiding so far. But the grim, simple fact was that, even if she made it down safely to the surface of Mars with her precious crew and cargo intact, *Zelda Gilroy* would not be rising from that dusty surface again, not with gravity nearly seven times that of Pallas.

Except for the proposedly interstellar *Fifth Element*, there wasn't a vessel in the Belt so far that was capable of that; there hadn't been any need for it—Emerson vowed to start working on the problem from this day forward. But for all practical purposes, this was a one-way expedition that half his children were planning to make. The rescuers would need rescuing. It might be years before he saw them again—*little Teal!*—he might never see them again at all.

He glanced over at Rosalie, holding back tears. He took her hand.

Yet it was their job, his and their mother's, to bring them all up and send them out into a frigid, hostile, uncaring universe, like fluffy seeds blown off a dandelion, where they could be killed or damaged in several million different ways. Maybe, the most important part of that job was not to let his fears for his children be seen on his face or heard in his voice. Emerson had done a great many difficult things in his life, but this was by far the hardest.

What he said was, "Well, what do you think Billy?"

"We'll take her! Thank you, Mr. Marshall!" They shook hands.

"Treat her gently," the big man told him. "She was my first."

CHAPTER SEVEN:
THE COLONISTS

"Sometimes, Desmondo," Conchita observed, "'This way to the Egress' is *not* a bad sign to see!"
—*Conchita y Desmondo*
in the Land of Wimpersnits and Oogies

Mohammed Khalidov was a good man; at least he believed that he was. He loved his little wife Beliita with his whole heart and with all of the soul he was certain he didn't possess. He worked as hard at his chosen trade as he could. (He was, he supposed, in some sense, a high-tech tinker.) He paid the many fines and fees and taxes that were demanded of him by whatever voracious state he happened to live in. He obeyed its many tangled laws. Sometimes, however, it became impossible to do all of those things simultaneously.

Times were extremely difficult for any individual from Chechnya who was not political in the slightest. So many of his fellow Chechens who were otherwise, regarded him as no more than a coward and a traitor (he was, in fact, neither), and the Russians simply didn't give a damn. Those bastards would kill you if they had the ghost of an excuse. Mohammed had long been more than a little careful never to give them one, but it was increasingly hard. In the bloodied realm that his native Chechnya had become, under the ugly succession of thugs and gangsters who had replaced the Marxists, *breathing* could be a punishable offense.

That was why he and his Beliita had volunteered to go to Mars, on the principle, "It is better to rule in Hell than to serve in Heaven," and why they were training here now, in what amounted to a rented desert in Mexico. There were, of course, many deserts in West America—the Mojave, or the Oregon Desert, for example, Alamosa or the Great Salt Lake. But, even if that nation (it amounted to that, although East America would never admit it) had been willing, East America wouldn't dream of asking.

It was a good day today; the sun was cheerfully smiling, and the sky was blue. Mohammed grunted, giving the screwlike metal tent peg a final twist into the dry sand and gravel which was the practice location's most Mars-like feature. Objects like this one were relied on to tie down the quarters they'd been provided with. On Mars, with its thousandth of a millibar atmosphere, it would be more than adequate—perhaps even unnecessary—at ghostly wind speeds up to 500 miles per hour. Here, a 50 mile per hour gust could easily undo all of his hard work. The fact that he was required to accomplish all of it in a space suit—*sans* expensive helmet, of course—with heavy gloves, made it harder. But, on to the next grommet.

"Move to the right a little, Khalidov, so the sunlight will fall on what you're doing." Mohammed looked up at the figure, backlighted by the desert sun. In that kind of illumination, her features were indistinct, but the woman's shrill, unlovely voice told him immediately who she was, and he believed she had a camera pointed at him.

"You're the one who needs to move, MiG," he answered her evenly. "You're casting a shadow on my work."

"That could be interpreted as insubordination, Khalidov. I'm planning to send these videos back east to the Agency as a progress report. Do you want me to tell them that you won't cooperate with the mission's political officer?"

Margaretha Inez Ghodorov, known by her initials as "MiG," was the original Congressionally appointed mission commander of the seventh expedition. She was a short, dumpy middle-aged woman with a Brooklyn accent and a natural inclination toward intrusive, counter-productive micromanagement. She knew nothing about space travel or colonization. Now, here in the Mexican desert, she was generally ignored by everyone because her superiors back in East America found her obnoxious to work with, too, and avoided it whenever they possibly could. Her responsibilities had been taken over, largely, by the mission's operations officer, Jack Reubenson.

Nevertheless Mohammed, whose inclination was toward amiability, obligingly shuffled to one side so MiG could take her pictures that nobody would pay any attention to back home. Who cared about screwing a tent peg into the sand? She "filmed" for a little while, gave him a pointless lecture about keeping the sand out of his helmet collar (he'd been struggling to do that very thing since he'd put the useless environmental suit on two days ago), and moved on to bother somebody else.

Sunny—and windy—Mexico. Its faraway mountain peaks looked purple. He wished that he had the time and energy to poke around a bit and to enjoy the spectacular scenery. He was accustomed to open spaces, but he'd never seen a place quite like this, except perhaps in an ancient John Wayne movie, nor shared it with a nearby curious iguana—which, he understood, the natives raised and ate, somewhat like chickens. He wondered if they gathered and ate the eggs, as well, and what scrambled iguana eggs would be like. This one was wild and roamed the red-sand desert freely.

The forty-eight colonists of the Seventh East American/United Nations Expedition to Mars (although those in charge didn't like calling it that, because it brought memories of the first six, which had been disastrous failures) would set their quarters up this way once they arrived there. The prefab shelters had actually been thick disks to begin with, inflated into longer egg-shapes with compressed air, lying on their sides. Everybody called them "Bigelow bottles, after the company that had invented and produced them, or BEAMs for "Bigelow Expandable Activity Modules." Early versions had been tested in Earth orbit and at the International Space Station. The hydrogen-bearing plastics they were made of were capable of repelling or absorbing the solar and stellar radiation that was thought to have killed the First Expedition. Each and every centimeter was monitored, each and every day, to detect the microscopic amounts of chemical poison within the plastic that some thought had killed the Second, or the slow leaks that were thought to have killed the Third. The truth was, nobody knew for sure.

There were only thirty-six of the colonists here in the training camp at the moment. The final dozen, all of them East Americans, he'd heard, were due in later today. Mohammed wondered what these newcomers would be like. Pushy and noisy, no doubt, being East Americans, wanting to run everything. Life is a damned soap opera, he thought, all about people. Location and setting didn't matter at all. From ancient Sumeria to the Moon—or to Mars—people are people. They have been busy thinking the same old human thoughts, feeling the same old human feelings, doing the same old human things to one another for a hundred thousand years.

Or more like ten million years. In the wild, chimpanzees, it was said, regularly stole from one another, raped one another, beat each other up to establish who the next Grand Wazootie would be, and kidnapped babies. Mohammed was willing to wager anything that *Homo erectus* or *Australopithecus* was much the same. It would all make great 3DTV.

It got pretty cold, here, especially at night, and especially at this altitude. It was sometimes difficult to breathe. But there was no adequate way that they could simulate the two thirds of Earth's gravity that should be missing. Less gravity might seem like an advantage to some, and in some ways, perhaps it was, but even screwing in a tent peg depended on the screwer's weight. People were accustomed to working against gravity, even to using it in their work. Other means must be found, and it was his job (among others) to find them.

Nevertheless, Mohammed felt almost lighthearted at the moment. It was Sunday, one of the future colony's two religious days. Most of the colonists were gathered for services in the colony's largest cluster of shelters, and there was nobody out here to get in his way. He could hear them singing. That he was a lifelong non-believer made him even more unpopular with his fellow Chechens, mostly Muslims and a handful of Russian-influenced Orthodox Catholics. The idea of a god had always struck him as absurd. He was, first and foremost, an objective scientist, not a believer.

Except, of course, in Beliita.

He believed in Beliita.

Nothing else, not even quantum physics, the first joy in his life, had ever made him happier than his sweet little wife, ten years younger than he was, and half his size, with her lithe, curvaceous figure, her dark eyes, and her dark, glossy hair. In their repressed, overly clothed native culture, her great beauty had gone for the most part unnoticed in their small hometown—or it was a cause for suspicion and disapproval. How he had come to win her love was a mystery beyond his ability to solve. He was a very funny-looking fellow; everybody said so. He could see it, himself. But he loved his Beliita with a passion that was all-consuming. It never occurred to the man that Beliita valued intelligence as much as he did.

Mars simply *had* to work for them, he mused; Beliita couldn't go home—not if she wanted to continue living. Winning her Ph.D. in physics in Paris, she had naively returned from France, not to the proud family congratulations she had expected, but to an attempted "honor" killing by three bearded savages—her uncles—outraged by her college degree, her atheism, her Western ways, and clothing. Her makeup alone, it appeared—a modest amount of lipstick and mascara by French standards—was a capital offense.

Her equally unapproved new husband, himself, Mohammed, had been forced to kill one of the men attacking her, with a shovel. It was by far the ugliest moment in his life. He shuddered to think about it, even now. Perhaps unwisely, he let the other two live. Now he couldn't go home, either.

A few feet away, a man with a gun in his hand snaked out through the peculiar, round door of his BEAM habitat. "I've got another one for you, Mo. It won't come on when I key the console."

The weapon was basically an unauthorized copy of a century-old form, the Fabrique Nationale P90 "personal defense weapon," chambered for 5.7x28 millimeters, a tiny .22 caliber cartridge that was the next best thing to useless in the overwhelmingly violent universe of warfare. Even worse, this version of the gun had been wired to be activated and deactivated from some central point. When it was turned on, it might make an enemy mad at you, but it wouldn't hurt him very much. Unlike the Belgian original, however, when it was turned off, it would certainly get you killed. More than anything, it had been designed, after a century of steep decline in East American self-respect and power, to prevent popular uprisings.

Mohammed shook his head. "It was an unspeakably stupid idea to start with, Jack, jiggering these little weapons so they can be turned on and off by some idiot Central Command somewhere." Jack Reubenson was a short, compact, powerful black man, officially the operations boss of the expedition—in reality, its leader. "The desk jockeys commanding troops from behind the lines don't directly suffer the consequences of a non-working weapon. These things are nothing but toys for throwaway troops, my friend. Tripwire guns, meant to create a provocation on demand. Plus, every part you add to a gun lessens its reliability by at least ten percent. This is probably worse."

The guns had been supplied to the colonists, not for fighting any imaginary Martian monsters, nor even for discouraging Mexico's *el tigre*, the ubiquitous coyotes, and the rattlesnakes. They were ballistic truncheons. Once on Mars they would theoretically prevent mutinies that had been known to happen when the strictures and privations of colony life had begun to make themselves apparent.

This wasn't his first firearms repair request. Mohammed usually "fixed" these guns simply by ripping out their added-on circuitry, rendering them fully autonomous. Nobody among the colonists had ever complained.

Beliita Khalidov knew that she was extremely pretty. Until recently, it had brought her nothing but grief. Concealed, for the most part, beneath meters and meters of heavy, dull-colored fabric, she had a fine, unblemished complexion, an upturned nose quite uncharacteristic of her people, a trim little figure—unlike her mother and her four big sisters, she'd remained slender as she grew—and dark, enticing eyes.

Others had courted her—or more precisely, courted her father—but her Mohammed was the first man to love her for her mind. He thought it was funny, and not a little bit sexy, that the classic Double

Slit experiment from quantum physics infuriated her. She took it personally. She was a mathematical particle physicist of some international repute (and thus an unforgivable embarrassment to her family), and she was inexpressibly glad that Mohammed, a sort of particle physicist himself, appreciated that.

Just now, her illustrious scientific work consisted of darning a sock, while the men outside talked about guns. How very wifely, she thought sourly. How very Chechen: they were the hillbillies of eastern Europe. She and Mohammed had been trying for more than three years to have a child. So far they had failed, although nothing wrong could be found with either of them. They'd both passed the expedition physical with flying colors. Now, she thought, turning up pregnant really would be a wifely thing to do, even if it got them rejected from the Mars expedition.

Instead, she darned a damned sock.

Or damned a darned sock.

The young woman arose from the folding cot where she sat inside the upper half of their cylinder (simulating the pressurized quarters they'd have on Mars—the lower half was for life support equipment and storage) and took the kettle off the camp stove, carefully keeping it away from the all-too meltable plastic partitions that separated portions of the BEAM. It was too bad, she thought, that no one had made a survival field samovar. It was a greater shame that they had to prepare and drink tea the English way. She blamed the Americans.

She would like to have listened to the radio, but all she could find was *mariachi* music and Spanish-language commercials for Spoonies: "Spoonie! Oonie! Oonie! Oonie!"

At that, it was vastly superior to drinking properly made tea while waiting anxiously for the Russian bullies—so like the Czarist Cossacks they were—who had troubled them for decades to raid their small town, rob them of what little they possessed, to rape them. Or, more recently, for the Army or the Secret Police, who added torture to the brutal, oppressive process. That was why she and Mohammed had volunteered for this Martian adventure, to get away from the constant persecution. Her own father had recently been murdered in broad daylight in the street.

In front of their house.

Doing pure science in Paris beside her wonderful Mohammed had been paradise, but it could never have lasted forever. And, of course, it hadn't. Returning to their homeland, to the birthplace they shared (that coincidence was what had first drawn them together in France), Mohammed had been forced to save her life and won her heart all over again. They had been required to flee, of course, assisted (for a steep price) by the local Mafiya.

Her two uncles had then pursued them to France to settle "unfinished business" and in despair she had asked Mohammed, "Is there nowhere on Earth where we can have peace?" Now, there was this Seventh Expedition, Mexico to Mars. Beliita hummed a tuneless tune herself, trying hard to forget (to whatever extent that it was known) what had happened to the first six expeditions.

If she had their baby on Mars, which seemed likely, she wondered what he or she would be like. They'd been trying for three years (back home, a capital offense in itself given their highly unconventional attitudes and beliefs) without success. Now, for the first time since they'd been together, they were trying to be careful. If she were to get pregnant at this point, they'd be ejected from the Mars program and have to go back to Europe.

"Beliita!" Mohammed suddenly shouted at her. "Come here! You must see this!" Having finished the sock, she folded it into its mate and put them away, standing up and stretching her stiff back. Through the circular open door of the BEAM, she could see the faraway horizon, where their future was just visible: a shuttle rocket of the kind that would take them up to the bigger ship being assembled and supplied in orbit was just hurling itself into the sky on a column of fire and smoke. This one, fully automated, was headed straight to Mars, where—if all went well—they would find its cargo waiting for them.

Even at this distance, the roar was momentarily unbearable, tearing at the eardrums, pounding at the temples, rattling the structure of the BEAM. Then it faded, accompanied by a thin sound of cheers from the colonists. At the moment, they were training, as they waited for the numbers to be right. Then, properly trained or not, they'd blast off on the first leg of a nine-month journey to the red planet.

A nine-month journey into the future.

Life, Beliita realized, looking at her flat belly, is a nine-month journey.

The gigantic flying machine could be heard across the desert long before it was seen, the pound, pound, pound of its jet-powered rotors filling the thin air over the simulated colony. It was a Russian Mil Mi-1006 heavy cargo helicopter, called "Halo IV" by the rest of the world. It was bringing in the last load of supplies, equipment, and the final dozen people for training. One of the last supply helicopters had been East American, the one after that was Indian. Mohammed was extremely glad to see this one; he was sick of curry.

The great eight-bladed aircraft set down, amidst a virtual tornado of dust and gravel, a few dozen yards away from the small cluster of half-buried cylindrical shelters. As the newcomers staggered under their backpacks, lugging suitcases into the artificial wind, the helicopter crew was offloading crates and boxes, roughly dumping them out onto the desert floor.

It's quite odd, Mohammed thought, how you pick up information. His people had been fighting Russians for at least two centuries. Without ever trying to learn such things consciously, he knew precisely where to place an AK-2150 metal-piercing bullet to sever a vital oil line, and just how to destroy the rotor hubs without damaging the cargo the helicopter carried. Mohammed didn't really want to know these things, but he did, nevertheless. It was almost in his genes.

Another part of him wondered what Comrade Santa Claus had brought them.

More work. It was always something. Fighting the horrible bulk of his training space suit, he levered himself painfully to his feet, leaned into the door, greeted his pretty wife with his eyes (she smiled back), tossed Jack's popgun—he wouldn't dignify it by calling it a rifle—onto his cot, and headed for the landing site to help with the cargo. Sometimes he thought about the horse in George Orwell's *Animal Farm*. "I will work harder," he quoted resignedly to himself.

The huge machine's whirling rotor overhead was more than a little intimidating, with its eight big blades. Although it was very tall, and the rotors were even taller, one's natural instinct was to duck, if not simply to cringe. The ground shook with the power of the two great engines.

They didn't stop. For some reason the pilots kept the helicopter's engines running as cargo was being offloaded. Mohammed could see bullet holes where he guessed the unarmed aircraft had taken ill-aimed fire from anti-government rebels. Ironic: a Russian helicopter being shot at by Marxist insurgents in Mexico. They were in that part of the country, after all. (That was another thing the feeble P90s were supposedly for.) The helicopter must have prodigious fuel tanks, he thought, to keep the engines running on the ground. On the other hand, fuel was relatively cheap; thanks to Thomas Gold's "crackpot" theories, everybody was an oil exporter these days, even Japan.

His first encounter at the landing site was a cardboard carton filled with broken glassware for their little laboratory. Useless. He gritted his teeth and glared at the idiot crewmen tossing cargo out of the helicopter. The half-dozen specimens he saw were slovenly at best, wearing soiled uniforms, one with a torn shirt pocket and a buttonless epaulet. Another wore a big, ugly grease stain. Even Mohammed's guerilla relatives would have been appalled by the sight. An unworthy enemy. Maybe the flight crew was better. He certainly hoped so. One of the sloppy unloaders looked back, grinned negligently, and shrugged. But they were a bit more careful after that. Good old-fashioned Soviet socialist worker "what-me-worry" mentality, Mohammed thought, and Russia wasn't even Soviet or socialist anymore. On Mars, it would probably get them all killed.

Where was MiG when she was really needed?

He organized a line of men—Reubenson was here, now— somewhat like a fire brigade, to hand the cargo down, and began assembling neat stacks of the cardboard cartons. Everything imaginable was in these boxes, including baby food (the expedition had no babies) and cheap Russian cigarettes, for an artificial atmosphere where oxygen was rationed.

Fine thinking, Russians.

Lackadaicality, he guessed the word would be, in the colony's official language. The trouble with Mother Russia was that, when she had rejected communism, she hadn't replaced it with freedom. Mohammed spoke four languages, his native Chechen, Russian, French, and English. He was working now on Mexican Spanish. His little Beliita was capable of fluency in nine and had promised to learn Martian. She made jokes like that, his Beliita did. He quoted Bradbury at her; *they* were the Martians, now. Or, at least, they soon would be.

Provided they got there in one piece. He thought about the broken glass.

And shuddered.

CHAPTER EIGHT:
BASIC

"The hardest thing to decide about other people,"
observed Conchita, "is, which ones actually know
something that you don't—they all insist they do, of
course—and which do not."

—Conchita and Desmondo
in the Land of Wimpersnits and Oogies

Julie knew certain strange individuals who would have loved
Marine Corps Basic Training, and even paid good money for
the experience. She recalled that there was a technical name for
folks like that: masochists.

From the moment they left their ragged, uncertain little formation beside the battered bus that had brought them all the way
down the east coast, they had endured the haranguing of their new
drill sergeant, who assured them that they were the lowest gaggle of
genetically unfit specimens he had ever seen—or smelled.

The small, wiry, intimidating black man could have recited the entire Declaration of Independence in that brain-splitting shout of his, or,
without a syllable of profanity, frightened some fresh boot out of his or
her statistical life expectancy with a look, or with one of his low growls
that could have ground glass. He was, Julie thought, a man of parts.

Following their initial browbeating, they all filed into the weathered one-story frame building that would be their communal home for the next dozen weeks, stowing their meager belongings where they were ordered. Almost immediately, they began to become acquainted with sand, dust, mildew, and mud—all of which northern Florida offered in abundance, along with every species and variety of poisonous plant, insect, and reptile known to North America.

The most recent of the United States of (East) America's many unfortunate foreign policy "adjustments" was occurring at the moment in the sweltering island jungles of the Southwest Pacific. Casualties were running high, and the attendant suicide rate was classified. Julie's group from the bus—her company, as it turned out—had been issued appropriate camouflage fatigues, which they also stowed. They were informed that the conditions here at Doolittle Field in the Panhandle almost perfectly simulated conditions in the islands.

Back outside, they were each given ("handed" would have been misleading; "caught as they were thrown at them" would have been more accurate) two ugly green plastic canteens—somewhat awkward, without a belt or any other gear to hold them—which they filled by turns from a rusty tap while the sergeant shouted at them, and were told they were "going to take a little walk" of about ten kilometers before they got an opportunity to eat. The fundamental idea, Julie calculated, was to determine which of the new recruits were going to present their sergeant with problems. Julie was grimly resolved that it would not be her. She reminded herself that she was supposed to be in hiding here. She meant to make herself as invisible as possible, and by doing just a little more than was demanded of her.

She was mildly surprised when that turned out to be relatively easy. Precious children raised by 3DTV and the public indoctrination system (neither of which ever expected anything difficult from them) were no match for a tough, skinny young girl who had grown up the hard way in the dark, lethal streets of Newark, performing dangerous tasks for illegal money.

In the end, Julie's experience of Marine Corps Basic Training was nothing to write home about—even if she'd had a home to write to.

She longed to write to her sister Millicente, but she didn't dare. She was supposed to be in hiding, after all. Military life disappointingly offered her very little that she hadn't been learning the hard way since she was a bright, hardened five-year-old, surviving the gritty life left to "peasants" in East America.

She was required, from time to time, to climb walls of differing heights and compositions, sometimes with the dubious assistance of her company members, the kids from the bus (the "rifles" they were eventually issued were far too fragile to stand on for this purpose, as she knew had been the practice earlier), to leap from platforms, to scale buildings of various sizes and shapes, and to clamber over random urban wreckage. The whole thing seemed pretty silly to her. She'd been doing that kind of thing for as long as she could remember.

If she had heard the pretentious word "parkour" she would have laughed out loud. Her acquaintances back at home played games that demanded all of the same skills and efforts: running, climbing, swinging, vaulting, jumping, rolling, quadrupedal movement, simply to avoid the cops, and it was considered fun. She'd generally avoided "playing," prudently saving herself for her work—in a trade where a sprained ankle might mean no food for a month—but she knew how to do it, better than most.

She went on cross-country outings with her barrack mates, along barely passable trails, up and down steep hills, laden with a fifty-pound backpack and other gear. Julie had been smuggling more contraband than that across a hostile city for almost a decade; the only difference now was when it rained (which it did almost every afternoon), she couldn't go indoors.

Climbing up a log wall was vastly easier than climbing a brick wall. Walking down a country lane inside a secured military installation was actually restful after the predator-filled alleyways and back streets of the city. Even the rucksack on her back was nothing compared to other bags she'd muled for the mob, full of West American currency, tru-metal coins, counterfeit IDs and license plates, and other such contraband.

You could never have printed such a thing on a recruiting poster, but how well a life of crime had prepared her for a career in the Marines!

For Julie, the mud was absolutely the worst. Over the following days, the ordinarily fastidious girl had been expected to crawl through it, to burrow into it. When the weather was dry; the mud was manufactured for them. Every inch of her was filthy, while live machine gun fire was sprayed over their heads. That exercise had killed two of them. It didn't seem to surprise anybody. She felt fortunate to have come from a neighborhood where death by gunshot was a more frequent occurrence than death by heart attack.

One young man—she hadn't known his name—died in eight seconds when he reached down to pick up a stick of firewood—and was bitten between his fingers by a coral snake. "Red On Yellow, Kill A Fellow." On the other hand, more than once they had all enjoyed fried meat from an alligator that had foolishly attacked them—it tasted like chicken. The jungle was full of delicious plants. They were beginning to learn that they, too, were creatures of nature.

Julie had tried to make friends. But it was as if her twenty-odd barrack mates had come from another planet or dimension altogether. They were nothing more than boys and girls, much more deeply concerned with their social media accounts and the audience-voted winners of several "talent" contests on 3DTV than with anything real—except for the food. It was surprisingly good, or at least it seemed that way. They all put plenty away after the first day.

The company's "natural" leadership eventually devolved upon a female from central Iowa named Beverly-Ann Salzman. At first, Julie couldn't figure out why. The "dirty blonde" young woman wasn't any brighter than anybody else in the group, or any bigger, or any stronger. She wasn't beautiful at all, and her figure was basically cylindrical. She performed in their military exercises at about an average level. Julie finally theorized to herself that nothing about Beverly-Ann was threatening—and that made her a popular person.

They had not been issued weapons yet. Their first weapons exercise was a class in fighting with a knife. They were each given a rubber dummy and ordered to hold onto them, neither lose them nor break them, because they were expensive. Julie had been threatened with knives, off and on, for most of her life. She saw the sergeant watching her especially closely during this knife-play.

Day after day, she and her new comrades crawled on their bellies under strings of razor wire, sometimes through gullies full of muddy, nearly frozen water (ice supplied artificially, like the mud), while live machine-gun fire whizzed by, just inches over their bodies. It wasn't all that different, she thought, from crossing through an intersection under dispute by rival street gangs.

On one occasion, however, somebody crawled over a ground nest of hornets, stirring the colony up, making the whole company consider risking the live fire (controlled by a computer) by standing up and running away from the vicious insects. Stung herself at least a dozen times, Julie was miserably sick for a week. It felt exactly like the flu.

Personal combat was more interesting to her. Julie had to remind herself constantly not to damage any of those she was thrown in with. While she had been muling Western money across Newark, they had all been attending prep school. Some even played a sissified form of football that the state had forced on them. One or two had learned martial arts from private tutors. Mostly they were here at a judge's order, to avoid jail for some childish offense they had committed, often for driving drunk, third offense. The one she enjoyed best was Reginald Frobischer III, a Connecticut aristocrat who fenced and played polo. Only he of all of them seemed to know how to hurt and get hurt without falling apart.

The others were learning.

"Pugil sticks" proved fascinating to her. Long, stout rods with ample padding on both ends, something like giant Q-tips, wielded the same way as quarter-staves in the Robin Hood movies. (In East American movies, Robin Hood always stole from the undeserving rich and gave it to the kindly government.) She'd never fought this way before, but took to it immediately, dunking each and every barrack mate she knew in matches fought on bouncing planks over a water-filled ditch, and never getting dunked herself.

Unarmed combat was merely a repetition of Julie's almost-daily experiences back home in Jersey, and it was here that she had to be most careful. The young woman had learned to snap a radius or an ulna—or a neck—long before she'd reached puberty. She could break an assailant's leg with next to no thought or effort. She did smash more than one expensively resculpted nose in Basic Training, entirely by accident. They had to learn the hard way that there's no crying in the Marine Corps.

There's no crying in the Marine Corps.

When they handed her what they insisted was a rifle, Julie felt very little but contempt. It was nothing but a fragile toy. Somehow, her family had managed, illegally, to hang onto her great-great-great grandfather's government-issued weapon from the First World War, a nine-pound 1903 Springfield meant to fire a cartridge called a thirty-ought-six, from which a bronze and lead projectile the diameter of a cigarette, weighing a third of an ounce could be launched at nearly three thousand feet per second, generating a ton and a half of kinetic energy. She had never had a chance to shoot it. Being hit by it must have been something like being hit by a truck.

That was a rifle.

By stark contrast, what they condescended to issue her was an FN P90 variant, a "bullpup" with its 50-round magazine lying atop the receiver, and a complicated system (highly prone to failure, she was willing to wager) for getting the tiny cartridges turned around and pointed in the right direction. It could hardly have made a difference, she thought. They were an inch and a half long, brass and bullet and all, and only .22 caliber. She could do more damage beating someone to death with the little gun than shooting them with it.

What was worse, was that the weapon could be controlled— turned on or shut off—*remotely* from some safe command-point not anywhere near the front. This was to avoid, they'd all heard it explained, "incidents" which might leave the diplomats and politicians embarrassed. Those in charge didn't seem to give a rat's ass that it might leave Marines dead.

Apparently, that's what they were for.

In an emergency, she might have planned to take the issue 20-round pistol away from one of the officers, but they were chambered in the same pathetically useless cartridge. She was grateful she now had her issue fake "Bowie" knife and wanted to thank the Marine Corps all over again. Not.

The form of her rubber foil had not changed since the 20th century's Second World War. It was weighted and balanced to emulate a seven-and-a-half-inch blackened blade, the M42, Camillus or Ka-Bar manufactured, with one long, sharpened edge, a pair of long "blood gutters" along the sides, and a much shorter, clipped and sharpened "false" edge up top. The real weapon would have a small steel cross guard, and a handle of stacked leather disks. A heavy steel pommel would complete the ancient design. This was an instrument made and tested for almost two hundred years, for fighting. Julie let the *faux* weapon spin across her palm and knew she had been born to do this.

"Saltzman!" the sergeant shouted. His name was Melvin Spanner, they had learned, but everybody called him "Sarge." His close friends called him "Wrench." He would not suffer being called "Sir" or saluted, because, he declared, as ancient tradition mandated, "I work for a living!" He was almost as small as Julie, and probably three times older, but a paragon of speed and energy. Julie could tell that he worked hard to keep the kindness from showing in his eyes. When he'd begun teaching them unarmed combat, everyone had received and worn proudly great blue-green bruises by his hands. He remained unmarked, although Julie was almost certain she'd landed a booted foot in his ribs.

"Sergeant, yes, Sergeant!" Beverly-Ann replied, snapping to attention.

"What's the Number One rule about fightin' with guns and knives, Saltzman?"

Julie could see she didn't know. "Use a spoon because it hurts more?"

"You young people and your movies. Latrine detail, all next week! Frobischer!"

"Sergeant, yes, Sergeant!" Reggie responded.

"What's the Number One rule about fightin' with guns and knives, Frobischer?"

"Uh, never bring a knife to a gunfight, Sergeant!"

"That's true enough," the sergeant said, "and good advice for all of us. But it's not the answer I was lookin' for. You'll be helpin' Saltzman out next week in the latrine. Segovia!"

"Sergeant, yes, Sergeant!"

"What's the Number One rule about fightin' with guns and knives, Segovia?"

Easy. "Run from a knife, Sergeant, and attack a gun."

"Very good, Segovia. I wonder who taught you that. Now, can you explain to the other boys and girls here why those are words of wisdom?"

"My big sister taught me, Sergeant. It's because anybody can easily run out of the reach of a knife, but you can't outrun a bullet."

"Your big sister, if available, could have a job in the Marines. Now, what's the only thing you can say for sure about winnin' a knife fight?"

Julie screwed her face up, trying hard to imagine what the sergeant was waiting to hear. Above all, she wanted to avoid latrine duty, if she could. She blinked. "Nobody ever wins a knife fight."

"And I've got the scars to prove it," he agreed.

"Segovia, we're here," said the sergeant, later that evening in the barracks, "'cause we're all they can get. There are rumors about you, why you enlisted. Trust me, the brass don't give a rat's ass what thug you eighty-sixed. They need you, that's all that counts."

Julie couldn't think of anything to say, so she didn't say anything.

"I called you 'cause I want to give you two things." He produced a document. "First, your orders. After you graduate, you're goin' to Officer Candidate School. The Marines—our Marines—need all the officer material they can get. Second, hold on just a minute, will you?" He went to his wardrobe closet and fished among the uniforms, producing an odd artifact: a very large knife in a metal-tipped black sheath.

"My eight-times-great grandfather carried this, when he was one of thirty thousand black men who signed on with the Confederate States of America to keep Yankee soldiers from molestin' their chickens and their women."

"Black Confederate soldiers?" Julie asked.

Spanner replied, "Never taught you that in Ding-Dong School, now, did they? That war didn't get to be about freein' the slaves till it was almost over. It was mostly about taxes. Bet they never told you Fort Sumter was a tax-collectin' station. I was gonna pass that blade on to another generation of Spanners but decided I didn't want to offer any hostages to history by havin' kids. It's all yours, now, so use it well."

She determined to look it up later. Meanwhile, she accepted the antique weapon from him, barely resisting tears, and drew it from its sheath. The 17-inch blade was darkened with age, but otherwise in perfect condition, and was two inches wide with a sharpened, clipped point just like the Marine Corps knife. The slim handle looked to be walnut, or some other native hardwood, and was pro-tected by a strap of steel that served as both guard and pommel, spanning the fingers holding the handle. "Hence the description 'D-guard Bowie' the sergeant explained.

Tentatively at first, Julie tested it in the air a little and tried a couple of thrusts. It was a worthy weapon, well capable of hacks, passing cuts, and point-work. More of a short sword than a knife, it most closely resembled a cutlass.

She said so.

"Just you be careful, young Marine. I honed it shavin'-sharp last night and wrote you up some MOS papers that'll let you hold onto it no matter where they send you."

CHAPTER NINE:
THE LANDING

As Conchita watched the ambulance go by, she said,
"You know, Desmondo, it's even worse to bring empty hands to a gunfight than a knife."
                                    —*Conchita y Desmondo*
                        in the Land of Wimpersnits and Oogies

T he makeshift little spaceship from the asteroid Pallas carried
       no acceleration seats or couches of any kind—they were just
       too heavy and took up too much room—but the four young
Ngu offspring sat on the plastic-laminated flooring, their backs
against the insulated inner hull, on what little padding their sleeping bags provided. They had all decided that, for only nine weeks at
merely one-tenth gee constant boost, they could endure it.

They had also decided among themselves, from the outset of
the undertaking, to travel to the red planet extraordinarily lightly, if
only for the sake of the valuable cargo that they bore—which was
presently fastened down all around them, and on the two decks
below them, in cardboard boxes and plasticized containers—and
the anticipated landing, only semi-controlled, after all, that they
were about to make, and for which they were all suited up, helmets
and all.

69

Not so much as the vessel's commander, but as his sister's older brother, Billy, nodded at Mirella, somehow long-legged and sensuous even in her baggy pressure coverall, who was acting as the mission pilot. She nodded back and smiled nervously at him. Her slender gloved fingers began to fly across her laptop's keyboard, strapped onto her thighs. Powerful gyroscopes beneath the little ship started turning and slewed them around—it felt just like a theme park teacup ride—pointing the engines in her flat stern in the current direction of her orbit around the red planet. All three of the recently refitted engines restarted simultaneously with an abrupt cough, jarring the ship and her anxious four passengers. The cough stuttered, becoming a rumbling roar.

Imperceptibly at first, they fell. At the proper moment, the small ship's engines still burning forcefully, an enormous fluorescent. safety-orange "balute" deployed high above them and inflated itself with heated helium gas, taking what advantage they could of the desert world's impossibly thin carbon dioxide atmosphere. For a while, Billy could watch the gigantic plastic balloon batting itself about through the thick plastiglass viewport slanted above his head where he sat on the deck. The balute seemed to be emitting brilliant yellow clouds that were lit up by the high-altitude sun. Billy wasn't overly concerned. Mirella had told him that it consisted, mostly, of a fine, dry powder that, among other things, acted as a lubricant, like talcum powder, helping the giant balloon to open freely. He kept his sharpest lookout—and his real concentration—on the virtual altimeter, and airspeed and fuel gauges on his own laptop.

The balute was partially ablative and was soon wrapped in a faint halo of flames. The underside of the spacecraft was protected by mineral tiles and its engines. Then, having performed its task perfectly to slow the falling vessel and moderate their descent, the balute was automatically jettisoned at exactly the correct predetermined altitude and velocity and sailed away on what little effective wind the nearly airless Mars had to offer at any altitude. Smokey the Bear might not have approved, Billy reflected, but on Mars there were no forests to set afire.

He heard Teal speak: "We thank you, Leonardo da Vinci."

As their ship descended toward the Martian surface, the four Ngu siblings felt little or nothing of the anticipated deceleration stresses—the stretched-out facial features, heavy pressure on their chests and spines—that they had been given to expect. The tough little Pallatian rocket ship did just about everything that they had imagined possible, and even more that they hadn't. It was performing its task admirably. Fritz Marshall would be proud of his *Zelda*.

She did rattle and shake them violently—Billy could hear stifled whimpers from his two younger siblings Brody and Teal—responding to various kinds of vibrations occurring simultaneously—different frequencies and amplitudes, in different directions—as *Zelda Gilroy* rapidly shed velocity and altitude. Several times solid objects of some kind—they may only have been high-speed grains of sand—struck the underside of the hull, startling them. She whistled and whined and keened loud enough to hurt their ears as fuel flowed through her hard-working propulsion systems, acting first as an engine coolant. And, of course, the thin Martian atmosphere—although it was more than a thousand times scarcer than that of Pallas or Earth—whistled through her undercarriage, along and through the hull.

Billy felt that his eyeballs were about to shake out of their sockets. He watched as a big cardboard storage container of computer printouts fell off a shelf it had been bungeed to, right onto Brody's head, and spilled everywhere. It was meant to be the ship's log, kept by the ship herself on their long voyage from their native Pallas. The box also contained careful records of her refit. Brody let out an indignant shriek, more in anger, Billy suspected, than fear. He was fully aware that Brody often felt the entire universe was out to get him—or his dignity.

On the other hand, his two sisters, Mirella and Teal, remained as stoically silent as they could and clung tightly to one another, Mirella's piloting tasks being completed. But nothing loose stayed in its place. Billy had believed he'd fastened everything down or put it away inside the vessel's many well-latched cupboards. But now, as a sharpened yellow pencil flew past his head, point first, and buried itself in the soft plastic safety rim of a viewing port, he knew that he had been wrong. It felt to him as if the spacecraft would flip herself over, upside-down, at any second. It was not unlike riding a beach ball supported by a fountain or a firehose. Or a flame thrower.

The engines cut off suddenly, a theoretically perfect three feet three inches from the gritty carmine surface beneath them, and the ship landed jarringly, bouncing slightly on her skeletal, spring-loaded landing structure. Red dust outside rose and fell again in only a second in the virtually airless environment. For an eerie moment, they sat and listened to the various clanks and ticking of the rapidly cooling engines, then the grounded craft lurched suddenly, as one of her four landing struts beneath them collapsed, or maybe sank into the powdery orange sand. The deck now stood at an odd angle, perhaps ten or fifteen degrees off level.

Outside, they could see their first "sandbow": multicolored refractions from superfine silica dust suspended in an extremely bright light. It was the very stuff the red planet's massive year-long dust storms were made of.

No matter the angle, thought Billy to himself. She wasn't going anywhere, ever again. Her overworked engines would never roar again. She would never see the unobstructed stars again. At best she would be a cherished museum exhibit for centuries to come. But the tough little spacecraft had done her job splendidly, almost without a hitch. They were, all four Ngu siblings, alive and perfectly uninjured. The good ship *Zelda Gilroy* had touched down on Mars.

Billy said, "Teal, communication with Pallas, please."

His younger sister flipped a toggle, switching signals from her earphones to the cabin speakers, cutting off a Spoonies commercial. "Spoonie! Oonie! Oon—" Teal started tapping keys on her laptop. "*Zelda* to Pallas," she told it. "*Zelda* to Pallas. We are here on Redball, down and safe, as planned."

"That's good to know, dear."

"Mom!" On the weeks-long voyage here Teal had spoken to her mother almost every day. They had all found it comforting.

"Yes, dear, your beaming father is right here beside me. Is there anything you need to tell us? Otherwise, I'll sign off now to avoid our being overheard by unfriendly strangers." They never knew who might be listening, occupation military and police of various kinds, including those, it was rumored, who were about to be sent to Mars—mostly United Nations agencies Pallatians knew as "Yoonies."

"Okay, Mom. Say hello to Dad. Thank Mr. Marshall for us. *Zelda Gilroy* over and out."

A strange quiet fell over them again. Damn! They were on Mars! Another stunned five minutes passed in sharply punctuated silence, then, curiously, they all heard a polite, even diffident knocking at the compartment's hatch. Billy cautiously shuffled the slide and recocked the hammer of the powerful Grizzly .45 Magnum automatic pistol that had been his father's parting gift to him, in the antique holster he carried on his belt, opposite a big, strangely curved Nepalese military knife called a *kukri*, the famous Gurkha knife. (He'd prudently emptied the chamber and lowered the gun's hammer just before the entry burn.)

He grabbed a handy stanchion and dragged himself to his feet, suddenly feeling incredibly heavy in the Martian gravity, which was six times more powerful than what he'd been born and grew up in. He had trained physically for this, but it was like climbing out after two or three hours in a swimming pool. Staggering from one brace-point to another across the slanting deck, he finally reached the hatch. Like many early spacecraft, *Zelda Gilroy* had no airlock. They would all have to keep their space suits on if they wanted to open the door. He left the thick inner, transparent plastiglass hatch in place—it was as close to a vacuum as it could be out there, and indescribably *cold*. Moisture began to condense and run down the inner surface of the door as Billy slowly cranked the outer door open.

Just outside, standing on an upper rung of the boarding ladder, was a fantastic figure. Billy tried to appreciate the historic moment properly, but it was just too funny. The valiant crew of *Zelda Gilroy* had just met their first Martian.

The strange apparition before him affected an atmospheric-style space suit, or rather, overlapping parts of several such space suits, displaying different colors: red, green, yellow, and blue, all patched, sewn, and glued together skillfully from what Billy guessed were the issue space suits of several previous expeditions—perhaps all of them.

The man's first- or second-generation helmet seemed to be filled with hair and beard more than head—it was a wild, grizzled blond—but it couldn't quite conceal the stranger's humorously sparkling blue eyes, and the warm, welcoming grin in his weathered, wrinkled face. At his waist he had hung—without a scabbard; risky in a pressurized garment—an enormous, gleaming, curved sword, obviously hand forged, edged with huge, jagged teeth. To Billy, it seemed very familiar somehow.

"Welcome to Barsoom, Earthlings!" the man proclaimed proudly. The radio frequency scanner on Teal's laptop passed the man's helmet-transmitted words along. Billy noticed that a hand-sized solar panel, glued to the back of his helmet, took the place of batteries, "I am John Carter, Jeddak of Jeddacks … no, no, that's not quite right … I'm actually … I'm … well, I can't quite remember who I am, today. It happens. I'll look it up just as soon as I get back home and let you know!" He eyed the outsized .45 Winchester Magnum pistol on Billy's hip, the big forward-curved knife on his belt, and gripped the grimy, cord-wrapped handle of his weapon a little tighter, possibly worried he'd brought a sword to a gunfight.

You're also about as crazy as a bag of frogs, thought Billy, who hadn't actually seen that many frogs. He'd practiced most of what came next over and over again in front of the full-length mirror on his bedroom door at home: "We are not Earthlings, sir. I'm William Wilde Curringer Ngu, the son of Emerson Ngu, of the Pallatian interplanetary spacecraft *Zelda Gilroy*. We have come to help the latest colonists to this planet—who are Earthlings—if we can."

The apparition replied, "Well, I ain't your latest ghudamned colonist, sonny-boy. I hiked all the way out here t'help *you* folks, if y'need it an' y'ain't too proud t'admit it. I don't need no help, myself, thankee very much. Over yonder, 'bout a dozen klicks or so, you'll find the latest croppa them newbies. Poor little kids don't know if they're shittin' or it's Wednesday, but they're gonna need all the help they can wangle, pretty damn bad, and soon. Understand me, it's Springtime hereabouts just now. Wind don't amount to all that much at its worst, but the bloody winters are a whole different kettla mudbugs. Whatcha bring 'em? Gotta tell ya, this here crate of yours don't look all that palatial. Where y'all hail from?"

"*Pallas*, my friend, a planetoid. The second largest of the Belt Asteroids. Historically, it was the first of what we call the Terraformed and Settled Worlds. My brother and sisters, here, and I were all born there, and there are four more of us Ngu kids back home. It's a very pretty place, even if I say so myself, with tens of thousands of deep-blue, perfectly circular lakes, white-crested mountains that you wouldn't believe, thousand-foot trees of all kinds so lofty it takes your breath away, and a brilliant, multicolored light show every dawn and sunset, caused somehow by the atmospheric canopy. It's where we're all from. Did you happen to remember who you are?"

Billy was beginning to feel more than a little self-conscious about leaving the poor old man outside in the cold, using up his oxygen, teetering on the top rung of the boarding ladder. What would his mother think? But *Zelda* had no airlock through which the fellow could be invited inside.

After several moments' embarrassed silence and a bizarre display of several tortured-looking expressions, the elderly figure standing before Billy informed him haltingly, "It's right here on the' tippa my brain. Just call me 'the Old Survivor,' son. Everybody else does.

"Who in the hell is Zelda Gilroy?"

CHAPTER TEN:
THE CAVES OF MARS

"I think there must be a difference," Conchita told
Desmondo, "between stepping outside your comfort
zone, and stepping onto the railroad tracks in front
of a locomotive."

—Conchita and Desmondo
in the Land of Wimpersnits and Oogies

"We're supported by my father, Emerson Ngu, and the
Pallatian spacelines founder Fritz Marshall, among
others," Billy explained to his hosts. They were all
crowded together in what seemed like a giant plastic bottle: Billy, his brother Brody, their two sisters Mirella and Teal, and several members of the UN/US Martian colony, located several dozen
yards inside the yawning mouth of a gigantic "lava tube" cave.

The entrance was at least a hundred yards across, and perhaps
seventy-five high. Jack Reubenson, the mission commander, assured
them that it was a rather modest example of such geological—
rather, areological—features. They could see, perhaps two miles
deeper inside, sunlight streaming down on a pile of rubble beneath
what was called a "skylight" where the cave roof had collapsed for
unknown reasons perhaps billions of years ago.

Billy wondered to himself what made the colonists believe that the cave-roof so high overhead wouldn't collapse again right here, where they were now. But he kept that question politely to himself. Using this areological feature was actually a practical strategy, he realized, to protect the colonists from the severe solar and space radiation that the ghostly Martian atmosphere failed to shield them from, as well as from a more or less continual shower of micrometeorites. In this way, it was much like the world-spanning, smart, plastic environmental envelope of his own native Pallas. To a degree, it also helped with the ubiquitous wind-blown Martian dust, which was unimaginably finer than talcum powder, a concern that ultimately need not worry the colonists inside their enormous cave.

His remarks about his father and Fritz Marshall earned him some suspicious and hostile looks from several of those present; to these Earth-people, or, more importantly, to the East Americans among them, as well as their Yoonie-influenced allies, thanks to a lifetime of government propaganda and bigoted mass media, all too delighted to spread politically useful falsehoods, William Wilde "Wild Bill" Curringer, for whom Billy was named, and his own father, the great Emerson Ngu, were branded "robber-barons" and legendary villains, like the Emperor Napoleon, Adolf Hitler, Donald Trump, or Vladimir Putin.

"They organized a consortium," he told the colonists nevertheless, "that helped us cobble together a transport vehicle capable of landing safely, *once*, in this planet's gravity, bringing you—the victims of what was certain to be the East American/United Nations space program's next 'regrettable tragedy'—as much of the stuff we calculated you would badly need, as we could."

"What's all this 'stuff' gonna cost us?" asked a heavyset individual whose name, they had learned, was Roger Leigh, apparently the machinist for the expedition. Except for his curly hair and massive beard, his features, including his expression, were indistinct, backlighted as he was by multiple dazzling floodlights mounted on the cave's ceiling high overhead. Billy could make them out through the translucent plastic of the bottlelike Bigelow BEAM. "None of us here has any money to speak of, or much of anything else that you rich Belter sonsofbitches would want."

77

"Yeah," demanded somebody else they'd introduced as Schulman, "why don't you just pack your crap up and go back to Pallas?"

There it was again, Billy thought with frustration: the prevailing attitude on Earth, or at least in East America. Lots of people from there suffered from the incorrect assumption that, because the Pallatian settlement had been founded by a billionaire, William Wilde Curringer (it was a bit, he realized, like being named after George Washington—or even worse, Christopher Columbus)—all Pallatians were rich. But, in fact, the asteroid's culture had been created by individuals and families no better off than these colonists.

Of course, the Ngu family were wealthy—now. Emerson Ngu had started literally with nothing but the clothes he stood in and a price on his head for having escaped from a Yoonie agricultural commune when he was eight years old. He had worked hard and smart ever since then to create what he and his family now possessed and enjoyed. But he and his wife, System-famous xenoarchaeologist Rosalie Frazier, had brought their children up to bear their good fortune with as much grace and dignity as possible.

"We do have 3DTV out here," offered Mirella, "including broadcasts from Earth. We have probes and telescopes of our own. For too long we had to stand by helplessly and watch your predecessors on this world die. After six failed expeditions we got sick and tired of it. We don't want anything from you, Mr. Leigh. We're doing it for ourselves."

"Not to mention jamming our dirty Belter thumbs in your government's eyes," added Brody, grinning. One recent candidate for President of East America had exhumed Hillary Clinton's ancient epithet, referring to the Settled Worlds of the Asteroid Belt as a "basket of deplorables."

"How the hell can you know what we need?" Jack Reubenson demanded, still unconvinced. Taking in the structure they had gathered in, it occurred to Billy that the expedition commander was not a happy camper. Despite half a dozen stringent exercise regimes Reubenson was attempting to follow faithfully, despite the improvised barbells now piled in one corner of his quarters, and the spider-web of bungee cords he'd likely exercised with assiduously on the way here—272 days in free-fall—the long, gravity-free voyage from Humanity's home world had severely wasted his musculature away. Nor had it been particularly good for his bones. His clothing hung limp on his once-athletic frame. He was far from alone in this unenviable condition, and only slowly beginning to recover now.

But sadly, sufficient protein to support his efforts to recover was in short supply. Against both practicality and principle, he probably hoped secretly that these intrusive strangers had brought him a T-bone.

Medium rare.

"Well, we couldn't exactly call you up on the phone and ask you what we should bring, now, could we?" Mirella answered Reubenson. "Because then your bosses back on Earth would know what we were up to. Instead, we brought you what *we* would need."

"Oh," said their previous detractor, Schulman, "caviar, then?"

"Yeah," Teal told him, "and no caviar for you!"

"Bosses?" Despite a lifetime spent struggling against the political and economic strictures of a collectivized society, it had never occurred to Reubenson before now to think of his superiors in the UN/US Space Program as "bosses." If anything, they were nothing but useless chair polishers, bureaucrats, deskbound bean counters to him, highly over-politicized administrators who cheerfully sent others out to take the risks. Secretly, when nobody but his comrades here were listening, he called them "pencil-necks."

"Somehow, they already seem to know, anyway," Teal added. "Not that they can do anything about it except generate a lot of irritating noise. On the way down here from Pallas, we had to listen to endless unbroken weeks of high-megawattage propaganda from Earth, rabid screaming, official outrage, and the direst of threats imaginable both to us and to you from the East American government, numerous enviro-crazies, and the Yoonies themselves. I can play you some recordings."

"No need," said Reubenson. "We've been hearing it, too." He and Mohammed and Roger didn't know quite what to make of "little" Teal Ngu, a slender female taller than they were, yet not quite a woman, who expressed herself like one of their college professors. Knitting quietly on a nearby cot, Beliita Khalidov discovered that she liked these four adventurous children very much. She hoped, if she ever had a daughter, that she would be like Teal. Maybe a little shorter. Somehow aware of the exotic ethnic makeup of the current UN/US mission to Mars, they had won her over completely by presenting her with a shining copper samovar and matching tea-glasses in wire frames.

"Given the obvious limitations of our little ship," said Billy rue-fully, "it was pretty much a one-way trip. For better or worse, our fate is now the same as yours. So try not to waste the effort, okay?"

The Old Survivor had offered to guide the four Pallatians to the makeshift, extensive cave-dwelling of the East American Seventh Expedition's underground settlement. "Sub-arean," they agreed should be the word, the equivalent of "subterranean." It had promised—and turned out—to be a long walk. The old man had explained that he appeared there at irregular intervals, bringing the current generation of suffering colonists food that he obtained from someplace he refused to talk about, and little bits of salvaged technology from the six previous expeditions. Billy and his siblings had worried about the ambient radiation.

As the four Ngus, their informal colonial reception committee, and the Old Survivor himself gathered in one of the cylindrical BEAM shelters, it became uncomfortably apparent that, under his brightly colorful patchwork environmental suit, the old man wore nothing but perhaps a loincloth—there was that "Jeddak of Jeddaks" thing again—and that he didn't seem to be much of a believer in frequent bathing or deodorant. His enormous, curved, jagged-toothed sword he had politely left outside the shelter.

He would share the colonists' meals and the alcohol they had learned to make, telling them tall tales from previous expeditions. All that was missing was a campfire. Then, after one of his enig-matic visits, the Old Survivor would disappear for days, weeks, or even months at a time. The Ngus learned that the Earth colonists all assumed that he, too, was a cave-dweller. Given the massive water flow in its deep history, and its once-violent volcanic activ-ity, the planet was riddled with one kind of cave or another. The only things they didn't have to worry about were the spiders and snakes—and bats—they'd encounter on Earth. None of the set-tlers had been able to spare the time or energy to track the Old

Survivor back to his lair. Right now, it was all they could do to concentrate on raw survival.

The colonists had only begun working on sealing off the enormous cave entrance and the "skylight" and the work was going very slowly. Moving from shelter to shelter within the huge settlement, the Ngus met several disillusioned would-be Martians. They had become fast friends with the Khalidovs—to their mutual surprise and delight, Mirella had actually read some of Mohammed's papers. Several others had invited them into their humble, cylindrical homes, half buried in the Martian soil inside the vast cave in an attempt to keep their occupants warm and reduce radiation and other hazards.

Each of the little shelters was served by small gas bottles—they reminded Billy of propane containers—brought by hand from the solar-powered oxygen refinery outside, that they had used before he'd brought them a portable cold fusion reactor.

Although Billy knew perfectly well that he and his three siblings would probably be stranded on this cold, forsaken, airless desert world for the rest of their lives, he had no regrets. But he was anxious to get on with what they had come here to do, especially after the Old Survivor's warning about the coming winter. To begin with, they would need help carrying their equipment and supplies from the inert *Zelda Gilroy* out on what he thought of as the prairie—the radiation-saturated prairie—to the settlement.

The Ngu sisters had also brought with them the seeds, spores, ova, and sperm of a myriad of organisms potentially useful for saving the Martian settlers—who had absurdly been prevented from doing the same for themselves by various religious-pressure groups back on Earth. The girls thought it would be especially nice if they had some chickens and pigs.

Next, Billy and his siblings revealed their biggest surprise to the already shocked and overloaded colonists. They had begun, the newcomers confessed, to distribute spores—when the balute had opened—of what the Pallatians knew assorted environmentalist fanatics back on Earth would soon come to denounce heatedly as an "unauthorized and environmentally damaging organism" across the red planet's cold, almost airless surface.

The spores were even lighter and finer than Martian dust. Carried by the high-velocity, but extremely feeble, winds, it was an organism potentially capable of transforming Mars—converting the little world to a welcoming shirt-sleeve environment—in mere decades, virtually by itself. The red planet was about to become the Orange Planet, and finally, the Yellow Planet. Within their lifetimes, these new Martians would no longer need to lurk in caves, no matter how capacious. They would eventually have an atmosphere overhead to protect them.

"It's a composite organism, you see," Mirella explained, "much like the lichen you find on mountain rocks back on Earth, which is a symbiotic partnership between a fungus and either an algae or a cyanobacterium."

"A what?" asked Roger Leigh.

"Commonly called 'blue-green algae,'" Teal answered, "unrelated to other algae."

"'A difference that makes no difference ...'" Leigh quoted James Blish.

"Unbelievably," she told him, "we found it on the asteroid Ceres, flourishing in hard vacuum and at near-Absolute Zero. It is tiny in its natural state, and has almost microscopic tubules, something like the rhizomes on strawberry plants, that it fills with oxygen, metabolized from water in the asteroid's carbonaceous chondritic soil, apparently as a defense against opportunistic virus and anaerobic bacteria, which also grow in extreme cold and vacuum. Apparently, there's an entire ecology out there, and this plant is at the bottom of the food chain."

"And this is significant to us, why?" asked Reubenson trying unsuccessfully to stifle a yawn. "I gotta tell you—a botanist, I am not. I'm an engineer. Plants bore me. I prefer creatures with eyes, human beings in particular."

"Because we took samples of it home to Pallas with us," Mirella explained, "and Teal tinkered with it genetically. She grew those tubules into the size of macaroni. We believe that, compared to Ceres, Mars will seem like a tropical paradise to it, and the organism should flourish here, maybe even explode, population-wise, producing enough oxygen to transform the whole planet. It will spread and grow completely without our help, and the biomass it produces will have hundreds of uses from foodstuffs to textiles. You'll be able to build roads with it."

Already, as they'd heard on the way here, furious critics, such as a powerful environmental group calling itself the "All Worlds Are Earth" society, led by its thundering chairman Timothy Strahan, were filling the airwaves between planets with tirades and threats in frantic anticipation of the Pallatians' evil influence on the colonists and their expedition. The society didn't know precisely what that influence would consist of—nothing had been said in public yet, about what the Ngus called "macaroni plant"—but Strahan and his fanatic ilk didn't want any settlement on Mars at all, and many of those in government secretly shared that opinion. Once the man learned about the revolutionary organism Teal and Mirella had found—or created: the current version was very different from what they'd discovered on Ceres and taken home to their genetic laboratory on Pallas—he'd likely have a stroke!

In her own way, Teal was just as impatient as Billy. She could be excused for that, perhaps. She was sixteen. She'd gotten her Ph.D. via the Solarnet when she was fourteen.

"Mirella ran across the original lichen," Teal offered, "whose characteristic tubules were almost microscopic, on our one and only trip to Ceres, so far, with Brody here, who was with the initial pre-terraformation survey team."

"If this were back on Earth," Mohammed interrupted, "East America—especially, the environmentalist wacko—would have stopped the terraformation cold, right there."

"Out here," Billy said, "we think people are more important than shrubs and lizards and dead, empty worlds. And we also understand the dual function of city lamp posts—half illumination, half political expression."

Mohammed and Roger laughed. Reubenson tried not to.

"But despite the hard vacuum," Teal went on, "temperatures approaching Absolute Zero, and the complete aridity, the stuff was thriving on what it took out of the ground. It was, as Mirella told you, an organism consisting of a partnership of fungus, algae, and perhaps even a photosynthetic bacterium."

"Sounds vaguely obscene," Reubenson observed. Roger laughed again.

"The really electrifying scientific news it represented," Mirella said, "was that, taking what it needed almost entirely from the carbonaceous rock it lived on, it inflated its tiny tubules with pure oxygen, apparently, as I said, as a defense against hostile microorganisms—which means, as I also said, that there must be an entire vacuum-based ecology out here that we never suspected. When I publish my findings, bacteriologists across the Solar System will begin looking for what the more sensationalist websites will be calling 'space bugs.'"

"Now they've found them," Teal volunteered, excited, "on the outside of several satellites and even at a space station!"

CHAPTER ELEVEN:
ECOREVOLUTION

"Coffee and tea are what they call 'social lubricants,' Desmondo," Conchita explained. "They've helped more people communicate than the telephone."

—Conchita y Desmondo
in the Land of Wimpersnits and Oogies

B rody spoke, "Our baby sister, Teal, however, took her genetic research in a completely different direction. Anything that can produce oxygen out in space, she reasoned, from practically nothing, is potentially invaluable to a population, like ours, who live in a place like this."

Teal replied, "Your 'baby sister' Teal's foot is going to be up her twin brother's ass, if he doesn't stop patronizing her. Tell me, sir, what degrees do you have, anyway?"

"Ooh! Touchy, aren't we? Shades of degreeism. As you know perfectly well, Sister Dear, I have my J.B.M.I. with Honors, from the U.H.K.—that's 'Just Barely Making It' from the University of Hard Knocks, Settled Worlds Division. Our own father doesn't have any hoity-toity degrees, nor Billy, here. I chose to spend my own precious college years getting dirty, growing calluses, getting a space suit suntan, and laboring with the proletarians of the Ceres

Terraformation Survey crew out in the cold and vacuum, just like your little moldy friend. That's how you and Dr. Mirella, here, ended up traveling there with me."

"Licheny," Teal muttered, almost to herself.

"What's that?" asked Brody, raising his eyebrows. "An ancient crime like loitering?"

"Licheny. It's only partly mold."

"Anyway," he misquoted, "she nursed it, rehearsed it, and gave out the—"

"I studied it," Teal interrupted, "determining its double-barreled genome. Triple-barreled in some cases. I played around with the stuff, producing Cerean lichen in every color of the rainbow. Most importantly, I greatly increased its size and the oxygen-containing volume of its tubules, until anybody who saw it lying in a Petri dish understood immediately why I decided to call it 'macaroni plant'. It was exactly the size, shape, and color of the stuff in the blue cardboard box—cooked pasta, slathered with melted cheese sauce. Very good, sprinkled with dill weed."

Brody said, "Ugh. I prefer it with ketchup." His own favorite comfort food was cream of tomato soup—admittedly with a couple of nice, fat grilled cheese sandwiches on the side.

The tubules of the final version of the altered organism (Teal would have been the first to admit that it was not, technically speaking, a plant) typically grew along the ground until they were one or two inches long, then split, like the letter Y, into two more tubules, this process repeating over and over until—on Pallas B, at least, the airless natural moon of her home world where she had safely conducted her initial experiments—they began to form a thick, yellow mat.

If there had been anything at all to hold it down—sufficient gravity, like the Earth's, or a plastic envelope, like that of Pallas itself—Pallas B would soon have possessed its very own oxygen-rich atmosphere. But the little moon's proprietors—a communications company that had begun with the asteroid colony in Curringer, Pallas's principal town, as KCUF, for many years the world's only radio (and later, 3DTV) station—drew the line at anything that might attenuate or interfere with their precious, highly remunerative signals.

Like, an atmosphere, for example.

"I understood perfectly, of course," Teal explained, "and I didn't really mind. It was their moon, after all, papers filed and properly claimed. And thanks to their physical presence there, conditions on Pallas B are slightly less hostile than those on Ceres. It's warmer—3DTV and radio transmitters throw off a lot of heat—and, thanks to our world's giant orbital reflectors—bathed in a lot more light."

"Get on with it, kid," said Brody, impatiently.

"Get on with yourself, Aloysius Brody Ngu. This is my damn story and I'm gonna tell it my own damn way. There's increasing evidence, too, that the original organism Mirella discovered was subsisting, in part at least, on cosmic rays. Just imagine—photosynthesis from the death-cries of dying stars."

"Teal!"

"Brody!"

"These young people," Mohammed observed in his kindly way, "could probably do well with something relaxing to drink, but alas, they are too young, are they not?"

"You'll have to ask them," Billy answered. "Pallas was built mostly by 'young people' who wouldn't tolerate the kind of laws and customs you're worrying about for a minute. The commonest age of "consent" is sixteen. But tell me. Dr. Khalidov, your expedition was actually issued a liquor ration by the Puritanical States of America and the Muslim-dominated United Nations?"

"Oh, my, no!" said Mohammed. "But did not a great Prophet once prescribe, 'Take a little wine for thy stomach's sake'? Is it not abstinence, then, that is blasphemy? They did force bicycles on us, one for every powered wheel we brought with us. Two solar-charged electric automobiles. We were stuck with eight bicycles, instead of an equivalent mass and volume of food or equipment. Look around at the terrain. Can you think of anything more useless than a bicycle on Mars?"

Reubenson laughed and added, "We have *six* bicycles now. We took the other two apart and built ourselves a carbon-fiber vacuum still. We have plenty of powdered potatoes that nobody wants to eat, but they do make pretty acceptable booze."

Roger Leigh nodded vigorously.

"When we run out of potatoes, we will try powdered corn or carrots or beets." Mohammed sounded enthusiastic. Billy wondered if there were such a thing as a "Jack Muslim."

In due course, a motley assortment of cups, glasses, and jars was assembled and passed around the cavernous tunnel, followed by an aromatic container of clear liquid. Billy took a first sip and struggled manfully to get his breath back. It reminded him strongly of the Irish drink *poteen*. It tasted absolutely terrible, but it was certainly alcoholic, which was what seemed to be called for.

Teal refused to be distracted. "No, I don't want a drink, thank you, but I would like to finish my story. My altered lichen had flourished on Pallas B. By the time Billy and my naggity brother, here, recruited me and Milly for their Mars project, I was confident that our macaroni plant would someday transform this entire planet and leave it a lot more pleasant for people who want to be free. Like the ancient philosopher Freeman K. Dyson said once, 'Who wants to live where somebody like Barack H. Obama—or was it Richard M. Nixon?—can turn off the air?'"

She concluded, "Which is why, everywhere I go on Mars, I am determined to spread macaroni plant spores."

"She's devised all kinds of clever means and devices to distribute spores," Brody said, nodding. "So I've taken to calling her "Johnnie Macaroni Seed.""

"Not seeds," Teal told him belligerently. "Spores."

"If it works," said Beliita, "I shall be very happy to call them anything, my dear. A frozen, airless desert world is no place to raise children. But the authorities will not be happy back on Earth."

"They're never happy," Mohammed observed. "Back on Earth."

"And there's even more, now," said Billy, "to make them unhappy. Although I am aware that your greenhouses here will soon be fully operational and productive, we've brought along about two tons of food that you can't grow easily, and many of the sweet surprises that make living worthwhile—the makings for a great chicken noodle soup, for instance, my mom's own recipe, and a great lobster bisque, which happens to be my favorite."

"And Spoonies!" shouted Teal, "Spoonie-oonie-oonies!"

"Several dozen pounds of chocolate!" Mirella exclaimed, "Like the Force, both light and dark.

"We've also brought you hot dogs, mustard, ketchup, and relish," added Mirella. "You'll have to supply your own diced onions. Deodorant, tampons, and other sanitary supplies. We even brought you a potato chip maker. You should try it with parsnips. We brought bacon and we brought frozen steaks—filets mignon—blue crabs, mudbugs—that's crayfish to you Yankees—and salmon. We also brought mustard *seeds*, salmon and crayfish eggs."

"Yeast for beer," Billy added, "and genuine whiskey making. Hops, too. Marijuana seeds, because tobacco—don't worry, we did bring a few pounds with us—is too damned hard to grow and there are domestic uses for hemp."

With a sour look on his face, Reubenson said, "We've learned to substitute dried spinach for tobacco."

Mirella carefully put down a coffee cup she had been given earlier and accepted a small jar of homemade vodka. The cup had been 3D printed out of some kind of tough, heavy, utilitarian plastic, but its contents had represented, she realized, an act of tremendous kindness and generosity on the part of the colonists, whose supply of the bean had to be severely limited. Happily, the brave little *Zelda Gilroy* had carried with her fifty pounds of fresh, Pallas-grown coffee.

Mirella preferred hers French roasted and black. With chicory.

"We first discovered macaroni plant's basic genetic material on Ceres, the largest of the Belt Asteroids, where, as a not-quite-microscopic organism, we stumbled across it—I'm a botanist. I was just along to keep my sister company—during a routine pre-terra-formation survey. To our surprise, it was thriving at Absolute Zero, in hard vacuum."

Looks of mild surprise on her listeners' faces surrounded her. It was a different group than before.

Mirella was retelling the story that had brought the four of them here, for perhaps the dozenth time, as the four Ngus traveled from shelter to shelter inside the great cave, being introduced to the colonists, of which there were forty-seven, altogether. One, a West American named Mama Sue, had died during the landing. She'd been buried with honor a few miles away, where their landing capsule had come to rest.

("Saved my neck," Roger Leigh had told them, "literally. Threw me down in my seat and told me to strap in. Landing came awfully quick.")

As she sat on a folding cot, Mirella leaned forward to emphasize her words, apparently unaware that she was communicating—with the expedition's males, at least, Billy thought—as much with her long, dark eyelashes, her gorgeous eyes, and her other physical assets, as her words.

Not that her other assets were all that visible, in her bulky, unfeminine environmental suit, Billy reflected, but interestingly, Mirella simply carried herself like the beautiful young woman she was, and people all around her noticed.

She would probably have been highly insulted, her older brother realized, if he'd suggested such a thing to her, or dared to call her a "girl," as he was naturally inclined to do. (He'd looked it up: in Shakespeare's day, the newly minted word had simply meant a youth of either sex—Mirella had just turned twenty when this possibly quixotic adventure had begun.) Or perhaps the young scientist was pragmatic enough to understand exactly what effect she was having.

Some questions, he realized with growing wisdom, are best left unasked and unanswered.

The world-changing organism that Teal and her sister were calling "macaroni plant," had been developed by Billy and Brody's gifted siblings, which was why they had journeyed to Mars with their brothers. The hardy not-quite-plant, they explained, grew from something like rhizomes, like strawberries, and cuttings, as well as spores. Immune to the Martian cold and lack of atmosphere (if the plant could speak, Teal observed, it would proclaim Mars to be a tropical paradise) it could be expected to proliferate thickly wherever there was the slightest amount of water and enough solar radiation and starlight to support it.

Through its fine, complex system of rootlike threads that penetrated the soil and burrowed down into the ubiquitous Martian permafrost, it also brought water to the surface. Mirella and Teal had discovered that it could be cooked and eaten in an emergency (they hadn't said what it had tasted like), rendered down to make lubricants and even fuel, or fermented and distilled to make a powerful whiskey. For a while they'd considered calling it "shmoo-gunk" after Al Capp's useful—and delicious—cartoon creatures.

Before very many months passed, Teal was convinced, the stuff would cover both Martian poles, and would steadily gain other territory, as well—like the caldera of Olympus Mons and the slopes and arroyos of Valles Marineris. Soon traces of oxygen—along with nitrogen and other byproducts of the plant's natural growth and decay cycle—would be noticeable with instruments, if not yet breathable, everywhere in the thin, cold atmosphere.

"A day will come surprisingly soon," she told them, "in the thickest patches out on the macaroni plain, in broad equatorial daylight, when an individual can walk without a helmet or a mask, his feet releasing oxygen from the tubules as he crushes a path through the macaroni plant. Of course, should he return and try the same thing at night, however, when there's no sun and photosynthesis isn't working, he would surely die."

"Before long," Mirella added, "in startling contrast to the planet's ancient red sandy deserts, huge patches of yellow macaroni plant will become easily visible by telescope from Earth. Mars will become the 'Yellow Planet,' and it will be shirt-sleeve inhabitable."

The scientific females confessed to their hosts that they had considered many other names for the peculiar stuff: "oxymold," "happygrass" (but that had sounded too much like something else), "tubeweed," "kudzuroni," and, as they'd said earlier, considering all the other uses to which it could potentially be put, "Shmoo-gunk," after the highly useful little egg-laying, milk-giving, whiskered meat animals in Al Capp's *Li'l Abner*. However, nobody around them got the two-hundred-year-old reference. The lichen was a recombinantly engineered, genetically tailored fungoid, highly photosynthetic, and, when it had grown from its spores, the size, shape, and color of its namesake, ordinary macaroni and cheese.

"What I'd really like to know," said a youngish woman who had been introduced to them as Dolly Policastro, the Martian expedition's agricultural expert, "is what effect this lichen of yours is going to have when we start raising crops. Does it grow on other plants? What does it do to the soil?"

Mirella blinked. "We did test it thoroughly. It has the same effect that lichen does at home on Pallas and Earth. None, whatsoever, unless you're a big old oak tree. But maybe you'd better tell me how you planned to raise crops on an airless world."

"Cold too," added Brody.

Dolly responded, "We're building a headquarters and community-center building inside the cave, here, for meetings, recreation, and our infirmary. Our first big building outdoors will be this greenhouse we're talking about with big, movable aluminized mylar reflectors. We have a lot of seeds and cuttings for special high-nutrition crops."

"Like broccoli!" Roger Leigh muttered.

Several people laughed.

The woman considered. "Maybe we can plant some of what you've brought, as well." She held a printout in her hand, a list of what the Ngus had brought with them. "We didn't bring any asparagus with us. Takes a couple of seasons to get started. An unforgivable oversight and entirely my fault. I love asparagus, and I'm not the only one here."

"Maybe they left it out," Brody observed, "because it makes your pee smell funny."

No one had an answer for that.

Teal said, "If we can figure out where to raise our animals, you'll have fertilizer, too. We could have guinea pigs and hamsters running around in a few weeks. Real pigs soon after that."

"Don't forget the chickens," said Mirella.

"You Pallatians actually eat guinea pigs and hamsters?" a man exclaimed. He had a pleasant voice and a middle-class English accent. Just now he wore a disgusted expression on his face.

"Not so far, Dr. Gabb," Teal confessed. Gabb was another Earth scholar, English, a prolific author whose individualistic works they were all familiar with on Pallas and had probably gotten him exiled here. "We actually raise several different breeds of cattle, and sheep and goats and ostriches and emus back at home. Llamas. And all kinds of wild game—it's what we're most famous for. But I'm more than willing to try eating anything that doesn't eat me first. I understand that the ancient Aztecs thought well of eating hamsters."

Gabb shuddered. "The ancient Aztecs thought well of eating chihuahuas—the original 'hot dogs' I assume—and of human sacrifice, as well, by the thousands."

"Well, then, I'm glad I'm not an Aztec," said Teal. "In this incarnation, anyway." Her siblings laughed. Teal didn't believe in reincarnation. She was the least mystical among them.

They were interrupted abruptly by someone squeezing through the flexible airlock at the front of the cylinder. When he took his helmet off, he revealed himself as "Moose" Holder, the expedition's communications officer.

"Sorry t'disturb you folks," he told them in a heavy Texas accent. "But I got us some bad news. The East American government an' the Yoo-nited Nations're sendin' a company of Marines our way 'cause they say we're ruinin' their plan. Booze insteada bicycles an' suchlike. They're callin' it a "punitive expedition'. Say they're gonna be here in two-hundred an' seventy-two days."

Billy stood, resisting an urge to hunch over under a roof that wasn't that low. "Maybe not as bad as you think," he told them. "We also brought you guns and ammunition. Lots of them."

CHAPTER TWELVE: THE AVENGING ANGEL

"Gosh, Desmondo," Conchita told her little cousin, "I hope they're wrong and that we won't grow up and give up 'all this freedom nonsense.'"

—*Conchita y Desmondo*
in the Land of Wimpersnits and Oogies

Timothy Albert Strahan sat back in his five-wheeled swivel chair behind the very large mahogany desk in his office at the Washington, D.C. headquarters of the organization he had created more than a decade ago and still headed: "All Worlds Are Earth." Its mission, generously supported by wealthy East American donors who shared their government's misgivings and distaste for adventures in space, was to prevent the despoilment of other worlds in the Solar System and beyond.

Strahan was an extremely large man, in his late fifties, slow-moving with a thick neck, blocky shoulders, and a big square belly. Late night comedians and conservative radio talk show hosts who dared to speak of him, mostly West Americans, called him "Gumby in a thousand-dollar suit," and sometimes compared him to a tree stump, but he made certain that there was nothing about his outward appearance that was not completely conventional.

AWAE (as it was sometimes called) was equally concerned with the importation of materials and products from offworld. A set of new and controversial equations from Penn State University claimed to show that the Earth's crust, burdened by the increased mass of these ill-conceived imports, could slow and crumple like tinfoil as the molten bulk of the world beneath it turned, destroying everything on the surface and killing every living organism on the planet with what were referred to as "super-quakes" and "super-volcanoes." Legislative moves were being attempted in various state legislatures, the (East) United States Congress, and the United Nations, to outlaw materials imported from the rest of the Solar System, but they were being stalled by all the usual deniers. As was to be expected, West America—which derived a considerable fraction of its GNP from trade with the rest of the Solar System—was stubbornly refusing to cooperate and even laughing about it.

The individual whom Strahan regarded across the aircraft carrier expanse of his desk was his direct opposite in many ways, fully as tall as the AWAE director, but very emaciated looking under his worn and faded yoked cowboy shirt, his frayed Levi jacket, and his almost colorless jeans, with long, stringy gray hair and an equally long, stringy beard. "Orrin Porter Rockwell" was the *nom d'guerre* the fellow Strahan had strongly urged the fellow to assume, from Mormon history, for the sake of the message it would convey. Strahan's research department had given him the idea. The man had been born Arthur Leander Malevsky of Rome, New York, but he had relocated to Utah with his parents when he was a child.

Rockwell/Malevsky was the reputedly ruthless commandant of "Gaia's Guardians" a guerilla organization that would do (and had done) practically anything to achieve their goals. In most jurisdictions, even the police were afraid of them. On his belt, tucked halfway into his right hip pocket, he carried a custom five-inch Bowie-style knife (illegal in the District of Columbia), designed by the legendary Elmer Keith and rumored to have been fashioned by the fabled bladesmith Gil Hibben, himself. It was said to have cut more than one throat. Rockwell's traditional Western attire included a bolo string tie—its slider was a tiny silver stick of dynamite, crossed with a miniature monkey wrench—that was invisible behind his beard. His favorite weapon was said to be a short-barreled revolver in .327 Federal Magnum. Like the original Porter Rockwell, he styled himself "The Avenging Angel."

Ordinarily, these two individuals, who happened to be political allies, took considerable care never to be seen or photographed together. Rockwell's radical and sometimes violent group was secretly associated with and funded by AWAE—and perfunctorily denounced by it from time to time. The current emergency on Mars, however, had moved the two leaders to cast their precautions aside momentarily. Their respective organizations and several other environmental socialist groups across the Mother Planet were publicly furious with what they imagined was happening on Mars and had referred already to the presence of the hated Pallatian capitalists on the red planet as a "disease."

Those heavily hair-sprayed "celebritators" whom various West American media referred to as "news floozies and gentlemen of the evening"—figures on the eastern nation's officially sanctioned 3DTV news networks—had eaten it all up like chocolate birthday cake. They had been deeply disgruntled several decades ago when no living organisms of any kind had been discovered on Mars that they could have condemned the colonists—or better yet, those detested spawn of the Pallatian criminal Emerson Ngu—for endangering.

But Strahan held a rage-wrinkled computer printout in his hand at the moment and shook it in Rockwell's weathered face, even though the fellow—and the way that his long-fingered right hand tended to hover over the conspicuous bulge under his Levi jacket on the left side of his chest—usually made him extremely nervous. Nobody he knew of was keeping count of the lives this man was supposed to have taken; nobody dared or wanted to.

But what Strahan had just read on the never-to-be-sufficiently-damned printout, filled him with a greater anger than he could remember ever having experienced over his long career as an ardent environmental advocate and strident public opponent of all irresponsible technological change. Which, for practical purposes, usually meant *any* technological change. Not for the first time, he wished that he could openly call himself a Luddite. If he worshiped anything, it was the spirit of Ned Ludd.

"Where the hell did *that* come from?" Rockwell asked. He'd had to suppress a reflex or two, to avoid drawing on the man sitting across the monumental desk from him. Unconsciously fulfilling the observation, made long ago, that, lacking other prey, the left would eat each other, he wondered how many rare and endangered tropical hardwood trees had died, just to provide Strahan with that ostentatious desk—it was no different, in principle, from displaying a tiger's head on the wall, or a zebra's hide on the floor—and what an appropriate punishment for that would be.

"En route, from the Seventh UN/US Mars expedition's designated political officer, Margaretha Inez Ghodorov. She was originally to have been the leader-in-chief of the Mars mission but suffered an unfortunate and fatal 'accident' on landing. Earlier, she had been its official commander, but as soon as they were underway, beyond reach, and nobody could do anything about it, she got shunted aside by this Reubenson thug and his minions, his henchmen, his buttboys, whatever you call them, in what was only the first of their many offenses to come. Poor old MiG, she was compelled to use her weekly personal slot on the vessel's comm system to contact us. The woman's sacrifices must not go unacknowledged, Porter. They're so arrogant in their insubordination up there, that they didn't even attempt to stop her sending this."

Reminding Strahan, somehow, of an old-fashioned undertaker, Rockwell shook his odd, oblong, cadaverous head, swinging his long gray, greasy locks. "Explain to me one more time what they're up to, again. Adapting mildew for life support, is it? I don't get it."

Once more Strahan repeated patiently to Rockwell, whom he had discovered long ago was not a particularly imaginative fellow, everything he'd been told about the sinister asteroid-born, yellow, branching fungus that generated oxygen. The amazingly maddening fact was that the two young female scientists who had discovered it and brought it to Mars were none other than the slut daughters of the notorious capitalist pirate Emerson Ngu. This whole series of disasters was becoming an environmentalist's worst nightmare.

"That little slant bastard again!" the famous Guardian Angel exclaimed angrily. There was that reflexive gesture, Strahan observed, Rockwell's hand hovering near his shoulder-holster. He

97

was beginning to believe that it was unconscious. "Why didn't that fucking loser, Gibson Altman, just put him down like the rabid dog he was, when he had the chance?"

During an era when most people still cared, a couple of generations ago, Altman had been the sexually disgraced United States Senator who had been placed in charge—more as a punishment than a reward—of the United Nations' experimental agricultural commune on Pallas, named after the 19th century socialist newspaper editor Horace Greeley. Half Vietnamese and half Cambodian, Emerson Ngu had escaped from it as a boy and begun making something of a splash with his inventions and other dubious undertakings among the criminals and anarchists who illegally occupied the rest of the asteroid. Numerous attempts to haul him back home to his peasant parents had failed in the corrupt and disputatious Pallatian environment.

"He did try, at least once—only the incompetent idiots killed Ngu's trollop, instead, turning a merely dangerous enemy into a fire-breathing avenger. But Ngu never really gave Senator Altman a sporting chance. He was usually surrounded by his fellow riffraff and rebels in Curringer once he got out. He still is. And the obscenely gigantic pistol he was infamous for carrying back then is now hanging on his youngest son's hip—on our once gunless and peaceful Mars!"

"Eldest," Rockwell corrected Strahan. "Intel says his second eldest, Drake, is about to sail off in that starship of theirs, and that his father is thinking about going with him, spreading his evil to the stars!"

"Whatever." Strahan shook his head. "I tell you, Rockwell, this 'macaroni plant' thing is a deadly insult to everything we've striven after for decades! It's the ultimate invasive species! It's a cancer that's going to spread like wildfire across the soon-to-be-formerly red planet, despoiling the natural surface of an entire world! It's what these people seem to be all about!"

"Save your pretty poetry for the 3DTV audience, Strahan," replied Rockwell impatiently. "That pistol—or a hundred more like it—shouldn't prove much of a problem to me. Matter of fact, I know that gun, the LAR Grizzly .45 Magnum, pretty well. Once manufactured in my home state: it's old, it's slow, it's heavy, and it's obsolete, just like the idiots opposing us. I swear I'm gonna go to Mars personally if I have to, to deal with these spoilers."

Horton Willoughby III, the sitting President of the (East) United States, sat—in the Oval Office, as usual—on one of the generous faux leather sofas ordinarily reserved for guests, watching a press conference on 3DTV. What made this particular press conference unusual is that it emanated from something like fifty million miles away, on the surface of the frozen desert planet Mars, and had been very skillfully edited to minimize the otherwise noticeable effects of the considerable lightspeed time lag between the two planets. Sitting behind the President's desk, as usual, the President's wife, Helen MacClellen Willoughby, made rude, snorting noises at the six video-screens they were watching.

"The rebellious colonists, blatant ingrates every one, whom the United States of (East) America and the United Nations had generously selected to be pioneers to the red planet," were being interviewed, after a peculiar fashion, on West American network 3DTV, an awkward and difficult technical undertaking, with the current fifty-minute transmission lag. To speed the process up, the interviewers' questions had been submitted over the Solarnet in advance, and were now being presented as inserts, answered "live" by the colonists standing in their space suits just outside the cave they dwelt in, and their new allies, the four deeply hated Pallatian transplants. Strangely, despite their suits, each of them held an umbrella over their heads. The dangerously subversive signal was being tightly censored in East America, of course. The nation's most powerful jamming transmitters were being overworked. The "Fist Lady" had seen to that, herself.

"To begin with, please allow me," disarmingly honest-looking Jack Reubenson had pronounced into the camera, what was actually almost an hour ago, "to take this opportunity to publicly declare that we no longer consider ourselves 'colonists' or 'visiting Earthmen'—"

"Or Earth*women*," interjected his agriculturalist, Dolly Policastro from under her parasol, along with several other females, present, on- and off-camera. Everybody laughed. Together, they seemed more than a bit like a bizarre Greek chorus—consisting of Harpies, Willoughby thought to himself. And he, of all people, ought to know a goddamn Harpy when he saw and heard one.

"And Earthwomen," a grinning Reubenson corrected himself. "We are all *Martians*, now, maybe the first in four billion years, maybe the first ever. And we are fully committed to changing this world of ours to suit us and those who will come after us."

How very fucking boring! Willoughby had already grown tired of listening. Senator Maxwell Promise and the rest of his East American government were as anxious to avoid the dire political consequences of their many failed domestic policies as any administration in American history, which was why they had stumbled into this mess. Willoughby didn't share their necessity. He thought of himself as a realist: as an objective student of history and human nature, he freely acknowledged that he was merely an apolitical placeholder, and that he had been chosen when Chen decided to arrange for a change of political regimes in Washington, as the man had previously done on more than one occasion, because of a widely shared perception that Willoughby wouldn't—or couldn't—do any further damage to the status quo.

As usual, the political players and their various operatives were all scrambling to find plausible scapegoats for East America's continued misery, safely outside of their respective spheres of influence. His own wife Helen, for example, who had inherited the interest, energy, and outright lust for power from her father, a former longtime United States Senator, already had the perfect victims in mind: these "Martians" who refused to behave themselves properly, and their execrable, despicable, *deplorable* Pallatian accomplices the Ngus, who, from Helen's perspective, had fallen onto the Martian surface like a gift from the Heaven she didn't believe existed.

Reubenson went on to describe openly what had already been started for them by the Pallatians with their lichen spores. Perhaps to spare his new friends the political and environmentalist fury from back home, he treated it as if it had been the "Martians" own idea, inadvertently confessing to conspiracy. Horton squirmed a bit nervously, hoping it wasn't too noticeable. He couldn't wait for this nonsense to be over with. The truth was, he didn't give a rusty fuck what happened on Mars.

Helen, it happened, had an appointment in New York City this afternoon with Senator Maxwell Promise, and afterward, she was planning to go shopping and stay overnight with her widowed mother. Thanks to this building's ultra-efficient filters and ventilators, he knew that, by the time she had been gone half an hour, no trace would remain in the White House air of her poisonous perfume. Best of all, he had finally found another attractive and compliant secretary, and had plans of his own for tonight.

His wandering mind snapped back to attention. It was that Reubenson fellow again: "Now we're aware of the detachment of Marines headed in our direction. You Earthfolks might as well order them to turn around and go home, if that's physically possible. You can't control all of the cameras and all of the telescopes in the Solar System. Everything your thugs do here is going to be seen by everybody on Earth. Is that what you really want?"

"Yes!" the Fist Lady answered the 3DTV image.

The President did wonder. Was this perhaps the time to rid himself of Helen? Her flight might suffer some tragic malfunction, and sympathy for the widower that he had become would cause his numbers to soar. Could he trust others to act for him in this? There were ex-Special Forces people who owed him favors.

Once again, using the United Nations as a front for the hundredth time, the Willoughby Administration (which spoke with a thousand voices, none of which was identifiably Horton Willoughby's) had angrily threatened to invade Mars, to arrest the colonists it now called "insurgents," and haul them "back" to an Earth, some of them—the Pallatian contingent— had never seen, to be publicly tried and imprisoned or even executed for the crime of "ecotage"— environmental sabotage. The Pallatians' nasty artificial organism transforming the planet was to be destroyed by any means necessary, forthwith, not because it was a bad thing, or because it was doing a bad thing, but because it was unauthorized—had been granted no official right to exist—which, in the administration's view, was the ultimate bad thing.

More concerned with satisfying a bloodthirsty public sentiment that they had manufactured themselves, than with accomplishing anything real, the administration had decided to send a "punitive expedition" to the red planet, consisting of the only major spacecraft East America possessed, a single, hastily converted "warship"—the same former heavy lifting freighter that had taken the colonists to Mars and dumped them there in the first place—recently refitted and rechristened the *US/UNSS Retaliator*, bearing a company of (East) United States Marines, commanded by the ruthless and controversial Colonel Mehetabel (meaning "God rejoices") Atherton-Nye and her second-in-command, the infamous Major Grenville Swope.

Asked about Timothy Strahan's recent public charge that the Martian colonists' "irresponsible plan" was to destroy the pristine natural surface of an entire planet, Reubenson laughed out loud and replied that their plan was simply to stay alive, and that the "pristine natural surface of Mars" mostly resembled a horrible case of acne, which—with the help of their new Pallatian friends—they were presently in the act of curing, using the macaroni plant.

CHAPTER THIRTEEN: OVER THE MOON

"It's kind of sad," Conchita told Desmondo. "People will go further, and do more, to punish those they disapprove of, than to improve their own lives."
—*Conchita y Desmondo*
in the Land of Wimpersnits and Oogies

Private First Class—soon to be Brevet Lieutenant—Julie Segovia, unlike her big sister Millicente, had never been much of a believer in superstition or coincidence. She had never so much as wasted her money on a lottery ticket.

Nevertheless, as she sat now, suited up and strapped down into the acceleration chair she had been assigned aboard the newly refitted *US/UNSS Retaliator*, she wondered about "synchronicity." She had originally enlisted in the East American Marine Corps to "get out of town" after executing her sister's brutal Russian "Mafiya" pimp, a necessary and simple act of extermination, like stamping on a cockroach, in her view, that left the world—or at least Newark, New Jersey—a better, cleaner place, and which she did not regret in the least. Now, through a series of bizarre and unlikely events, she was about to "get out of the planet."

Julie reflected on how it had all begun, eleven weeks into a seventeen-week Officer Candidate Training program. In many ways, it had been a lot like Boot Camp, only far more strenuous and physically demanding, with a lot of classroom time and homework thrown in for good measure. Julie had enjoyed that; it was the first chance she had ever had in her life to "go to school." The washout rate was an intimidating fifty percent. Marine officer candidates were supposed to have four years of college education under their uniform web belts, but thanks to a dozen "brushfire wars" across the battle-scarred face of the Earth that the East United States was waging, the Corps was desperate for mid-level leaders.

Julie, who had been taught to read by her sister, and who read everything that passed before her eyes, had no trouble keeping up.

For the rest of it, she obligingly hiked, climbed, performed clambering exercises, rappelled, jumped from fixed-wing aircraft on parachutes and from helicopters on ropes, and generally excelled at anything resembling acrobatics. The rifle practice was a bit of a joke, however. Marines were currently issued a tiny "carbine" of Belgian design that she was sure was delayed revenge on the world for Brexit. It fired 5.7x28mm ammunition, hardly more powerful than ordinary sporting-use .22 Magnum. What was worse, the weapon could be turned off remotely, from behind the lines, to prevent "unfortunate incidents."

In between, she read, studied, and went to class. She even found an instructor willing to fence with her, he with an Olympic saber, she with an *epee* cut down to 17 inches, with a fat button swaged—forged—for safety, onto the blade tip by a friend of his in the Motor Pool. This served to emulate the enormous Confederate D-guard Bowie knife her D.I. had given her in Boot Camp.

Then, late one evening, there had come a diffident knock at the door of her quarters. At her little desk, in a warm pool of lamplight, Julie sandwiched the yellow pad she was taking notes on into the textbook she was studying from, closed the latter, and put her pencil down. She stood, pulled her blouse down straight, and took the two steps necessary to reach the door.

She opened it.

"Segovia?" asked a tidy young man she didn't know.

"That I am, Private: Segovia, Corporal, Julia Conchita, one each. What can I do for you?"

"You're to report to the Colonel's office immediately, without telling anybody where you're going."

"The Colonel" was the commander of this training base. A glance at her watch told her it was 11:15 in the evening, just fifteen minutes before Lights Out. She grabbed her issue flashlight off the desk, only to notice, halfway down the hall, that the Private already had one. "Oh, well," she told herself, " 'Be prepared' should be the Girl Scouts' motto, too."

The young man escorted her across the graveled road circling inside the compound to a large frame office building she knew well. It was where she attended most of her classes every day. They climbed the stairs. One floor higher than she'd ever been before, she was conducted to the reception area of the Colonel's office, noisy and crowded now with other OCS students like her. She wished briefly that she'd had a chance to change her uniform.

The bosses didn't care. The Colonel entered the crowded room. He was a tall individual with long, flowing blond hair and a goatee like General George Armstrong Custer. He was accompanied by a real General, a Marine Corps Brigadier Julie didn't recognize, a Navy Rear Admiral, and a sinister-looking civilian. But after military rituals involving standing at attention and saluting, it was the Colonel who spoke first: "Marines, what I tell you in this room stays in this room. Anyone who breaches security will be summarily executed. This is not a joke."

A shudder went through the crowded office.

"You may already be aware from various unsecured sources that a crisis of interplanetary proportions is looming over our newest colony on Mars. A group of interlopers from the outlaw settlements on the asteroid Pallas has arrived there and is stirring up trouble, as Pallatians are inclined to do. Our colonists were already guilty of having unjustifiably altered the modified Zubrin Plan that had been laid out for them in advance, making unauthorized use of the expedition's assets, for example, to brew and distill alcohol."

A muffled undercurrent of stifled laughter went through the small crowd. These were, after all, Marines. Military men of every historical era had found unconventional and unexpected ways to make themselves a drink. Submariners were once famous for imbibing the fuel of torpedoes—until the weapons were switched to hydrogen peroxide.

A Marine himself, the Colonel didn't even try to silence them, and he refrained from telling them that the expedition's idiotically inappropriate bicycles had been used to manufacture the liquor, which would only have turned the laughter uproarious. He simply continued. "Now these Pallatians, a small group consisting of four children of the rogue industrialist Emerson Ngu, have introduced a semi-artificial organism they maintain will transform the planet into a—well, you can't exactly say 'an Earthly paradise,' now, can you?—at the expense of the natural environment. This, the government has decreed, in conjunction with the United Nations Council on Environmental Ethics, cannot be permitted."

Julie wondered why. From everything she had learned about the angry red planet, any change to Mars would be an improvement—including blowing it up to make more asteroids.

"Your President," the Colonel intoned, and everybody knew they were in trouble, "has commanded that this mission be carried out as promptly and aggressively as possible: pack your lightest. You will be transported to Mars aboard the *US/UNSS Retaliator* to restore discipline and good order to the colony there. Mr. Rockwell, here"— he indicated the civilian—"is going with you. If you are resisted, even in the slightest, you will be authorized to employ deadly force."

Together they had trooped aboard the spaceship in their hastily cobbled together red-brown-and-black camouflage, fully armed and heavily laden, jogging up the boarding ramp for the sake of half a dozen 3DTV cameras trained on the otherwise secret mission, possibly for future propaganda use.

It wasn't much different from getting aboard a commercial airliner: the *US/UNSS Retaliator*, resting in the winged cradle of its booster, would take off horizontally from an ordinary runway. Their weapons, of course, were unloaded—and taken from them as soon as they were through the hatch and out of sight. Rockwell held onto the small revolver under his left armpit. Julie kept her swordlike Bowie knife, presenting the Specialist credentials Sergeant Spanner had given her at various checkpoints on her way to her seat, midway along the aisle in the passenger section. Not for the first time, she wondered who the man had known.

There were no enlisted personnel aboard. Some genius of a Roddenberry fan had decided that this was a job for the officer class only, both full-fledged and larval, peasant armies having proven increasingly unreliable in several theaters of combat recently. Julie knew it was a big mistake. Her sergeant had advised her that fresh officers had to spend a couple of years *unlearning* what had been drilled into them at OCS or the Academy. Certainly everything that she'd learned so far in the Marine Corps, everything that was worth knowing, she'd learned from an NCO.

One of those things was to keep her mouth shut, which she did now.

When the ship began to rumble and gather speed, Julie didn't feel it as much as she'd thought she would. Perhaps because the takeoff was essentially horizontal, like that of an airplane. The process did seem to go on forever, though, interrupted only once when the vessel's giant booster wing assembly ran out of fuel and dropped away. It was piloted, and made its way, gliding downward, to the landing field below; The Chief Pilot would announce when it was home safe.

They had learned, somehow, that people cared about things like that.

As soon as the great wing was clear, the ship's main engines fired, filling the hull with head-splitting noise and almost unbearable vibration, driving the *Retaliator* into orbit, where it met the refueller and replenished itself. As a part of the redesign, the central section of the ship began to rotate, sparing its passengers the muscle- and bone-eating ravages of freefall which otherwise would last for nine months. Those aboard the ship would not be directly aware of its rotation, except for the mild illusion of gravity it provided. Looking out one of the windows would show the observer a rotating star field. But there were very few windows in this converted freighter's hull.

Julie knew that, from the bow and aft sections, where the pilots and, respectively, the engineers were located, massive aluminized mylar photon sails would be unfurling as soon as the acceleration phase was over. Perhaps half a mile across, they would help propel the ship to its destination a couple of weeks sooner than anyone was expecting.

Maybe they could use that couple of weeks to their advantage.

As soon as the *Retaliator*'s seat belt light went out and its rotating hull-section restored the feel of gravity under her feet—Mars standard, one-third gee—Lieutenant Colonel Mehetabel Atherton-Nye (known behind her back as "Meh"), commander of the United States Marines' First Punitive Expedition to the planet Mars, regarded her image critically in the mirror before she left her quarters to address her troops.

She approved of what she saw.

Atherton-Nye was a slender, wiry, surprisingly strong woman. Her skin was darkened and leathery from many years of difficult military service in tropical environments. She liked to tell reporters that she'd been named for some ancient and obscure female leader of warriors, but the disappointingly mundane fact was that her mother and father, both plain Ohio farmers, had named her for an early 20th century cartoon cat, although in ancient Hebrew it meant "God rejoices." Her deepest regret in life was that she hadn't been born British. Her second deepest was that, at this point in her career, she wasn't yet a general. She thought of herself as a victim of the "brass ceiling."

Atherton-Nye's right eye socket was discreetly covered with a kid-leather patch on a band around her head. She owned several of these, in different shades, to match her various uniforms, although she also owned a perfectly presentable artificial eye. This patch was sand-colored, from her recent campaign in Persia. She would switch to red when they reached Mars. That, and her English-style swagger stick—twenty-one inches of polished Equatorial hardwood with decorative ends made from large-caliber cartridge cases—were enough to identify her for the average 3DTV viewer as the controversial "Terror of Persepolis."

She had lost her eye to a native assailant with a double-edged, curved dagger in North Africa. A large and livid scar protruded from the bottom edge of the eyepatch and curved down and around to her right jaw. She owned that dagger now, called a *jambiya*. It was at home resting in her trophy case. She wore the attacker's teeth on a strand of cord around her neck, under her uniform jacket and shirt. She'd killed the man, herself, with four soft, heavy slugs from the antique .455 caliber revolver she always carried in a large, flapped holster at her waist. By her order, the would-be assassin's corpse had been publicly wrapped in the gutted carcass of a pig before burial.

Before she exited, she turned to her second-in-command, Major Grenville Swope, who had just arrived. "How is everything out there, Grenny? How are the troops taking to acceleration, zero-gee, and artificial gravity?"

The man looked up from his keyboard. "Well, ma'am, they are Marines. And quite a few of them are women. That is not entirely an unmixed—"

"Very good, Grenny. I'm asking about their health. It wouldn't do at all to have this uniform plastered with gobbets of vomit. I just had it cleaned. Bring your keyboard along. We'll go and talk to them."

"Yes, ma'am."

Swope, unlike his commanding officer, was probably better off having left Earth. There was a fabulous price on his head—an even billion dollars in gold, currently on deposit in Switzerland—offered by the people of several Pacific nations where he had directed the murders of millions of men, women, and children. He was a shortish, lumpy fellow in a perpetually wrinkled uniform, with bulging eyes and deceptively stubby-looking fingers, who went everywhere with a computer keyboard suspended on a narrow ribbon of Kevlar around his neck. He played it like a musician in a rock band. This, among other things—among many other things—was the device that could determine whether or not the Marines' 5.7x25mm carbines would operate. They, he thought, were his orchestra, and he was their conductor. He was their organ-grinder, and they were his monkeys. He also carried an FN 5.7x25mm pistol that had not been slaved to the keyboard.

Their orders—which they had just unsealed and were about to pass along to those who would be expected to carry them out—had been extremely simple. The most important parts had been delivered face-to-face, nothing "sensitive" written down. On paper, and on 3DTV, they were going to Mars to "help" the struggling colonists. After all, the American west (at least in the movies) had always had its palisaded fortresses and its rescuing companies of U.S. Cavalry. Off the record, Atherton-Nye and Swope had been commanded to batter the insurgents back into line with the Congressionally modified Zubrin Plan, no matter what that required. Porter Rockwell had been sent as the President's personal liaison.

In certain quarters, Colonel Atherton-Nye was known—in various non-Indo-European languages, which seldom got translated in East American media—as "The Village Burner." The West American media were onto her, however. They revealed that she had faced investigations for brutal and sadistic war crimes, more than once, and four court-martials (which had acquitted her). She was also known as the "Butcher of Burlington," for having led a savage but successful military expedition to keep Vermont and New Hampshire from seceding from East America, following the example of West America. To people like the Willoughbys, she was a hero in the Civil War mold of Ulysses S. Grant and William Tecumseh Sherman. Many in the current administration questioned how appropriate it was to place her in charge of this mission. Others felt that her past made her the perfect individual for the job.

Exiting her tiny office/quarters, she stepped out into the area holding her troops, beret on her head, swagger-stick under her arm. She was grateful for the spin on the ship. It was difficult to maintain dignity and discipline in freefall. They were an outsized company of Marine officers and officer candidates, thrown together for this unique purpose. They were remarkably young and, for the most part, abysmally undertrained. Swope had divided them into platoons, with an older, more experienced man (or woman, she thought approvingly) to tell them what to do. They would be up against amateurs, albeit armed with the same weapons they had. This expedition should be a piece of cake and might just win her full colonel's birds.

One step away from general.

CHAPTER FOURTEEN: LOST IN SPACE

Conchita said, "Desmondo, what are you going to do when we get home to where there have been no governments for three hundred years? I'm going to take a very long, hot shower,"

—*Conchita y Desmondo*
in the Land of Wimpersnits and Oogies

Those aboard the *US/UNSS Retaliator* were compelled to practice an odd variation on "hot racking." On many a naval vessel, bunks were constantly occupied, in rotating eight-hour shifts. In East America's one and only interplanetary passenger spaceship at the moment, the acceleration chairs could be folded down flat, but there wasn't room enough to flatten them all at once, so only a third were flattened at a time, and sleeping shifts arranged accordingly.

Marine Brevet Second Lieutenant—a very different thing, indeed, from a naval lieutenant—Julie Segovia was not altogether dissatisfied with this situation. As a little girl in Newark, she and her big sister had sometimes suffered much rougher accommodations, in burnt-out and tax-abandoned buildings, for example, one of them standing guard over the other, by turns, against night-predators of every imaginable variety.

One good thing: now that she was farther beyond reach of the long arm of the law than anybody in history (it never occurred to her that this expedition, of which she, ironically, was a part, was an extension of that long arm), she could use the ship's facilities to send e-postcards to Millicente, and let her recuperating sister know that she was okay. She'd even heard back, once, so far. Also, on this trip, unknown to anyone around her (she had lied about her age to get into the Marines), she would pass her eighteenth birthday. She wished she had an address for Lafcadio, too, but it was probably a lot healthier for him that she didn't.

Julie had given up any expectation of physical privacy when she had enlisted in the Marine Corps. Showering aboard this interplanetary vessel, for example, was done in large, transparent, zippered plastic bags, invented by NASA long ago for zero gravity, half a dozen of them hanging on the walls of a common bathroom area. There was only one place aboard ship where she could be alone, but a person could only go to the toilet so many times a day.

One morning, about three months into the nine-month voyage, there appeared to be no water for the showers. She had turned the tap, and nothing came out but groaning noises. As she'd been instructed, Julie got dressed again and made her way forward, pulling herself through a forest of upright acceleration chairs, past flattened furniture with sleeping Marines strapped to it, to the tiny cubicle that served the Colonel's aide, Major Swope, as an office.

Where the man slept, she had absolutely no idea, and didn't care to know. To her, he resembled some kind of crouching, evil toad, and she had caught him leering at her more than once when she was trapped in a shower bag with only her head sticking out. She didn't really understand why he was interested. It was just remotely possible, she thought, that he saw her as somewhat attractive, even if she herself believed she had a figure like a boy.

As she raised her fist to knock on the flimsy panel, it flew open abruptly. She was almost knocked aside by another young female emerging from the office as quickly as she could. It was a girl named Holly Archuleta, an OCS classmate who did not resemble a boy in any respect, crying, sobbing, with a little trickle of blood trailing from her nose. She held her clothing up in front of her shapely body.

Her uniform was torn. She sped away down the aisle, pulling herself along, her back and bottom uncovered, and vanished. Julie glanced into the office, Swope didn't see her. He was too busy zipping his pants. She left before he could look up. Let somebody else—preferably somebody male, and very large—complain about the goddamned fucking shower.

That evening, she traded a week's dessert servings for a small, pocketable "assisted opening" knife she could wear on a cord around her neck as a companion to the giant Bowie she couldn't carry in the shower. Holly Archuleta almost belligerently refused to talk to Julie about what had happened to her. She ached to reach out, to somehow help, but respected her choice to not speak about what had happened.

As with most good things aboard the *US/UNSS Retaliator*, time spent gazing out of one of the ship's few portholes was strictly rationed, and there were always long lines formed up in anticipation of one's jealously guarded turn. Video—which was available much more easily on the back of the acceleration chair ahead of yours— was not quite the same, somehow, although, unlike the view out the portholes, the picture came from up forward, in the non-rotating control spaces, and didn't roll space-sick-inducingly with the ship's rotation.

Over the weeks, and eventually months, that the Marines' voyage went on, Mars changed from a small, vaguely reddish star in the sky to an orange dot, then to a sphere on which major features like the North Polar ice cap, Olympus Mons, and Valles Marineris could be made out—another advantage to the video. However, their time was far from empty. It never is, in the military.

Before long, Julie could let herself be blindfolded and then take her issue carbine apart—not just "fieldstripping" it into sub-assemblies, but reducing it to a pile of parts and pins, held down by a magnetic cloth, so that not one component was left sticking to another—and putting it back together in under a minute. This could be a vital skill in as dusty an environment as they were headed for.

She took good care of the little weapon. It might not be much, but it was what she had, and possibly better than throwing rocks.

And there was, of course, the usual housekeeping and cleaning. The sergeants, whom they did not have with them, would have been horrified and disheartened that there were no cots to make up every "morning," tight enough to bounce a coin on. When she was not busy with a spray bottle of cleaner/disinfectant and a cloth, Julie spent every spare moment she had asleep or on the Solarnet, learning what she could about the planet Mars—so different, with its sweeping desert vistas, its dust storms that lasted for months and covered half the planet, its bottomless canyons, and its towering volcanoes. So very different from New Jersey, where she'd grown up, and yet no more demanding that you stay alert to stay alive.

Before she was ten years old, she'd heard of at least one occurrence a year of cannibalism in Newark. There was no place in the whole, wide universe, she thought, that was truly safe.

Meanwhile, aboard the *US/UNSS Retaliator*, what Julie had witnessed, what Holly Archuleta had been put through, was not the first, nor would it be the last case of what she assumed had been rape. But who could it be reported to? The Major controlled access to the Colonel. The girl she saw didn't want to talk to her. Swope went on leering at her speculatively, every time they passed, but there was nothing she could do except keep her little knife sharp and handy.

By the time they had established orbit around Mars, Millicente reported to Julie that she was up and around, on a walker, and that Lafcadio said hello. In carefully guarded language she let her little sister know that no one had been around, neither the police nor the *Mafiya*, concerning what had happened to her pimp. So, Julie thought, she had enlisted in the Corps, essentially, for nothing. Still, she could not remember being happier with where she was or what she was doing—or prouder of herself for what she had achieved. It was clean and warm here, and she always had enough to eat. If she could just stay out of Swope's repulsive reach, everything would be as perfect as it could be in a highly imperfect universe.

The landing, when it came, was simply horrible. There was no other word for it. After what seemed like hundreds of orbits, the ship's pilots photographing, measuring, surveying, and planning, poring microscopically over the thousands of photographs they had taken of hills, valleys, craters, dunes, and caves, the Marines prepared themselves to head for the surface. Their "landing craft" consisted of four big discoid units, theoretically hardened for atmospheric entry, that had been used for food storage on the way out. If the Marines made it down in one piece, the same structures would provide the foundations for their living quarters.

A set of six big strap-on retrorockets fired, and the Marines in the landing units no longer had a choice. They were committed to whatever came next. Julie sat, strapped down, hugging her stupid little carbine, in a chair like she'd spent the last nine months in and out of, only much more flimsily constructed. Her combat space suit was colored and mottled to resemble the Martian surface. Her name patch, unit markings, Marine and rank insignia, and the East American flag (still stubbornly displaying fifty-five stars) were all "subdued" to match the uniform. There was a United Nations rocker on her right upper arm, however, foolishly bright blue and white. It was a target; she planned to peel it off as soon as she could. Her giant Confederate hand-guarded Bowie knife hung off her chair, at her side. She thought Sergeant Spanner would be happy it had made it to Mars—if it did, of course—maybe she would write to him.

Julie thought it was something like descending in a round egg-carton, inside a plastic grocery bag. A few seconds after the *Retaliator* released them, and they began to drift away, the six rocket engines in the "handles" of the "bags" fired, reducing their orbital velocity, then slowing their descent. When the engines had exhausted themselves, four enormous parachutes blossomed in their places, snatching at the almost non-existent atmosphere. She watched it happen to the other three descenders. They were all going to land fairly close together.

Second by second, the reddish-orange surface beneath them grew closer and more filled with daunting details, craters, bumps, and hills. Finally, the parachutes were released, six smaller rockets roared briefly, followed by a *thump!* and an odd, crackling noise, transmitted through the structure they were sitting in, as the bottom half of the "egg-carton" crushed, exactly as it had been designed to do. Word came from the orbiting *Retaliator* that all four "birds" were down safely and that they were no more than ten kilometers north of the colonists' underground settlement.

Colonel Atherton-Nye, anxious to gain a name for herself (and silver birds for her shoulder-tabs) had decided to strike immediately and decisively, before her Marines could even establish a camp for themselves. If they'd arrived aboard oceangoing ships, she would have ordered them burned, like Cortez at Veracruz. They would begin by making a feint, using half of her command, at the colonists' yawning cave entrance, figuring to impose themselves on the recalcitrants before anybody could react and bottle them up, at least, underground.

The remaining half of Colonel Atherton-Nye's forces would come down two miles behind the colony through the "skylight," where the roof of the colossal lava tube had fallen in millions or billions of years ago. There was a theory among the "experts" aboard the spaceship that the collapse had resulted from a small meteorite strike. Nobody seemed to notice that it looked ominously like a giant ant-lion pit. Nobody but Julie who, sometime during the hike to the colony, unfolded her bayonet. It was a recent addition to the little weapon, copied from the old Soviet AK-47 and the SKS, that was integral to the carbine. She looked around. She was not the only one, after all, who had flipped her auxiliary weapon forward.

When they arrived at the "skylight" they sat beside its edge and waited, worrying about their suit dosimeters. Some of the older, more seasoned Marines actually nodded off, having learned long ago to get rest whenever they could. The coming battle would be whatever it was, whether they worried about it or not. They would not be able to hear gunfire from the frontal assault on the colony in the Martian lack-of-atmosphere, but they would be informed by radio when the "pincer movement" (as the Colonel had called it) had started. Meanwhile, some of them began paying out and anchoring ropes, the same color as their suits, one to a Marine, that they would descend upon, once the signal came. Julie swung her carbine around on her back, but she did not fold the bayonet.

At last the go-signal came. Julie grabbed her rope and, in much less gravity than she'd grown up in, slid gently down the long, sandy slope on her helmeted face and her belly, into the "skylight" seventy-five yards above a rubble pile below. When she was just ten feet from touching down, the man beside her grunted into his helmet mike, released his hold on his rope, and fell lifeless to the ground. Another man, further away, fell, too, this one with a scream, and Julie knew that they had been ambushed and were under fire. She let go of her rope and fell the remaining few feet, landing softly on the rocks and sand below on slightly bent legs. As another of her company collapsed, she aimed up the enormous tunnel and let a burst of tiny bullets go where she thought the enemy fire might have come from.

Looking around, she took cover behind the biggest rock she could find. It wasn't much bigger than a loaf of bread, but it was cover. Although there were bullets hailing all around them and rock chips flying everywhere—she thought something might have scratched her helmet visor—she couldn't hear any gunfire, only her people dying around her. Nothing had prepared them for that. The atmosphere of Mars was only seven tenths of a millibar—less than a thousandth of that of Earth. No sound would carry here.

Suddenly, they were taking fire from behind them down the cavernous lava tunnel, as well. She could tell by the way the bullets were striking. And they weren't all 5.7mm, either. Some of them had to be *big*. She turned cautiously and saw several individuals not in military suits, advancing on them, pointing a combination of 5.7mm rifles and much larger-bore pistols at her and her group. Muzzle-flashes flared from them soundlessly. Some of the weapons she'd been trained to recognize as Pallatian Ngu Departure 10mm pistols, the brainchild of Emerson Ngu, laminated together like padlocks. She lifted her carbine, prepared to die as expensively as possible, and aimed it straight at the colonists' apparent leader, a very large man, wielding a huge, old-fashioned-looking automatic pistol with an enormous hole in the end. It looked like a 1911A1, but it was much larger.

117

Major Swope, who was in command (Atherton-Nye was at the colonists' dwellings near the entrance), raised both his arms and started waving and yelling, "Hold your fire! Hold your fire! We surrender! We surrender!" He must have meant the message for his own troops because the colonists were clearly on an entirely different radio frequency. They stopped shooting as the Marines raised their hands.

Nevertheless, abruptly, a young Marine—Julie thought it was Holly Archuleta, the girl she'd seen abused by Swope—dashed down the rubble pile and tried to thrust her bayonet into the colonial leader. He easily stepped aside, like a toreador, parried her thrust and seemed to swat her with something he carried in his left hand. She screamed into her suit mike and went down flailing. The colonists kept their weapons trained on the Marines.

The big man put his huge, curved Asian knife away, knelt, and snatched the suit-fabric of Holly's thigh, rolling it tightly. He yelled something into his suit mike and someone else brought him a small green cylinder of adhesive tape. He held the suit material he'd rolled up, while another person applied the duct tape where it would do the most good. This one Marine, at least, would not die today.

The big man looked up at Julie and their eyes met, just for a moment. He grinned broadly at her. Then, on the Marine frequency, she heard a voice that she didn't recognize. She could see it was not the big man talking.

"This is Seventh Expedition Leader Jack Reubenson. I'm above you, on the surface. Your people up here are our prisoners." They looked up and saw a man high above them in a civilian suit, waving at them. "If you surrender, drop your weapons."

Julie grudgingly complied—but she held onto her Bowie.

CHAPTER FIFTEEN:
THE BOY NEXT DOOR

"Don't touch those coprolites, Desmondo!" shouted
Conchita. "You don't know where they've been!"
—*Conchita y Desmondo*
in the Land of Wimpersnits and Oogies

The Battle of the Rubble Pile, as it came to be known forever afterward, like many a historically famous battle, was
over in only a few minutes. Somehow Jack Reubenson and
Billy Ngu had anticipated Colonel Atherton-Nye's "clever" strategy
and out-pincered her. The Marines left their weapons where they'd
dropped them, and the Martians let them lay—it wasn't as if they
were going to be damaged by the rain or anything.

The big man Julie had noticed turned out to be William, elder son
of the hated industrial baron Emerson Ngu himself. He appeared
to be somewhere in his mid-twenties. She didn't get it straight
until a long time afterward, whether his middle name was Wilde
or Curringer (it was both, as it turned out), but apparently he'd
been named after the infamous plastics billionaire who had illegally
founded the human settlement on Pallas, the "capital" of which—
the little town of Curringer, half dive-bars and half whorehouses in
the beginning—was named after him, too.

119

She didn't learn until much later that it was also the spot where the man had died in an ultralight aircraft crash.

The big man had simply introduced himself to Julie as "Billy," adding that he was a Pallatian and a civilian. As the defeated Marines were "marched" off to the colonists' encampment (it's hard to actually march in a space suit in a one-third gravity environment) inside the cavernous mouth of the giant lava tube, he simply strolled along beside her asking her questions. The escort was chiefly to get medical attention for their wounded, of which there were six—bullet holes in their environmental suits neatly taped over by their adversaries.

It didn't feel at all to Julie like the kind of interrogation she had been trained in Boot Camp and OCS to resist. Handsome sandy-haired, crewcut Billy Ngu asked her what her name was, but neither her rank—which was clearly painted on the rigid shoulder-yoke of her environmental suit, anyway—nor her serial number or function. He was extremely curious about her enormous knife, however—no move had been made to take it away from her, but she prudently left it in the Kydex/fiberglass replacement scabbard she'd had made for it, hanging at her side.

He showed her his own edged weapon, calling it a kukri. He said it was the traditional household and everyday working knife of Nepal (he had a theory the design had been introduced by Alexander the Great, although this one had been made in India, from a cast-off truck leaf spring—which was also traditional—and was the official sidearm of the famous Gurkha warriors, feared and legendary fighting men of the former British Empire. The formidable blade was leaf-shaped, very wide, and at least a quarter of an inch thick, about a foot long, and bent forward at a forty-five-degree angle, halfway along its length. It was highly polished, but clearly showed the marks and ripples of hand-forging. From the way that it had easily sliced through her company-mate's environmental suit, she could guess how sharp it was. She didn't quite reach out to touch it, and he didn't quite offer.

Billy seemed utterly fascinated that her weapon was a genuine antique, owned by a family of former slaves defending the South, that had actually been involved, somehow, in what he alternately referred to as "the historic War Between the American States" and "the Second

American War of Independence." Half of her Marine company were Southerners, so she understood the references and was not in the least offended by them. From his own accent and body language, she would have guessed that he was a Midwestern American, himself, rather than some exotic "Asteroider" as they were portrayed on East American 3DTV. (The actors invariably used coarse Russian accents.) She suddenly caught herself wishing that she could see his hands, took it as a warning, shut up, and let him talk, replying monosyllabically, only when it seemed absolutely necessary.

The colonial "settlement," when they got there, consisted of two dozen outsized plastic Bigelow BEAM bottles half-buried in the sand, fifty yards inside the giant, yawning cave-entrance formed by the ancient lava tube. Powerful floodlights had been strung at intervals along the underside of the cave roof. A little further back in the cave, a somewhat larger structure, consisting of four highly modified bottles coupled together was where they took the wounded.

Alerted by radio, a doctor and her medical volunteers were waiting.

Julie found herself a round-topped rock the right size, jutting up from the cave floor, and sat down wearily, wondering what was going to happen to her and her fellow Marines now. Thirty of them had survived the weird Battle of the Rubble Pile unwounded. They hunkered together now, on the ginger-colored sand, almost unguarded (the key word being "almost"), still unable to believe how easily they'd been taken by an inferior force of raw civilian amateurs armed no better than they were. Only a few minutes went by before expedition leader Jack Reubenson emerged from one of the translucent bottles with Billy Ngu—Colonel Atherton-Nye trailed behind them, a grim look visible through her helmet's face; the woman would never get her full-colonel's eagles now—and approached the subdued group, of which Julie was a part. The young Marine noticed immediately that the antique .455 caliber Webley revolver the Colonel had worn at her space-suit hip was gone.

"Okay, Marines," said Reubenson, addressing the group. He seemed very uncomfortable without pants pockets to put his hands in as he spoke. "Here's what's gonna happen. What you see around you here, is all there is, I'm afraid. It's everything we have. None of us came here to fight a war or take prisoners; we came to get away from all that. The simple fact is, we can't afford to keep you folks, as POWs, or even as guests. Just like us, you're all stuck down here on this godforsaken ball of rock, probably for the rest of your lives."

From their gasps, it was clear that some of them had never considered that possibility.

"So we're gonna top off your oxygen bottles—see our cute little fusion reactor over there? A gift from our new friends from Pallas, who are also stuck here forever—we'll give you all a hot meal, a few in quarters at a time. You'll have to sleep in your suits. Sorry about that. Then, tomorrow morning—after breakfast and more oxygen— we'll escort those of you who can still walk back to your landing site. Might even trust you with a shovel or two to bury your dead."

He nodded at Colonel Atherton-Nye in acknowledgement. "We understand that your four landers are readily convertible into habitats. We'll try to co-exist, then, but we'll hold onto your weapons, at least for a while, until we see how that works out. It's not as if you need them to hunt big game on the lone prairie."

Nobody laughed.

"And if you're still wondering how this happened to you," Reubenson added, "Anthropologists inform us that defenders on their own territory have a two-to-one advantage over aggressors. Also, for what it's worth, I used to be a member of the First Air Commando Group."

Apparently, Jack's "defenders" had suffered no losses, no casualties or fatalities in the battle, of any kind, except for some expended ammunition which could not be replaced at the moment. Nor was it by any means the worst night that Julie had ever spent. Snug inside her suit, cushioned by a bed of sand at one-third gee, she slept like a baby—but then, she always slept like a baby. She could tell that the meals the colonists generously shared with their defeated enemy had stretched them to their very limit. These were hardly the heinous *refusenik* villains that had been described to her and her comrades in so many of her pre-mission briefings. Mostly, they seemed to her like hard-working old-fashioned farm couples, very proud of what they'd accomplished so far, and eager to show it off.

The Bigelow bottle that Julie had eaten dinner in belonged to a Mohammed and Beliita Khalidov, both of them Chechens and from a Muslim background, but dedicated scientists and not religious in the slightest, who had fled, they told her, from Neoimperialistic Russian oppressors and murderous fanatics among their own people, as well. Pretty, dark-eyed Beliita proudly served Julie tea from a shiny new samovar she said the Pallatians had brought her. She was happy to be with her husband Mohammed and *free*. It didn't matter much to her if it was on Mars or in Oklahoma. She did miss Paris, she confessed. Beliita may have been the most rational individual Julie had ever met, and the young Marine automatically liked her, very much. If these people were going to be her neighbors for the foreseeable future, Julie was determined to be the best neighbor she could be.

Breakfast Julie shared with Dean and Tam Deutsch, a friendly, cheerful, outgoing couple whose long-term goal, once the basics of survival on this planet had been dealt with, was to establish the first restaurant on Mars. They were leaning heavily toward Basque cuisine, they admitted. They had been drafted from their university positions by the East American government to come along, Julie learned, by Congressional decree, as official expedition historians— every bit as useful as the bicycles the mission had been saddled with—but they were very handy with tools, they said (they were the ones who had built the distillery), and enthusiastic campers who were experts in all things having to do with "living rough."

Somehow, the couple managed to offer her scrambled eggs and French toast with maple syrup. Bacon and sausage had been strictly forbidden by the politically correct US/UNSS space agency committee in charge of avoiding any possible offense to various repressive religious groups. (The colonists were damned lucky, Tam told her, that they weren't condemned to vegetarian or vegan diets— she greatly looked forward to activating the pigs and chickens that the Pallatians had brought fertilized ova for.) Interestingly, there were no practicing Muslims among the forty-seven colonists, and the Jewish colonists were more than willing and able, as they had always been, to look out for their own religious dietary observances.

At last, laden down with a generously packed box lunch and plenty of extra water, their oxygen bottles topped off once again, and more bottles carried behind them on little improvised sand-sleds, the Marines were ready to begin the ten-kilometer trek back to their landing site. They'd left a skeleton crew behind, who had been contacted and told to prepare for their arrival. Julie looked forward to getting out of her environmental suit for the first time in forty-eight hours.

The Pallatians had agreed to come along. Julie had, of course, met Billy Ngu and couldn't seem to stop thinking about him. It annoyed the hell out of her, she thought. She was free, now, she argued with herself, and didn't need any entanglements in her life—especially with one of the presumed enemy. He was very nice to look at, though. And he had a nice voice.

Julie also met Billy's beautiful sister, Mirella, who had immediately noticed Julie's reluctant interest in her older brother but had commendably said nothing. She'd been named, she told Julie, for the famous ethicist and novelist Mirelle Stein, author of the infamous Stein Covenant, which was the founding document of what they all four grandly called "Pallatian civilization." Stein had been like a grandmother to Mirella's father.

Julie met "little" Teal (they all called her that), brilliant and heartbreakingly cute, for all that she was nearly seven feet tall. She's been named for Raymond Louis Drake-Tealy, a paleontologist and writer as famous as Stein, who had been married to Stein, and who had discovered what were believed to be billion-year-old alien artifacts among the Asteroids.

And Julie met young Brody Ngu, a quiet, pensive, perhaps even brooding young man who disturbed her somehow—named for Aloysius Brody, a frontier judge notorious for conducting court in a Curringer bar.

Billy told her that, if they ever got back off this planet, he planned to become an asteroid hunter. He was already a capable astrogator, he claimed, who had gotten his brother and sisters across space in what amounted to a homemade ship, and, with Mirella's help, down safely to the surface of Mars in the first place.

Any metallic asteroid more than a kilometer in diameter, he informed the lieutenant, mostly composed of nickel and iron, contained, as a "trace element," more gold than had ever been mined and refined on Earth in human history, along with proportionate amounts of silver, platinum, iridium, rhodium, and other rare and valuable metals. It had been the iridium in the Matterhorn-sized rock that had fallen on the Yucatan coast, sixty-five million years ago—scattered around the planet—that had given away the solution to the great dinosaur whodunit. Thirty percent of the asteroids circling the Sun, he said, were the metallic kind.

A few scientists even believed that there were diamonds out there, too. "Some as big as your head." He laughed, as the old English saying about coconuts went, contained in a different kind of asteroid he called "carbonaceous chondrites." Pallas, he added, was a carbonaceous chondrite.

Mirella intrigued her. The elder Ngu sister was fully a head taller than Julie, maybe more, with a model's straight, slightly up-tilted nose and prominent cheekbones. It was impossible to tell beneath her suit, but she appeared to have long legs. Nonetheless, the young woman was all about botany. Not only had she discovered the Cerean organism that seemed to be at the center of this conflict between Mars and Earth, she had selected and adapted other crops for the Martians to grow in the future, attempting to predict, as she did, what could be done with the worn-out iron-heavy Martian soil. Julie believed that she had been cursed with a "black thumb," herself, and could kill houseplants with a single glance, but she was more than willing to learn from Mirella, if that became possible.

It took a great deal of energy to converse with Teal. She was younger, but even taller than her sister and at least twice as active. Younger people tended to grow taller every generation on Pallas, possibly owing to the mild gravity, which was only one twentieth of that of Earth. Still, her siblings all called her "little Teal." Yet she could not be dismissed as the mere teenager that she seemed to be. She was the ingenious geneticist who had manipulated the Cerean organism's innermost workings, turning the macaroni plant into something useful.

And somehow extremely threatening to the bosses back on Earth.

CHAPTER SIXTEEN: DERBYVILLE

"See that nice old bald man over there in the yellow robes?" Conchita asked her little companion. "He just told me that sometimes, defeat is all you need to achieve a victory. What do you suppose that means, Desmondo?"

—*Conchita y Desmondo*
in the Land of Wimpersnits and Oogies

Once they had reached the Marine landing site, the Pallatians didn't linger. The skeleton crew who had stayed behind to work on the encampment were fully armed and hostile. Julie thought that Colonel Atherton-Nye was going to order the Ngus arrested, but perhaps she took another look at that enormous battle-worn pistol hanging off Billy's thigh, at those Ngu Departure 10 mm pistols carried in gun belts slanted across the hips of his three siblings and gave the idea up. Instead, she extended a suited hand to Billy and thanked him for his courtesy.

The young Pallatian took the Colonel's uncharacteristic cordiality with more than a grain of salt. He had prudently looked the "Butcher of Burlington" up on the Solarnet.

He looked around for her murderous henchman, Major Grenville Swope, but couldn't see him anywhere. That one bore careful watching, he thought. Swope was unquestionably better off having left Earth. Billy—and everybody on Pallas—knew that the man was a field operative for a violent environmentalist splinter group, "Gaia's Guardians," back on Earth.

Nevertheless, Billy reciprocated the Colonel's smile and handshake, however insincere, and then reached into a zippered outer pocket of his environmental suit and handed her an odd bundle. "This, I believe, is yours, Colonel. As this unit's Commanding Officer, you ought to have it." It was her antique Webley revolver, in its British Army issue canvas holster, wrapped in the Web belt it was attached to. The lanyard ring hanging from the weapon's butt would have tinkled in a decent atmosphere. Wordless, she accepted it. He reached further into his pocket for a small handful of shiny objects. "Here are the cartridges. Six, I believe."

She took them in her other hand but didn't move to load the gun.

In the end, Billy's tolerant and kindly attitude was what set the tone for relations between the colonists, their Pallatian allies, and the Marines. Nye's people would grudgingly trade with their neighbors, he expected, for supplies (he wondered what they'd find to sell), but otherwise keep to themselves.

The skeleton crew remaining at the Marine landing site had not been idle. The four large, disc-shaped UN/US landers, fashioned from some ablative black composite material, had been fairly close to each other when they'd come down, but not close enough. Lacking any work-vehicles or heavy machinery, the crew had driven anchors deep into the ground, then used ropes and differential hoists to crank the landers across the sand, until they were in contact with each other. A flat, circular solar array now surrounded the base of each unit, and a black plastic heat-absorbing dome had been inflated above it. Through no intention of the designer, the habitats looked exactly like four gigantic derby hats, resting together on the Martian surface.

The Pallatians soon departed, among themselves naming the place "Derbyville."

127

The habitats each had a series of thin interior radial partitions running halfway from the circumferential wall toward the center, creating a couple of dozen alcoves, or niches, all around the inside. Each of the Marines claimed a niche, and as soon as the "derbies" were pressurized, and survival-kit sleeping bags distributed, Julie climbed gratefully out of her environmental suit and, her Bowie knife resting beside her, got a few hours' surprisingly comfortable sleep on the floor. One-third gravity, she was discovering, is very good for that.

Meanwhile, on their way back, the four Ngus discovered that the Martian Communications Officer, Moose Holder, had established something he called "HRN"—the "Helmet Radio Network," a little broadcast every evening, just before bedtime, over the frequency of the communications rigs in their environmental suits. Listeners would stow their suits under their cots, their helmets beside their pillows, and stretch their earphone leads to their heads, where they would hear the latest news and gossip, some of it directly from Earth (their preference turned out to be West American), and sometimes a bit of music some individual had brought to Mars with them. When Holder learned the frequency the Ngus were on—in the middle of their return from Derbyville—he had added the Pallatians. He planned to add the Marines as soon as possible. It was a warm little touch from home.

It reminded Billy fondly of KCUF, "the Voice of Pallas" which, in his father's day, had been a tiny 50-watt breadboard lashup in the corner of a Curringer bar. It had slowly expanded, and when they sent up a pair of orbiting repeaters so that that signals could be heard all over the asteroid, eight-year-old Emerson had been able to tune them in at the Greeley United Memorial Project on a little razor-blade receiver he'd made in secret, from instructions in a discarded hobby magazine, even winding the tiny earphone coils by hand.

Later, KCUF had added a television signal, broadcasting from the asteroid's moon, Pallas B, then converted it to 3DTV. Today the Pallas station could be seen and heard all over the Solar System, even on Earth's Moon. The Martian colonists sheepishly admitted to listening to it back home for news untainted by government propaganda. Who knew what kind of future awaited HRN?

Billy was absolutely determined to persuade Holder to rebroadcast some news of Pallatian content. It was good to have news from home, but he had a prophetic intuition that the pioneers on what he thought of as the "Settled Worlds" ought to stick together somehow. There were no copyright problems; under Pallatian "law," if you flung it out into space, you couldn't put any restrictions on its use.

Another of the questions in Billy's mind was answered on that evening's broadcast. Where had the Old Survivor gone during the colonists' conflict with the Marines? Apparently, he was back. The Communications officer and "disk jockey" had asked the old man directly.

"Oh, not very far," he told his interviewer. "Just plain common sense t'stay outta the line of fire. Hadda go home an' see how m'tomato crop was turnin' out. It's just fine, happy t'say, an' so're my other plants, celery an' carrots an' suchlike. Ain't no tomato worms on Mars."

"And exactly where *is* your home?" Holder asked the old man with exaggerated innocence. His tone told Billy this was a well-established ritual of some kind that he was listening to.

The Pallatian could hear the Old Survivor grin behind his beard and chuckle as he said, "You'd sure like t'know, now wouldn't ya, sonny?"

The Avenging Angel (he never thought of himself as "Porter Rockwell," and it wasn't his real name, anyway; it had mostly been Strahan's idea) had not left the colonial settlement with Atherton-Nye's defeated substandard fighters. He had means nobody knew about, to avoid unwanted attention. He had used them to hang back during the rubble-pile fight until he saw clearly that there was no hope of winning it. The overly celebrated Colonel may have been Hell itself against Fourth World savages, armed only with spears and bows and arrows, but the damned fool woman didn't know the first thing about fighting real warriors.

He did know. Being an ardent student of Sun Tzu, he made almost a religious practice of avoiding battle assiduously unless it was absolutely necessary. This war that he waged was not going to be won by any direct confrontation, but by making each member of the other side terribly, personally afraid (Gaia's Guardians' strategy of choice), or so angry that their leaders made fatal mistakes. Keeping his eyes wide open among the colonials after the fight, he thought he'd seen the perfect way to accomplish exactly that.

Which was why he waited, now, lurking deep in a side-crevice of the great dark lava tunnel, about three miles from the entrance, where the colonists had become accustomed to dumping their "honey pots" in a deep hole they had laboriously dug for that purpose. They would scour them out with sand, afterward, like North African nomads. Someone would eventually come along, sooner or later. It didn't really matter who it was. After he had dealt with them, as brutally and horrifyingly as possible, leaving a terrifying corpse, a suit full of blood, and an expression of startled fear on their dead face if he could, life among the rest of them would never be the same again. They would feel the terrible wings of the Avenging Angel cast a shadow over their lives, and they would waste all of their precious time and energy worrying about who was next, even if nobody ever was.

He felt somebody coming, rather than heard them, through the soles of his boots. He opened the small control panel on the left forearm of his suit and pressed a series of virtual buttons. The suit, which had been the color of the lava tube walls during the battle, scanned the wall he stood against now and adjusted itself to match. He became invisible.

He reached into his left chest pocket and extracted his weapon. It was tiny, especially held in the palm of his glove, with just enough grip—for this trip, he had replaced the original neoprene with a more durable polymer—to wrap two fingers around. It looked like one of the short-barreled "snubby" revolvers traditionally carried by police detectives for over a hundred years in murder mystery stories. But it was not a five-shot .38 Special, it was a six-shot high-pressure

.32 ultra-magnum, almost as potent as a .45. And it was not from Massachusetts, or even Arizona, where the famous gun companies had moved after the West seceded, but from Brazil. The frugality of his choice still pleased him.

Despite its diminutive size, he knew the weapon hit *hard*, driving its 0.312" projectile to exceed .357 Magnum velocities. It might give his intended victim just time enough to realize they were going to die.

Camouflaged and ready now, he waited in the dark.

He watched his prey pass by, unidentifiable in the low light. From the figure's size, he guessed it was male, probably the older Ngu brother, carrying a waste container bucket in each hand. Perfect. He stepped softly into the middle of the passageway, raised his revolver, and, without saying a word, fired one shot, silent in the Martian "atmosphere," into the back and through the heart of his prey, who collapsed immediately, dropping the buckets and spilling two big pools of human waste across the floor. Advancing on the victim, he saw from the Pallatian belt it wore, that it was indeed one of the Ngu siblings, lying face down. He pulled the 10mm Ngu Departure pistol it wore out of its holster, took aim, and fired it point blank into the bullet wound he'd just inflicted with the .327. Then he let the stainless weapon drop into the filth beside the body. Let them figure that one out, he thought with a mental chuckle.

Mildly curious, he rolled the dead body over with a toe.

At the embryonic Marine base, now that their fallen comrades were buried beneath the red soil, the first task at hand for Julie and her company was building doors of some kind for the small, wedge-shaped spaces that would become individual quarters. In an un-characteristically cooperative mood, the aerial survey crew of the *Retaliator* guided a hunt, by the Martians, for the parachutes that the Marine landers had jettisoned just before touching down. The tough material would be useful in helping them to make a home on the lifeless prairie. There were a dozen of them in all. They managed to find ten, Colonel Atherton-Nye offered four of them to the colonists for their help.

The next afternoon, Julie was in what would eventually become her quarters, trying to make a door out of parachute material. She was having difficulty with the heavy aluminum wire frame she'd created but was unwilling simply to hang up a curtain like some of her mates. Drapery didn't work the same way in one third gee. Her Bowie knife was stuffed into her space suit, lying on the floor under her cot, to keep it out of her way in the cramped space. She had bent all the way over facing away from the center of the structure when she heard an unpleasant voice behind her.

"Now that's what I call a pretty sight," remarked Major Swope menacingly, as he stood not more than a foot behind her. "You ought to be bent over more often, Segovia, it would be good for you!" Before he finished the sentence, he pounced, landing on her back. She could smell his foul breath coming hot and damp past her neck. One of his stubby, pawlike hands grabbed the neckline of her T-shirt and yanked it down to her waist. The other groped for a breast.

Her small knife swung free on its lanyard. She ignored whatever he was doing to her, got her hand on the weapon, jerked it free of her neck and switched it open, then somehow turned around—she said afterward that it was the hardest physical thing she'd ever had to do—and thrust the little blade deep into his solar-plexus, withdrawing it with a twisting motion that had become reflexive in Boot Camp. He let go with a "*whuff?*" and sat back on the floor, his hands over his gushing wound. His fly was already, she assumed, in anticipation. The look of astonished indignation on his fat face would have been worth the trouble alone.

Breathing hard, she got hold of her helmet mike. "Security? Who's being Security today? Major Swope just assaulted me." He looked up at her stupidly, his life draining away. "I think I've killed him."

CHAPTER SEVENTEEN:
THE PRESIDENT'S MISTRESS

"Movies and books have taught us all the wrong things, Desmondo," Conchita reflected. "They have stolen the joy from our lives by conditioning us to expect that, just as we've achieved the happiness we've always sought, some calamity becomes inevitable."

—*Conchita y Desmondo*
in the Land of Wimpersnits and Oogies

Melanie Wu sat on the edge of the luxurious bed, trying desperately to figure out how she should be feeling this morning.

Item: it was only six months ago that she'd been just another secretary—"Don't ever say that!" she'd been lectured sternly by her colleagues, "Say 'Personal Assistant!' "—one of dozens, hovering around a prestigious Washington, D.C. law office like fruit flies. When one of the younger partners, Maxwell Promise, the extremely handsome son-in-law of the multibillionaire philanthropist Richfield Chen, had "noticed" her. And noticed her. And noticed her again.

At the time, Melanie had wondered whether it was because Max's wife, a rather unattractive woman whom he pretty clearly loathed, was also Asian. That would have been something to worry about. She'd later learned Mrs. Promise didn't care what he did sexually—she may even have been pleased to be relieved of a duty she considered burdensome—and he'd turned out to be so very kind to her and extremely generous, an untiring and attentive lover, gentle when she needed him to be, firm and implacable when that was most exciting. He had never given her a single reason to be afraid of him. He made her feel safe.

She stood up, stretched, and regarded herself at length in the big vanity mirror across the room. The sight of her own slender yet curvaceous body, draped in a nearly transparent "Teddy" nightgown, punctuated by the dark, twin points of her nipples, was strangely arousing to her. Narcissism? She didn't think so. Whatever social anthropologist it was who'd observed that the general hailing sign that sex is on the menu (the actual quotation was that "the fucking lamp is lit"), is the sight of a naked, or near-naked woman, hadn't been far off the mark.

Item: Max told her constantly that she was beautiful. He said that, among other things, he loved her smooth, soft, flawless, lightly tan-colored skin. She had her doubts about his taste. Merely five feet two inches tall in her bare feet, as now, she was hardly statuesque. She was quite slender, she admitted, with a narrow waist, gently rounded hips, and a flat belly, but she didn't know why: given a chance, she ate like a horse. She possessed the usual big, dark, "almond" eyes (highly exotic to somebody of Max's rural Connecticut background) and the shiny black hair of her people—red highlights in the bright sunlight—with just a faint sprinkle of freckles across her nose and cheeks. Very plain, she thought, very ordinary. She did have a nice pair of unusually large breasts for an Asian female, she knew—firm and "perky," with areolae and nipples that were nearly black. Every day, Melanie hoped and prayed that they weren't why she had attracted Max's attention.

Item: when she had awakened this lovely morning, following her very first election-night party in the nation's capital, she had found herself in the bridal suite of an extremely expensive downtown Washington, D.C. hotel. the mistress of the President of the United States.

Well, she conceded, the President-Elect, technically.

She picked up her little cell phone, another gift from Max, no bigger than the size of her thumb, from where it lay on the night table. He had warned her it was highly likely to be "tapped" and to be discreet. (He'd never told her that the fact that he didn't have to explain it to her further, and could count on her to do it, was one of the many reasons he loved her.) She let its holographic address book and telephone directory fan out before her, and selected the entry for Francine Carmody, her fellow secr—personal assistant—at the law firm and her former college roommate. The girls had known each other well for seven years.

"Frannie? What are you doing today?" It was Saturday. They had been celebrating election night for three days! She was glad she'd caught her friend and not her answering system.

"Mel?" came the surprised answer, "Why the hell are you calling me? Today you should be doing something fun with your friend."

"The poor man has meetings scheduled all day long." Melanie didn't tell Francine that this was probably the most thoroughly planned political succession in American (East or West) history.

Soon-to-be former President Horton Willoughby III was extremely anxious, it seemed, to retire, Max had informed her, since his horrible wife had suffered her fatal traffic accident. Willoughby had already arranged to be appointed president of a highly respected midwestern university, which he apparently regarded as Heaven on Earth of some kind. For all practical purposes, Maxwell Promise was already President of the United States.

She shifted to alleviate some very sore and stiffened muscles. Max could be utterly relentless. "We celebrated plenty, believe me—after he shook loose of Her and her father. I think I have a three-day hangover. I want to go for a ride, Frannie. I want a drink—a mimosa or a bloody mary. I want some lunch—*croque-monsieurs*, I think—and most of all, most of all, I want some friendly company I don't have to lie to. You game?"

She had especially wanted to tell her father what was happening with her, but he lived in the country next door, West America, and she didn't think he'd be particularly proud of her.

135

"In that sexy little yellow convertible of yours? Honey, you do know that it's winter, don't you, and there's snow all over the ground out there and nasty mud wherever there isn't?"

"Yeah, Frannie, I know. But the sun is shining and it's almost warm. The snow is melting. The goddamned car will wash."

"Okay," Francine said, "Breakfast cocktails. Grilled ham and cheese between thick slices of French toast. Powdered sugar and strawberry jam. You had me at 'the sun is shining.'"

"First things first," said Melanie, sitting down at a table they'd been shown to on the verandah. "How is that handsome brother of yours?"

Fran feigned innocence. "Hale?"

"How many brothers do you have?" Melanie asked, pretending to be stern.

"Just the one," she admitted.

The chic restaurant overlooked the river, and, although it was cold outside (a small Navy vessel of some kind was breaking a pathway through the ice for smaller vessels) the stone-flagged terrace featured at least a dozen infrared heaters, standing tall on shiny metal poles. The brilliant sun and blue sky helped, as did a lack of wind. At least there were no bugs this time of year. Melanie thought it was an especially good day to feel alive.

Hale—Space Force Captain Nathan Hale Carmody, Ph.D., currently on loan to NASA—was Francine's big brother, a geologist specializing in the "Planetary Sciences" who had attended the new Space Academy near Warner Robins, Georgia, and earned his advanced degrees while serving with the military. It was a constant joke among the three of them that Hale and Melanie were "carrying on" behind his baby sister's back—except that Frannie strongly suspected it wouldn't be at all pretended, if Hale had his way. Melanie was a strikingly beautiful, winsome creature, and she had brains. She was also thoroughly spoken for.

Frannie assumed a conspiratorial expression, lowered her voice, and leaned over the wrought-aluminum table toward Melanie, excitement filling her voice despite the fact that she was whispering.

"This isn't exactly a state secret, or I wouldn't know about it, myself," she said, "but it won't hurt to keep it quiet anyway—although what with the election and all, I've been dying to tell you for weeks. Melanie, my brother Hale's on Mars!"

"Mars?" Melanie repeated the word quietly. She did remember vaguely that another mission had been sent to the red planet. How many did this make, six? Seven? She said as much.

"This isn't a regular colonizing effort, Mel. Those are up to seven now, I think. This is something quite different, apparently. I don't really know the details. Something about the Marines quelling a colonial uprising, of all things. As you know, Hale is Space Force, Chief Scientist for the expedition—or he was meant to be, until somebody went and murdered his boss, the Second-In-Command, a Major Swope. Now Hale has that duty, too."

"Francine, how do you *know* all this?" Melanie demanded, the centuries-old name and face of the doomed movie star Marilyn Monroe passing momentarily through her mind. She shuddered. It is possible to know too much, through no fault of your own, and to be punished for it.

Frannie looked at her with big, wide eyes. "Are you gonna tell Max?"

Melanie laid a hand on top of one of Frannie's. "I kind of think I have to—but I won't mention you or your brother."

"Well," Frannie told her, sitting back but not particularly relieved, "each member of the expedition has a few minutes every week to speak with their families back home. That's how I know."

"You'd think they'd censor you." There was that shudder again.

"You'd think," Frannie agreed. "Only we peppered our conversation with *Boontling*—that's an artificial language made up in the late 19th century, in Boonville, in the Anderson Valley where we were born, in Northern California. I'll tell you more about it sometime, so you won't be a 'back-dated chuck'—a person who is ignorant or behind the times. You can look it up, really. Anybody asks, we just say it's baby-talk between a brother and sister."

She'd never asked, but Melanie had always suspected that her best friend came from some extremely bucolic background of some kind: West American, Boy Scouts and Girl Scouts, Little

League, and 4H. Now little Francine Carmody was another stylish, sophisticated East American career-girl living in a Georgetown apartment with forty pairs of expensive shoes.

"Lieutenant Segovia," Colonel Atherton-Nye intoned, "you have murdered a superior officer. For the time being, you will be restricted to your quarters and reduced to basic rations until you're told otherwise. I don't know what's going to happen, but I don't think this is going to end well for you, no matter what you claim."

Julie was mildly surprised that the pretentious woman hadn't pronounced her rank "lefftenant." She felt indignation swelling, hot inside her, but she had long ago learned the hard way never to let it be seen. "I did not *murder* Swope, ma'am; I acted strictly in self-defense, ma'am. He was behind me, ma'am, covering me like a dog in heat. He had pulled my shirt down and placed a hand on my bare breast. He had unzipped his fly and pulled his penis out, *ma'am*."

The Colonel cleared her throat. "That's for your court-martial to decide. And you are insubordinate to the last cell in your body, Segovia. I am well acquainted with your kind. Captain Carmody, kindly relieve the lieutenant of that barbaric instrument she carries. I'm going to bump this ugly situation back to Earth for instructions. We have a new administration down there, in effect, and I need to know if there are any changes in policy."

"Policy? What in this world are you talking about? That bastard tried to rape me! I know of at least one other Marine officer he did rape." Julie stood, swatting Carmody's fumbling hands away from her waist. A Marine might have decked her; Carmody didn't know what to do. Julie unfastened the long scabbard from her belt and handed the knife to him. "Take good care of that, Space Force," she advised, but looked the Colonel in the eye as she added, "You'll be giving it back to me, with apologies, when all is said and done."

She couldn't comment on how weird it felt, having joined the Marine Corps and come to Mars to avoid prosecution for murder, only to be accused of another once she had gotten here.

The light was very dim, this far back in the lava tube. The "skylight" lay between Billy and the "bright lights" of the colonists' settlement near the tunnel mouth. The helmet lights on these suits, as usual, were inadequate. He was looking for his sister. He hadn't been able to raise her on the radio, but she'd been having trouble with it recently.

The floor of the tube, like everything else on this miserable forsaken planet, was covered with fine dust. He wondered if the macaroni plant was going to change that—something else to ask his sister once he caught up with her. Aside from making certain that she was okay, he wanted to know when they could start looking for signs that the macaroni spores had started taking hold.

He had gone a few more dozen yards, when he spotted what looked like an abandoned laundry bag, lying on the dusty cavern floor. As he reluctantly drew closer, he perceived that it was an inert human figure instead, in a space suit. Another few steps and he could discern that the space suit was Pallatian. He never remembered taking the last few steps.

Before he knew it, he was on his knees, looking into the dead, empty eyes of his baby sister, Teal. His heart broke.

CHAPTER EIGHTEEN: THE SMOKING GUN

"There's something evolutionary about all this, something genetic," Conchita observed, as they watched the funeral. "Do you realize that everybody living in the world today is descended from the ones who got revenge?"

—*Conchita y Desmondo*
in the Land of Wimpersnits and Oogies

For just a moment, an eternal moment filled with searing pain, Billy looked down at the cold, dis-animated face of his beloved sister, his little Teal, lost in despair, trying not to weep into his helmet. *Weep?* He wanted to wail at the stars. The universe had failed—what else was the goddamned thing for except to provide a safe and decent place for wonderful creatures like Teal to exist?

As his mind slowly began to function again, Billy's reasoning came down to: little Teal was dead and some sonofabitch had killed her. He could do nothing for his sister, now. Her life was over. She would never smile again. She would never laugh again. He would never hear her voice again.

Never again.

Never again.

But he could do something for every other baby sister in the universe. He could find that fucking sonofabitch and *erase* him.

Teal had been shot through the heart from behind with a medium-caliber weapon, possibly her own 10mm. There was no visible exit wound, but environmental suits are tough and the inside of hers might have stopped the bullet. Blood was still bubbling and steaming out of the entrance hole into the unpressurized environment. Her Ngu Departure pistol was lying on the ground beside her, her name lovingly engraved on the frame entwined with their dad's, who had given it to her. Billy knew that, sooner or later, he was going to have to tell his parents what had happened. He'd rather have been shot himself.

The killer: Billy wondered briefly how he (or she, he reminded himself) had accomplished that, shooting adroit, alert, quick-handed Teal in the back with her own weapon. Guessing from her position, she'd probably died instantly. But her cowardly murderer must have come from some overly urbanized environment, probably on Earth or in the Moon, because he (or she) had overlooked one supremely important thing that no Pallatian ever would:

Tracks.

Back home on Pallas, which, under the "infamous" Stein Covenant, had deliberately adopted a hunter-gatherer economy deemed healthier for humanity and human society, Billy, and practically every other Pallatian, from early childhood onward, had spent countless hours following the tracks of wild game animals. Their first big-game kill was a publicly celebrated rite of passage. The only difference was that here, at the end of this particular chase, the animal he planned to put down would be the one that had murdered his sister.

Using the control panel on his suit forearm, he made sure he was on a frequency that only he and his siblings shared. "Mirella. Brody." He heard them both click acknowledgement. "There's no way to say this gently. Teal is dead. Somebody shot her. I'm going after them. You'll find her about a mile up-tunnel from the Skylight. Mind the tracks."

He switched off before they could answer and detached Teal's oxygen tanks—they were nearly full—from her suit harness.

He felt bad doing it, a little like a vampire or a vulture, but his sister had no further use for them, and he would have to have them for what he planned.

Peering closely in the sub-arean twilight at the dust-covered tunnel floor, he followed a set of tracks, bigger than his own size tens, that led him to a rope ladder hanging from a lip of the Skylight and out onto the sunlit surface where a spot on the roof had collapsed a billion years ago or so. A meteorite strike, he believed, although he wondered what you call a rock ejected by a volcano that returns to the ground at terminal velocity.

Tracks in the now-desiccated honeypot leavings and dust became places where the sandy surface had been stepped on and disrupted. They led him in the direction—ten kilometers northwest of the colony, as he'd known they would—toward Derbyville, the Marine Corps encampment.

What seemed like an eternity later, after two oxygen bottle changes, when he was almost there, the tops of the derby-shaped shelters just in sight, he saw his quarry, the tracks from the lava tube leading straight to him. Billy recognized him and switched frequencies.

He shouted, "Porter Rockwell! You killed my sister!"

As the Avenging Angel twisted around, his hand going for his weapon, he shouted back, "One down, three to—"

Rockwell never completed the sentence. Billy's enormous pistol was already cocked, its safety locked, in its holster. He drew swiftly and stroked the safety off in a single fluid motion, firing twice— enormous 260-grain hollow-points at 1200 feet per second—not quite soundless as the expanding muzzle gasses passed his helmet. The weapon came down out of recoil, and just as the man fell, Billy could see daylight through his wounds. He gently pushed the safety back up, twirled the weapon backward, around his trigger finger— technically a very bad habit, he was aware (he'd been trying to break himself of it for years)—and reholstered the big .45 Magnum.

Within a minute, Billy found himself surrounded by a dozen Marine carbines. Their effect on human flesh may have been debatable, but he reasoned that they wouldn't have done his space suit much good. Besides, they had their bayonets fixed. His hands were empty anyway. He raised them high above his helmeted head. No matter what happened to him now, it had been worth it for Teal's sake.

At least ten of East America's finest came to take the pistol-belt and pistol off his hips. With it, they took his kukri, the foot-long Nepalese camp tool and survival knife he'd carried since he was a boy. With their little bayonets, they urged him toward what must have been the biggest building on the planet, a sort of pressure-tight pavilion between the four derbies, constructed of the same parachute material they'd used elsewhere, apparently stiffened and sealed with glue of some kind. That was a good idea. If he ever got back to the civilian colonists he'd tell them about it. It stood in the curve-sided square formed between the four derby-shaped shelters, about forty feet by forty feet, and perhaps fifteen feet tall.

The Marines took him through one of the flexible airlocks they had contrived and immediately moved to relieve him of his helmet. They almost had to fight him for it, but they threatened to shatter the faceplate with the butts of their puny rifles, so he relented.

"Mr. Ngu," pronounced an imperious female voice behind him. He turned to see the eye-patched Colonel Atherton-Nye accompanied by two Marines in battle dress and a young man in a very different kind of uniform that Billy guessed (incorrectly) was Navy. "You are under arrest for committing murder within an American military reservation."

"It wasn't murder," Billy replied evenly. "Check your security tapes, Colonel. It was self-defense. And the dog had just murdered my sister."

"As soon as your sentence is carried out," she told him, "we might allow you a trial. Or what's left of you. Men, bring him over to my desk and get him out of that suit. Captain Carmody, bring in the other prisoner."

When the captain came back, he was escorting the young fe-male Marine Billy had noticed—and who had noticed him—after the lava tube battle. Atherton-Nye's "desk," a couple of crates shoved together, stood at the extreme end of the room. On it lay Billy's gun belt and the huge Bowie knife he'd seen the lieutenant carrying. The Colonel pulled Billy's kukri from its sheath, idly examining it. She was familiar with this kind of Third World weapon.

143

"William Wilde Curringer Ngu, meet Marine Lieutenant Julia Conchita Segovia. She killed my second-in-command, Major Grenville Swope, also claiming it was self-defense, although I don't believe he intended to *kill* her. Julie, meet Billy. I am reviving herewith the medieval custom of trial by combat. Your sentence, both of you, is that you will fight each other … to the death."

Julie tried to avoid gasping audibly. This was lunacy, she thought, and in any decent military would cost the celebrated Colonel her career. Julie thought the prospect of a duel to the death somehow aroused the one-eyed woman. Sick.

Julie's opponent was a big man, she thought, with just a trace of Asian in his eyes, now that she looked closely. She thought this whole thing was ludicrous, but here she was anyway, the big knife they'd just returned to her in her hand, swinging her slender arms to loosen them up, reluctant to kill the man, but prepared to hurt him if she could. The great trick would be to remain unhurt herself. It might not be that easy. As her old drill sergeant had observed, "Nobody ever wins a knife fight." There was an unfortunate amount of wisdom in that.

Her own weapon, of course, was the Confederate "D-guard" Bowie knife that her old sergeant had given her, and that she was officially authorized to carry at all times—except, apparently, when she was under arrest. Its blade was two inches wide for most of its length and seventeen inches long. It would almost be fair to call it a small cutlass. The business end featured a "clipped" top edge, to bring the point back to the centerline, a typical Bowie feature. The blade was mid-19th century Sheffield English steel, age-darkened and seasoned by three hundred years of existence and tender care. What was not typically Bowie was the protective bow, or knuckle-guard, like that of a sword, fashioned of polished German silver. The weapon was a bit blade-heavy, something like a light hatchet, but she was thoroughly used to it. The edges, both top and bottom, that she had carefully honed and rehoned herself, gleamed in the available light.

"This is perfect," Billy told her quietly, grinning. "Since the first moment I arrived on Mars, I've wanted to meet the most beautiful girl in the world."

What the hell kind of trash-talk was that? She ignored him.

Billy had brought his kukri to the fight—rather, the Colonel and the Captain had given it back to him. Julie remembered it was of native Nepalese design, the signature weapon of the fearsome and famous Gurkhas. Briefly, Julie wondered if Billy had fashioned it, himself.

Billy was well over six feet tall, she had noticed, and sort of handsome in a brutish way. She had never seen a proper crew cut up close. Those apish arms of his gave him an extra-long reach, and she was very grateful that her Bowie knife was a full five inches longer than his kukri. She noted that he snatched a heavy space suit glove from the table, for his left hand, which meant that she would have to watch out for a quick grab at her blade.

Her opponent assumed what she recognized from her martial arts classes in Basic as a "horse stance," both of his feet pointed forward, his knees as far apart as his shoulder-width, slightly bent. Julie herself was a mere five feet something in height—if she stood on her toes—and weighed less than a hundred pounds on Earth. He probably weighed two-fifty, but she guessed he had never been to Earth. He'd been born and grew up in a gravity field only one sixth that of Mars. She had been born and grew up in three times that amount of gravity.

He was a sickly bear.

She was a hardy mouse.

He'd be a grappler. Again, she reminded herself to avoid his reach.

He moved first, taking a silent, shuffling step, his shiny blade before him, edge down. She declined the implied invitation, and simply stood, waiting, her feet forming a T, her right toe pointed toward him, raising her big knife to an *en garde* position. He went for it, attempting to hook it out of her hand with the kukri. She took her point in a circle, letting his heavy blade slip off. At the last moment, she struck the kukri aside, hoping to slap it out of his hand, but, not surprisingly, he held on. They repeated the whole exchange, exactly. This time, slapping his blade away, she lunged, catching her point in his T-shirt, and tearing it.

First "blood" to Julie, then. She had already killed a man with a knife. Was she going to have to kill another? Grinning, Billy hopped backward hastily, out of her reach, an effective retreat in this gravity.

"You see how it is," she told him. "I'm better armed and faster than you are. Surrender now before I have to hurt you. It won't cost you anything."

"Better armed? I doubt it. You think these stiffs will let either of us surrender? I admit, Lieutenant. That's some toadsticker you've got there. Have you ever seen a real toad? I haven't. I've always wondered, though, kukri versus Bowie. I sure wish you were bigger. It would be a truer test."

Suddenly he surged forward, surprisingly fast for his size, slapped her knife out of the way, and feinting at her neck, just where it joined the shoulder. She ducked and turned, letting his knife fall away safely and slapping at the heavy back edge. On its way back up, the sharpened false edge of the Bowie nicked his jaw. He held on, dripping a little blood, and retreated again.

This time, it was she who took the offensive, pressing him hard, following him with two lightning steps, going for the unguarded hand holding the knife. She drew a little more blood from his knuckles. No victory. It cost her a lacerated thumb. So he shucked off the glove—at her face—tossed the knife into his left hand, and lunged at her like a classic fencer. It was Julie who had to back up this time.

"Ambidextrous," he explained.

"Shortened," she replied, swinging at his neck. The oversized Bowie tasted flesh. But instead of being decapitated, Billy only looked like he'd cut himself shaving. "Will you surrender, now?" she demanded.

"Two cuts," he answered cheerily, "Nine hundred ninety-eight to go."

"If it takes a thousand, then that's what you'll get," she responded, abruptly ducking as low as she could, and pushing, parallel to the floor, past him, to stand behind him. The move wouldn't have been possible in Earth's gravity.

She kicked the back of one knee, heard it *craaack!* painfully, and then landed with both of her feet on his right shoulder. He fell, turning onto his back. She slapped his knife away with a *claaang!* jumped onto him, straddling his chest, her knees pinioning his biceps, and held the point of her knife vertically at his throat, her left hand on the back of the dark blade, supporting it. A tiny pool of blood gathered where the knife tip pressed a dimple into his neck just below his Adam's apple.

She sat up, shifting her weight to gain leverage for the final, fatal thrust.

"Now, goddamn it," she hissed grimly, between her teeth. "Will. You. Surrender?"

He fluttered his eyelashes up at her.

"Will you respect me in the morning?"

CHAPTER NINETEEN:
THIS WAY TO THE EGRESS

Conchita sighed. "The saddest thing I've ever learned,
Desmondo, is that most people would rather control
their neighbors than be free, themselves."

—Conchita y Desmondo
in the Land of Wimpersnits and Oogies

"Lieutenant Segovia!" Colonel Atherton-Nye shouted. "Kill
me that renegade at once!"

"No, ma'am!" Julie remained where she sat, somewhat
absurdly, on Billy's chest, but the pressure of her knifepoint left his
throat. She let the weapon lie harmlessly across her lap. "I'm not
obliged to obey an illegal order. This whole farce is illegal as hell!"

Atherton-Nye turned to the men flanking her, her favorite pair
of Marine guards and the Space Force officer. "Shoot her!" A heart-
beat passed. Two heartbeats. Nobody stirred a single finger. "No?
Then—" The woman reached for the antique weapon that Billy had
returned to her. Julie wondered whether she could throw her knife—
she'd never tried. Sergeant Spanner had maintained that throwing a
knife was simply handing the enemy a weapon.

Billy, in the meantime, had been looking the other way, away
from the Colonel's crate-table, toward a corner of the room between

two derby units, where he saw a pair of bright lights shining through the transparency. He abruptly surprised Julie by shrugging her off his chest with ease—Atherton-Nye's eyes grew large—leaped to his feet, shouted down at the girl, "Hold onto your knife and *exhale!*" And he dashed for the table where their belongings lay.

At that moment, something that was all headlights and crazy mechanical clutter *crashed!* through the corner wall. This, Billy thought, I know how to do, from dozens of drills and a single previous emergency. He refrained from trying reflexively to catch a breath, relying, instead, on speed and the oxygen already dissolved in his bloodstream. He knew that it takes three minutes to die of anoxia. The Marines and the Space Force were getting in each other's way, comically, trying to exit through the back airlock.

He snatched up his gun belt, and grabbed the kukri from the floor, where it had landed near the desk, turned and ran toward the electric rover he could see Roger Leigh was driving. On the way, he scooped up his former antagonist, who by this time was looking a little blue around the lips, along with her giant knife. She was going to miss that scabbard.

A big box of heavy transparent plastiglass had been installed around the upper portion of what was essentially an electric dune buggy, but equipped with four, complicated, independently powered wheels. Roger and Mirella were properly suited up. Between them, lying on the console, he saw a couple of cheap, flimsy, bright yellow emergency suits neatly folded.

As they closed the makeshift door and the "cabin" began to pressurize again, Billy drew a grateful breath, snatched a roll of duct tape from a tray of tools, tore off a piece, and sat behind the other three riders in a competition shooting position, facing backward, his forearms resting on his knees. As he'd guessed, the Marine guards were back, in space suits, leveling their pathetic little rifles at the rover. Before they could fire, Billy shot two of them, right through the plastiglass, and immediately slapped the strip of tape over the two overlapping bullet holes he'd made. His ears rang. By that time, they were well out of range, headed back to the settlement, and Julie was halfway into an emergency suit.

149

"What if you hadn't had that roll of duct tape handy?" she demanded of Billy. "Speak up, because you've damn near deafened me with that goddamned hand cannon of yours." She wriggled a little finger in one ear, a highly unsatisfactory undertaking since it was gloved.

"Shucks," said Billy, "I was just getting used to having an entire planet as a silencer. I was gonna put my finger in the dike, if you'll pardon the expression, until we got home."

Julie said, " 'Home' being the colonial settlement in the lava tube?" It was more a statement than a question.

Roger turned to look at Julie directly. "You have anyplace else to go, Lieutenant? They haven't built a Little America truck stop on Mars, yet, or even a Motel 200. Anyway, you won't be the first. Your little friend what'shername ... Holly-something ... Archuleta? The one that Grenville Swope raped? She officially defected yesterday morning."

Mirella put her gloved hand on Roger's suited arm. "Hold on. I've got something on the GPR." She, too, turned where she sat. "That's 'Ground Penetrating Radar,' Lieutenant. Can't be natural; it's a fist-size bit of nearly pure steel. Hats on."

It was very good advice. When she opened the door, it evacuated the whole vehicle.

Reaching for a carbine mounted on the inside of that door, she told Julie, "Just in case your former friends catch up to us. Brody souped this thing up a little bit." She turned to Billy. "Back at Derbyville, I was just getting out to rescue you with it. I'd forgotten that you'd taken vacuum-breathing lessons."

"He did what?" Julie asked Billy. It appeared to her that human cultures were beginning to diverge. To her, the expression "souped it up" was slang, two centuries out of date.

"He tweaked it," Billy attempted to explain to her, without really explaining. "Where is Brody, Mirella? I thought the two of you were—"

"I tried to help him," Mirella told him. "He wouldn't let me. Just told me to get you a pickup and took off."

Billy nodded, but still Julie sat, looking perplexed.

"He doubled the power, somehow," Roger translated for her, without looking back at them. "Tinkered with the vehicle, too. It feels like I'm driving a ticking time bomb."

Mirella turned and only walked a few steps out into the desert. She stooped and picked something up from the ground, returning with it to the car, then climbed back in, shut the door, and initiated repressurization. Roger set the car in motion again, generally southeast, toward the colony. Then Mirella showed them all what she had retrieved, and, automatically, Julie reached out for it.

"Unh-unh!" she warned the Lieutenant, pulling it back out of reach. "Don't touch it—damn thing's so cold it's sure to burn you. Billy, I believe, by rights, this belongs to you."

Billy looked down, a bleak expression on his face and a hollowed-out feeling in his chest as he put on his gloves to take it. It was a small black six-shot revolver (most pistols this size were five-shooters) that she had recovered, with an extremely short barrel. Yet it couldn't have been the gun that had been used to murder their little sister. The caliber was too small. With gloved hands, he pressed the Smith & Wesson-style cylinder latch forward, rolling the cylinder out and to the left. Six brass cartridges glinted up at him. One primer of the lot was dimpled, meaning that there had been a single fired shot. The headstamps on the back ends of the cartridge cases all said FC .327 FEDERAL MAG.

In the earliest years of the settlements on Pallas, Billy explained to Julie, it was the custom that the winner of a duel—of which there were a surprising number back then—took the loser's weapon. The loser was usually in no condition to object. However there hadn't been a real duel on Pallas for at least fifty years and the custom had largely been forgotten. Now it appeared to have been revived here on Mars.

He said grimly, "This is what Rockwell shot our little Teal with. At least I think it may be. The evidence at the scene was a bit confusing. Later, he tried to use it on me, and flung it away—an involuntary nervous reaction, I believe—when I shot him first. I'll make sure this is never used by bad people for evil purposes again." He put the weapon in his pocket.

"You going to destroy it? Julie asked.

"I'm going to carry it," he said.

Every step seemed to speak her name into his head. And now Brody could see her, helmet-down in the rust-colored soil, her air tanks already scavenged from her skinny body.

He could only hope it had been Billy that took them. He could only hope—

"God, Teal."

Before he could fully process what he was doing, he had broken into a jog, closing the distance between his mindless feet and her lifeless form.

He'd thrown the keys at Mirella, telling her to make tracks and find Billy, wherever their crazed bastard of a brother had gotten off to—he'd left them high and dry on the comms channel and even now, Brody wasn't sure where he was.

And now as he threw himself into the dust at his twin's side, he wasn't sure how much anything mattered anymore. Her Ngu Departure pistol was still on the ground at her side, cold steel in the dirt.

"Teal, sis, I'm so sorry," he breathed, reaching out for her, and then, as if stung, pulling back—his Teal, his twin sister, lay where she had fallen, ignominiously covered in human excrement, which had frozen onto her helmet and stained her suit. And it was this, more than anything, which brought the ache of tears to his eyes, such that he had to sit back on his heels and wipe uselessly at the helmet which covered his own face.

"Shit, get it together, Brody," he told himself, his gaze once again coming to rest on his sister's body—consciously replacing his sorrow with anger, he pulled from his belt a folding knife, which he fumbled open with a clumsy gloved hand. Finally it snapped locked and he began to vainly scrape the layer of ice from the exterior of Teal's helmet.

As soon as he'd cleared away a patch of it, he wished he hadn't even begun; her face was pale and sort of gray, her dark eyes open and her lips parted in something like surprise, perhaps even pain.

He couldn't hear the footsteps behind him. But he felt them, and immediately he dropped the knife, his hand going to the gun on his hip—prettily engraved just like his sister's, with his name and their father's in delicate script. He pivoted where he sat, still cradling Teal's body in his other arm, smoothly drawing the pistol; it was raised to shoulder-height by the time he locked eyes with the suited interloper, small and dark-eyed, petite—

"Mrs. Khalidov?"

Of course, she couldn't hear him, either. But she put up her hands in a gesture of surrender, and slowly, his shoulders shuddering, Brody lowered his weapon.

Beliita Khalidov approached slowly, as if afraid the young man might change his mind about the pistol, but when he slid it back into its holster, she sank to a crouch beside him, a gentle arm finding its way around his shoulders until they sat helmet-to-helmet upon the ground.

"Brody," she said, and though her voice was muffled by the plastiglass of their joined visors, he could hear it, warm and soft and sort of motherly, in the pressurized space inside his helmet. "I was out for a walk, and I saw you—what happened?"

And now Brody could feel the tears beginning to collect in his eyelashes, the world around him growing sparkly and distorted through the watery lenses gathering over his eyes.

"My—my sister," he said, the words staggering out a little stupidly. "She's ... Teal is *dead*, some—some sonofabitch put her down like a goddamn dog!"

Beliita nodded, holding him close against her side to speak to him, her other hand going to his, where it still gripped Teal's suited arm. "Come. Let's take her inside, Brody. Dr. Bonney will get her cleaned up and you can hold her properly."

"Colonel Atherton-Nye," purred the smooth, calming voice over the radio, "it isn't true that your government is cruelly refusing you—and the fine men and women under your command—a ride home. Although I suppose people could be forgiven if they believed that you're being punished for the complete mess you've made of things up there." He paused for a moment to let the words sink in, then started talking again before she could reply, apparently unaware of the huge time-lag between the halves of their conversation. "It's the laws of physics, you see. Or at least as I understand them. The *US/ UNSS Retaliator* has already left Mars orbit. You and your people are on your own until and unless ... "

"Until and unless what?" the one-eyed woman demanded. "Er ... sir." There would be that infuriating 45-minute transmission lag, she knew, all too well, before he could receive her message and reply to it.

Time passed.

"That's better, Colonel. My experts inform me that it's quite impossible to turn that ship around and come back for you, even if I were to give the order. We might be able to mount another mission when it comes back to Earth." She could hear the paper he was reading from rattling in his hand. "Given travel-time between Earth and Mars, that's at least 544 days, add more for refit and resupply. The better part of two years. Do you think you can you hold out that long?"

"We will hold out, sir," Marine Colonel Atherton-Nye told President Maxwell Promise. "For as long as we have to."

"Here's an interesting one," Reubenson observed, looking up from the holographic monitor display. The Ngus had bought half a dozen small, sophisticated computers with them to Mars, powered by solar cells, and the equipment necessary to put the colonists in touch with the Solarnet. Somehow, news of recent events on the red planet was getting to Earth in any case and generating comments from various figures there, public and private. " 'Timothy Strahan,' " the expedition leader read, " 'President of All Worlds Are Earth, a conservation organization' "—Ha!—" 'offered this comment on the violent murder of Porter Rockwell, AWAE's representative on the planet Mars, by the son of renegade capitalist Emerson Ngu.

" 'Although we disagreed occasionally with Mr. Rockwell's radical approach to solving social and economic problems, his energetic spirit will be sorely missed by his family, friends, and comrades in the environmental movement.' "

Billy snorted, "Yeah. His approach: 'There is no problem that can't be solved with a sufficient amount of high explosives, right, *comrade*?'"

"Roger that," said Reubenson.

"That's my name," said Roger Leigh. "Don't wear it out."

"Billy," Jack ignored him, "I understand your people have a lot more experience dealing with pushy Earth governments and the UN. You think they'll leave us alone, now?"

"I couldn't say. We just quietly threatened to divert a small asteroid their way, a generation or so ago. Even if it hit in the middle of the Pacific, the tsunamis alone …. But we were only bluffing, Jack. Pallatian ethics don't allow 'collateral damage.'"

Reubenson raised his eyebrows. "Makes it tough if they know that."

"That's not even a serious risk." Billy shook his head. "They'll go to any length to avoid understanding our concept of integrity."

"So you're out, now, too." Holly Archuleta looked up at Julie from the makeshift hospital bed where she was slowly recovering from the effects of sudden decompression. She complained that every joint ached, and that her lungs hurt. Both her eyes were blacked. The doctor had said that she was lucky. "From the Corps, I mean. Because you killed the bastard who—no, please, I need to say it—the bastard who raped me. I guess I owe you, Segovia."

Julie shook her head. "Please call me Julie—we're both civilians now. You don't owe me a thing, Holly. I killed Swope because he tried to rape me. I'm out of the unit because I wouldn't obey Atherton-Nye's order to kill Billy Ngu."

"He's the dreamy hunk who disabled me," said Holly, "after I tried to kill him and then he saved my life. He could just have left me lying there, to freeze-dry in that creepy tunnel."

"I tried to kill him, too," said Julie, "but I couldn't do it. And he saved my life, anyway. If he's any example, Holly, I think the brass back home, and on the way here, lied to us about these people. I saw Lieutenants Kennesaw and Natchez down there at the cave mouth working on the new greenhouse. They were part of the skeleton crew and weren't at the battle. Apparently they both lit out sometime before I did, taking their weapons, suits, and some supplies with them. Something tells me, as Atherton-Nye gets nuttier, they won't be the last."

"She's in a pretty bad place for a Marine," Holly admitted. "She can't move forward and there's no place to retreat to. All she can do is dig in where she is, and there's no future in that."

"Why, Holly Archuleta," replied Julie, "I had no idea you were a tactician."

They both giggled.

A shadow appeared on the plastic partition. "Lieutenant Segovia? Jack Reubenson said to tell you that another four Marines have just shown up, with their weapons and some food, saying they're seeking asylum."

"And so it goes," said Julie, getting up from where she sat. "I'll see you later, Holly."

"I have no idea if he ran out of oxygen or simply tripped and fell and cracked his helmet." Mirella knelt by the space-suited corpse they had found a few yards from the *Zelda Gilroy*, which was still heavily loaded with supplies for the Martian colony. The little ship's main hatch had been broken into and some of her lighter cargo was missing. It was several weeks after Mirella's new friend Julie Segovia had defected from the Marines and come to the colony. The man's tracks told them he had broken into the little spaceship and stolen some of the supplies. The absence of those supplies now also said he'd had help.

"It's too bad he wasn't alone," said Dean Deutsch, obviously annoyed that his helmet denied him the useful gesture of scratching his head. "We're gonna miss those three crates, whatever they were. Do you know what was in them?"

"Not until I check the manifest," Brody told him. "They must be starting to get desperate over there in Derbyville."

Reubenson replied, "We've told them a dozen times that we're willing to trade with them. I'm even inclined to be generous, extend credit."

Ever the cynic, Brody said, "Yeah, but that would mean admitting what's really happened here. They're still whining to Mommy back on Earth to come and save them from the nasty old colonists—who aren't doing a damn thing to them!"

As it was on any frontier, Earthside or elsewhere, sunrise on Mars heralded, not the time for pioneers to wake up, but the time for them to begin work. Being a true child—and grandchild—of the frontier, Billy was alert, vertical, and dressed, breakfasted, and environmentally suited up, by the time the sun peeked over the red planet's horizon. Squeezing the weapon from muzzle to trigger-guard with his thumb and forefinger, he examined the chamber of the mighty Grizzly Magnum—you never know—one of the fat, shiny cartridges was in there, exactly where it ought to be.

The only real difference between the son of Emerson Ngu on Mars and the historical frontiersmen back on Earth who came before him was that his morning meal—cheese and grits and something vaguely bacon-flavored, with coffee—had been prepared in a microwave cooking device, powered by yesterday's sunshine. From the moment that he stepped through the circular door (he thought of it as the "hobbit door") of the BEAM he'd been assigned to, his trusty anti-radiation parasol swung at his elbow.

One of the notorious solar-electric Mars-buggies environmentalists on Earth loved to hate so much, it seemed, had developed a serious problem. Its right front wheel was making a horrible noise which Billy thought was probably a bearing. It could only be heard through the metal and carbon structure of the little car, not through the non-existent air. For all intents and purposes, there wasn't any air on Mars. Nevertheless, left untreated it could mean the beginning of the end of motorized transportation on Mars. The local material the bearing was likely impacted with was iron-bearing quartz, eating its abrasive way though the motor shaft. The environmentalist crazies back on Earth would be so happy. Mars was getting its revenge! Billy had a momentary mental flash of himself trying to ride a bicycle through the local sand, gravel, and dust in a space suit, carrying a parasol.

Come to think of it, those bicycles would eventually suffer and die the same mechanical death, as well. They were dependent on bearings, too, however valuable they may have been as virtue-signaling.

Why he had to be the one to effect the repairs—he was a spaceship mechanic, damnit!—was beyond him, but he never really questioned it. His father, as relatively tiny as the man was, lived well-ensconced in his head. He began to gather the necessary tools for the job ahead. Keeping delicate parts away from dust in an environment *made* of dust was going to be something of a challenge.

It was as if the entire planet had been constructed of jeweler's rouge—about the same color, too—and not for the first time he wondered if the macaroni plant was going to change that. Cursing the astrogational necessity for tools made mostly of polymers and fiberglass with steel and titanium contact- and stress-points—like the huge spanner he was wielding—he began to take the wheel-hub apart.

Billy found what he needed in the outdoor motor pool cabinet—there was no need to keep the tools indoors in an oxygen and water-free environment—and took them to the buggy, extending his umbrella's telescoping handle, pointing it in the optimal direction that its radiation-counter indicated, and planting it in the sand where it would protect him from deadly emanations from the sun and stars.

His own environmental suit had been manufactured especially for him back home on Pallas (as an aspiring space pilot and asteroid hunter, he ordered a new one every year) and was several times more impermeable to radiation and micrometeorites than the regrettably shoddy government-made outfits the colonists had been forced to bring with them—the poor folks *needed* the umbrellas—but he and his siblings, he thought, ought to set the best example that they could. All part of the service!

He grinned.

He wiped the hub off carefully with a special solvent-wetted paper towel. Real water didn't last very long in this environment, boiling away almost instantly in the hard vacuum. Then he unfolded a large plastic bag, put the business end of his huge wrench into it, along with both hands. Two long plastic tubes went with them and connected him to supplies of water and compressed air. He carefully washed his hands and the wrench in the tiny boiling storm within the bag. Then he inverted it over the loosened hub and pulled the wheel apart. As he thought, fine dust was caked all around the inside of the hub. It looked like a devil's food doughnut. Using the air and water he blasted it all out, relying on the Teflon it was made of to lubricate it, reassembled it, and covered it everywhere he could think of with quick-setting polymer sealant. He lifted the corner of the cart with one hand and spun the wheel, feeling no friction.

Sensing unexpected movement just inside his field of vision, he glanced up. Two rough-looking individuals, only vaguely familiar, shambled toward him from around one end of a big ochre boulder. Their environmental suits, he noticed, were badly worn, faded, and patched, although they made the Old Survivor's look downright artistic. Their helmet faceplates bore a thousand little scratches—and some not so little. They bore United States Marine Corps markings. *East* American Marines, Billy corrected himself. They also both carried weapons, those nasty little FN 5.7s they'd all been issued, Billy thought he'd rather have a bad head cold.

One of them spoke over the colony's suit frequency. "We came down here to give you the good news, Pally." Apparently it had become their nickname for Pallatians. "Poor old Colonel Atherton-Nye is dead, and you killed her!" These men were the Colonel's bodyguard who'd helped supervise his duel with Julie.

"*I* killed her?" Billy deeply regretted that the hammer-thong of his Grizzly was looped securely over the massive weapon's hammer. One way or another, he wouldn't make that mistake again.

"Sure you did, Pally. After you and your goddamn Mexican chippie crashed out of our place, and that Space Force fliegleboy deserted her, the Colonel had some kind of a fit and lay down and never got up again. And it's all your fault, Pally, it's your fault!" The man was close to tears.

The other fellow made a show of examining his carbine idly and added, "So Joe and I just thought maybe we oughta come over and kill you a little bit, too. It's only fair."

"Kind of a long walk," somebody observed wryly, "to get dead." It was hard to tell directions in these suits, but the voice sounded like

Holly Archuleta's. "And I'm not Mexican, numb-nuts, I'm Puerto Rican!"

"I wasn't talking about you, chica," the bodyguard snarled, pointing somewhere behind Holly, presumably at Julie. "I was—" Suddenly he raised his carbine. Holly's was already up. Its bright green laser painted itself across the man's forehead. She pulled the trigger, shattering his helmet, then fired again, instantly killing the other gunman, who had raised his weapon, as well. Holly carried no umbrella, Billy observed. He'd have to get after her about that—never.

Billy's Grizzly was already halfway out of its holster. Now he put the thumb safety back up and let the weapon settle in its worn old holster again. He left the hammer loop alone and would never use it again. He looked back behind Holly. Julie wasn't there. Nobody was.

"You saved my life, Holly," Billy told her gratefully, noticing for the first time that she was leaning on a crutch. "I guess that makes us even."

"I'm not counting," she told him sweetly. "Are you?"

CHAPTER TWENTY: SONG OF THE VULGAR BOATMEN

"Desmondo, cheer up!" Conchita demanded. "Do you really want to get home again, or have you given up?"

—*Conchita y Desmondo*
in the Land of Wimpersnits and Oogies

"**L**eft!" Julie tried not to shout. "Two more paces left!" The sixty-odd space-suited figures at the other ends of the ropes, denied their vision forward by a canopy of radiation-proof umbrellas, dutifully obeyed her radioed instruction, and moved slightly to the left.

It was a very good thing, she thought, that the Ngu siblings had brought plenty of rope with them from Pallas. It had been formulated for asteroid hunters, they said, to withstand hard vacuum and extreme cold. Between them, Billy and Jack had "stolen" an idea from the Marines who were their neighbors now. They had suffered a theft and now would protect the precious cargo still stored aboard the *Zelda Gilroy* by dragging the little spaceship the ten kilometers or so that separated her from the settlement. This was several times the job that the Marines had undertaken, merely winching their four landers closer together. But the colonists had some advantages, too.

"You know, Billy," Mohammed Khalidov had observed, shortly before this unlikely project had gotten under way, "we really ought to leave a flag or a marker behind of some kind. I assure you, history and historians will want to know exactly where this spaceship landed."

Billy had snorted. "That's dead easy, Mo. They can tell from all the crap I'm dumping here to make this damn thing light enough to drag!" And with that, the last of the three engines had fallen to the ground as its final support had yielded to his cutting torch. It was strange to see an open flame on this planet, but acetylene comes with its own oxygen supply.

Julie looked down from where she perched now, as high atop the derelict vehicle as she could climb, beneath her own parasol, unable to use binoculars with her helmet (there was a technical problem to be solved), with Brody's modified carbine across her lap. It shot ten-millimeter pistol cartridges now; Fritz had sent him half a dozen barrels fresh from Emerson's Ngu Departure factory where the field redesign had been accomplished. She felt a bit guilty about that, with other people hauling her like freight. But somebody needed to keep an eye on where they were all headed, trying to follow the footprints and tire tracks of everyone who had come from the camp to the ship or the other way around and avoiding craters and gullies. She had excellent eyesight, was a good shot, and was by far the lightest.

One of the colonists' advantages was the pair of solar-charged electric four-wheel drive vehicles they'd brought with them, to the utter dismay and disgust of Earth's prissier environmentalists. The cars weren't remarkably powerful, and they would be useless for days, after this duty had dragged their batteries down to nothing, but they were helping to pull the broken spaceship across the sandy ground. Somewhere on the planet, there were a dozen more just like them; the technology had not advanced perceptibly. All forty-seven settlers would take part, too, plus the sizable handful of Marines who had recently changed sides, plus Brody, and Mirella Ngu—neither of whom was accustomed to the pull of Martian gravity—doing the driving. Billy, who was having the same gravity trouble, had been "ordered" by Reubenson to stay behind to defend the empty camp from potential marauders.

As they advanced, Reubenson and his aides fed wide pieces of sheet metal, salvaged from their own lander, under the craft and fastened them on so it could skid across the sand in the lighter gravity. It would have been impossible on Earth. Whenever the whole thing *lurched!*, Julie had to be careful not to tumble to the ground. Everybody else had hold of a rope and *pulled*. It reminded the child within her of the memorable illustrated scene from the written version (Millicente had insisted) of *The Wizard of Oz* when mice by the hundreds had towed Dorothy and her sleeping friends out of the nearly lethal poppy patch.

Unlike those mythical field mice, however, somebody had decided that what they all needed was a "work song" to get the job before them (actually behind them) accomplished properly. It was impossible to tell who the culprit was, precisely, with everybody using the same communications frequency. Ironically, it turned out that the only song everybody knew in common—colonists, Marines, and even Brody and Mirella alike—was a bizarre birthday dirge, sung to the somber Russian tune of "The Song of the Volga Boatmen."

"Happy Birthday! (pull!) Happy Birthday! (pull!)
Now you've aged another year!
Now you know that Death is near!
They say that cancer's caused by beer!
Happy Birthday! (pull!) Happy Birthday! (pull!)

"Happy Birthday! (pull!) Happy Birthday! (pull!)
People dying everywhere!
Women crying in despair!
Death, destruction, and despair!
Happy Birthday! (pull!) Happy Birthday! (pull!)"

There were a lot more like that, dozens and dozens of verses. Julie didn't know a single one of them. Growing up among the shattered ruins of Newark, New Jersey, struggling every day just to

163

survive, she'd never been to a birthday party, not even her own, and the likelihood of death had never been a joke. But she soon caught on and sang along gaily with everybody else.

Billy stood atop the defunct spaceship, where Julie had sat, several yards inside the yawning entrance to the lava tube. It was almost like the indoor baseball stadiums he'd seen on 3DTV. Brody and Mirella stood down below, on either side of the widely opened main hatch. The people of the colony began to gather 'round. He could see that someone in the back was making a video recording. Whether it was for posterity, the East American government, the Yoonies, the Solarnet, or simply Moose Holder's Helmet Radio Network, he didn't care. Maybe West America. He wondered if his family on Pallas would see it. The hardest thing he'd ever done was tell his mother and father about Teal. It was the absolute lowest point in his life—he'd talked to Julie for hours about it, afterward. He'd far rather have died, himself.

He began addressing the colonists, "My family and I discussed this back in Curringer on Pallas before we came here. We talked about it more or less continuously on the weeks-long flight from there to here. We hashed it over one final time just last night. The contents of this vessel are a gift to you—as individuals—from our families and friends back on Pallas who didn't want to see you die like your unfortunate predecessors. In a few minutes it will all be given to you—as individuals—no strings attached. We've also talk-ed it over with Jack Reubenson and his staff."

"I have a staff?" Reubenson asked, looking around.

"You have a very good staff," Billy answered him. "Everything is going to stretch a little thinner, so we can share it with the brave souls who've defected from Derbyville. There will be no administration of it; you will each have no one to answer to. You are absolutely free to keep, consume, or trade whatever you receive.

"But, as you line up—single file if you please—to take your gifts away, I want to risk boring you all by telling you why it is we've de-cided to do it this way. You see, it's all about history ..."

There were a couple of boos and even more groans. When it was possible, people let Brody and Mirella toss crates down to them. When they'd each received three, they carried them back to their quarters where Billy, of course, could still be heard.

"I don't have an appropriate story for you from the founding of the settlements on my home world, but it might surprise you that Thanksgiving, the West American Autumn holiday, is a fairly big deal on Pallas, too. We time it to share the event with them, about twice a Pallatian year, if only in spirit. But the stories that they tell you about it in East America: those noble Indians saving incompetent and evil Pilgrims from starvation and all that, just aren't true.

"Among the pioneering Europeans to settle in North America—which was no less an alien world to them in the 17th century than Mars is to us today—were the members of the Plymouth colony, in Massachusetts, at the edge of the Atlantic Ocean, which came under the leadership of a Governor William Bradford after the old governor died—possibly of starvation, as you'll see.

"At first, they had all tried working on a share-and-share-alike basis, you know, the old 'From each according to his ability, to each according to his needs' nonsense. That's a silly idea that has proven wholly incompatible with real human nature, which, in its true Darwinian manner, wants to know 'What's in it for me?' Individuals who worked hard received little or nothing for their efforts, with no hope of bettering themselves; parasites who loafed got a free ride, for as long as it lasted. Pretty soon the few workers left gave up working, and the Plymouth colony was about one bad week away from starving or dying horribly of some poverty-induced disease like the old governor.

"But then the new Governor, Bradford, did something that socialist dictators three hundred years later, like V.I. Lenin and Josef Stalin, Hugo Chavez and Nicolas Maduro were incapable of. He saw correctly that the socialist model didn't work at all, and so he jettisoned it. He divided the colony's land up into private plots, parceled them out, and told the people, 'You're on your own.'

"Thanksgiving Day is the celebration of the first successful harvest after the Plymouth colony was saved from socialism by the intelligence and integrity of Governor Bradford. That's why the Left despises it so much and tries to turn it every year into a national guilt-fest using the excuse of the poor Indians that they, themselves, still mistreat and exploit.

"Think of what we brought you as your plot of land. You're on your own. The system of trade instead of dealing with currency has made Pallas successful—helped it grow through honest bartering and working together. Try to make the most of our gift."

The moving process had required three grueling days, during which hundreds of oxygen canisters had been emptied and refilled, and thousands of gallons of water dispensed, but was a great success, in that not a single individual had been injured or killed. By the last day, what remained of the *Zelda Gilroy* now sat, emptied out and lonely looking, a few yards inside the mouth of the enormous cavern that sheltered the colonial settlement from the powerful solar and cosmic radiation that made Mars such a dangerous place to live. In the end, there had not been enough room for the sixty-odd people and even the cars to pull the ship into the cave; they'd imitated the Marines, instead, using ropes and hoists to do the job.

Julie found Billy in the gloomy, twilit depths of the upper lava tube, crouching like Rodin's *The Thinker* where his sister Teal had fallen. It was not her grave, but the place where her brother had found her. The young Pallatian's grave had been added beside that of Mama Sue at the landing site. Near Derbyville lay fifteen more—another Marine had died in treatment. Thanks to the stupidity, insanity, and evil of authority, Mars had claimed more martyrs.

"Hey," Julie said, to avoid startling him as she approached him from behind. She didn't want to startle a man who carried that damned Grizzly artillery piece around. For that matter, she was armed, herself, with that "tweaked" Marine carbine Brody had now made her a gift of. And, of course, they both had their big knives. One of the recent defectors had very kindly brought her the fiberglass scabbard she'd unwillingly abandoned at Derbyville. It was possible that the poor guy, hardly more than a teenager, had anticipated some token of affection as a reward. If so, he'd departed disappointed. She'd immediately cleaned and polished her ancient knife. They had all been waiting for Atherton-Nye to drop the other combat boot.

"Hey, yourself," he answered, looking up at her. He was pretty clearly not unhappy to see her, she thought with a rising feeling. "What brings you this deep in the tube, Lieutenant?"

"I told you, Billy, it's Julie. I was looking for you," she said softly. "I never got to tell you that I didn't really know your sister, but I'm very sorry she died. My big sister Millicente—she's my only family— almost died last year, so I think I understand how it must feel."

Billy paused before he answered. "Thank you, Julie. Teal was murdered. The murderer's dead, too. That account's closed. But I'm going to miss the little twerp every day for the rest of my life—what should have been the rest of hers. For Mirella, it's going to be like having an arm sawed off—be a friend to her if you can. I'm especially sorry that Teal won't be here to see the macaroni plant bloom or get a foothold or whatever it does. Once it does, it'll change the planet, and my sister will have largely been responsible. By the way"—he indicated the spot on his throat where Julie's blade-tip had rested—"thanks a lot for not killing me."

She chuckled. "Now why do I suspect, Mr. Wild Bill Curringer Ngu, that it wouldn't really have been an option, no matter what happened?"

"Well," he answered, "my dad did teach me to be devious as hell."

"Your dad was actually *the* Emerson Ngu. I can't quite get over it. That's like meeting Neil Armstrong's son, or Thomas Edison's, you know?"

"How could I? To me, he's just always been 'Dad.' He still is, for that matter. You know he's planning a trip on humanity's first starship, the *Fifth Force*. My mom's going with him."

"Wow!" She shook her head. "And he invented the Ngu Departure pistol, the Pallatian motor tricycle, and the wonderful Pallatian flying belt."

"My favorite." Billy laughed. "And best of all, he invented *me!*"

She laughed, too, but deep inside, and despite herself, she was beginning to agree with him. She still hadn't thanked him for saving her life—the truth was, she didn't know how.

A figure shambled up to them in the low light. "Mr. Ngu?" she asked.

"Yes," he replied, "what can I do for you?"

"I'm Dr. Bonney." She was an attractive middle-aged blonde. "We haven't met yet. I performed the autopsy on your sister."

"Yes?"

"I have some questions about the ballistic evidence. It looks like you may have shot the wrong man."

CHAPTER TWENTY-ONE: CRIME AND PUNISHMENT

"What do you suppose it means, Desmondo?" Conchita asked, peering at the piece of paper in her hands, " 'You are much more like you are now than you were when I knew you before'?"

—*Conchita and Desmondo*
in the Land of Wimpersnits and Oogies

"You do realize, don't you, Mr. Ngu, that there are no lawyers on Mars?"

Her name, as it turned out, was Naval Lieutenant Junior Grade Spring Comity. She was one of several East American personnel who had recently defected from Derbyville, asking the civilian colonists for asylum. Spring was a pale, perfect platinum blonde of almost painful beauty, with a flawless complexion, and her hair pulled up off her long and lovely neck, not out of any fashion sense, but simply because it worked better with her space suit helmet. She also had a perfectly straight nose, extremely long eyelashes, and languid eyes of pale, pale blue, the kind that had defied photographers' lenses since the time of Mathew Brady. The young woman's voice was soft, her Southern accent gentle. She was slender and almost as tall as Billy.

Apparently, Billy realized, somebody suspected him, absurdly, of having murdered his own beloved sister. He felt heat and tension rise within him, but it wouldn't do any good to get mad about it now, he reasoned. He would get plenty mad about it later. Lieutenant Comity was not a lawyer, she admitted; she had worked, she explained to Billy, for two and a half years as a legal secretary in the Marine Corps' Judge Advocate General's office, under the Department of the Navy, back on Earth, and had been requested by Reubenson to defend him.

"Defend me against precisely what, Lieutenant?" he demanded angrily. "And against whom? And under what legal authority, exactly? In what court? I have a basic human right to know these things, and above all, who's accusing me! Is it that damned doctor?" He remembered hearing about his father's legal troubles.

"We are still awaiting discovery on that," she informed him. "And rulings from the appropriate authorities. Meanwhile, you are requested and required to turn your weapons over to me for safekeeping." She reached a hand out. Even in this gravity, her movements toward him across the floor of the infirmary "building"—little more than a plastiglass contrivance duct-taped together on a spindly frame of aluminum tubing—were liquid and sensuous. She didn't have many curves, he observed. She looked even more like a fashion model than his sister, Mirella.

"Absolutely not!" he told her. "There are fewer than a hundred human beings on this world. On mine, there's no such thing as 'authority.' Even if you were a real lawyer, Lieutenant Comity—which you yourself admit you are not—we're not establishing that precedent here, or there was no point in coming to a new world in the first place. If Jack wants my gun and knife let him come and try to take them!" The ancient Spartan king Leonidas, he recalled, had thought quite well of that position.

There was a long pause, as she obviously attempted to control her own temper, then: "Call me Spring, Billy. I can call you 'Billy,' can't I? He won't do that. Actually, he agrees with you: you don't strip a man of his defenses on a frontier world unless he's proven guilty of something. The precedent is well established. Also, the presumption of innocence necessarily includes an absence of anticipated punishment or rights denied. You realize we're making case law for a whole new world, here." Her nostrils flared slightly as she said that, and her cheeks acquired a slight flush. Obviously, the whole idea stimulated her in some way he found unhealthy.

She leaned toward him. "Billy," she said huskily, "this whole business rests on the ballistic evidence, as opposed to any inconsistent statements you may have made when you came back from the, er, Derbyville. You said that Porter Rockwell carried a 21st century Brazilian .327 Magnum revolver. You showed it to Reubenson and the others. I'll bet anything it's in that space suit pocket of yours, right now. And yet the good doctor tells us that the bullet pathway is more in keeping with a ten millimeter. How do you account for that?"

"How the bloody hell do I know? I'm not a ballistician! That goddamned doctor again! I can't account for it, Lieutenant. I wasn't there when it happened. I found my poor little sister lying dead in a pool of shit. If it wasn't to dump honeypots, then I have no idea what she was doing up there. The twenty-round magazine of her Ngu Departure autopistol was missing one cartridge. Did Jack or anyone bother to look for the spent case in that tunnel? One shot had been fired from Rockwell's revolver, too, but of course it retains the brass. If I believed in an afterlife, I'd bet you anything that Rockwell is off somewhere laughing his ghostly ass off at us right now."

She uncrossed and recrossed her long, smooth, graceful legs, where she had sat on the table she used as a desk. She was not wearing her environmental suit—a dangerous practice, he thought—although he hadn't seen a woman without a space suit in what now seemed like years. Hers was hanging up in a corner of her makeshift office. Instead, she wore a soft, green dress with a skirt that could be crumpled up and made to fit beneath the protective garment, at need. Despite himself, Billy felt something stirring inside him. She was unquestionably a beautiful young woman, and she smelled terribly good.

She said, "What you're suggesting, Billy, is that Porter Rockwell shot your sister with that antique weapon of his—we're going to need that, too, for evidence—and then, once she was dead or dying, he shot her again in exactly the same wound—just to muddy the waters and confuse us?"

"And it's worked perfectly, too, hasn't it, Lieutenant? That's exactly what I'm 'suggesting.' This way, All Worlds Are Earth and Gaia's Guardians can still sabotage us from beyond Rockwell's well-deserved grave."

"That's a mighty fine theory you have there," observed Jack Reubenson, squeezing in through the flexible airlock. He entered the room and took his helmet off. As he did, he had to set down the 5.7X25mm carbine he was carrying to do it. "You understand that I don't have any choice in this matter, don't you, Billy? As Expedition Leader, I'm officially placing you under arrest and confiscating your weapons for the sake of public safety."

"Mr. President," announced the Secret Service agent *du jour*, "the area is clean."

Maxwell Promise pulled his coat collar up around his ears. He even saw a single snowflake fall before his eyes. Wasn't the District of Columbia supposed to be in the South? Then why the hell was it so fucking cold? Unlike many of his predecessors, he was as kind and friendly to his bodyguard as it was in him to be. To him, it seemed like an elementary precaution. "Very well, Winthrop, please tell the Secretary I'll speak with him now—and make damn sure that *he's* clean. Melanie, I'm very sorry, but we'll need some space for a few minutes."

The agent replied, "Yes, sir!" Melanie didn't say anything at all, but the disappointed look she gave him spoke volumes. She turned and started walking across the frozen grass.

It was perfectly ridiculous, Promise thought, that the President of the (East) United States couldn't have a reliably private conversation in his own goddamned office or quarters, or even go for a quiet walk outdoors with his girlfriend without fear of being listened to or recorded. Instead, he had to venture out onto the White House grounds, in the middle of a cold, humid Southern winter, into a little copse of trees that constituted Somebody-or-Other's Garden, and even then, he had to have it swept electronically before he could speak freely. He also had to keep lip-readers with telescopic lenses in mind. It made him feel like a major league baseball player. Maybe what he needed was a big catcher's mitt to hide his face behind.

Melanie had walked away, all bundled up and looking to him like a darling little Eskimo, to sit on a child's swing-set left over from some previous administration. God, he thought, she was adorable. She made his blood feel carbonated. With a Secret Service escort, his Secretary of the Environment, Beauregard Spottiswood, approached. No matter how southern it sounded, the man had been named, he had explained to Promise when they first met, for a California community that had been utterly obliterated in the "Big One" of 2023. That devastating earthquake had killed over twenty million people, in all. crippled the entire American economy for decades and led directly to the balkanization of the country. In essence—and practical reality—the Canadian border, pivoting around Chicago, had been rotated ninety degrees.

After shaking hands and exchanging various pleasantries, Secretary Spottiswood cleared his throat and began. "I don't know how much you've heard lately, Mr. President, from our colony on Mars."

Promise was taken somewhat aback and momentarily confused. Fucking Mars, of all things. Shouldn't this sort of business be coming from the space agency or the military or somebody else? "Oh, that. Well. I do have my sources, Spotty. What do yours tell you?"

"Please don't share this with anybody, sir, I entreat you. I have it straight from Tim Strahan, himself, the president of All Worlds Are Earth. The news, I'm afraid, is not terribly good."

Promise grinned. "And you drew the short straw and were appointed to tell me."

The man grimaced. "Something like that, Mr. President. The Marines, under a distinguished combat veteran Lieutenant Colonel Mehetabel Atherton-Nye, boldly assaulted the renegades, crouching in their caverns within the first few hours that they, the Marines, were on the ground. They had to cover ten kilometers on foot before they could fire a shot. However, against insurgents who know the territory, and the Pallatian agitators, who grew up with weapons in their hands, Colonel Atherton-Nye's forces didn't acquit themselves very well. The colonial rebels sent them home with a bloody nose, and fifteen fatalities. Most of them have never gotten more than a few hundred meters from their landing site since then."

"Except for the dozen or so who have since changed sides." Promise inserted unexpectedly.

The man's face colored. "Except for them, sir, yes."

Promise looked around, reflexively reassuring himself that he couldn't be overheard. Even then, like the major league baseball players he'd been thinking about, he put a gloved hand in front of his mouth. "You may personally assure Mr. Strahan for me, that I have been giving this matter some considerable thought. Hard, practical thought. However, nothing can be done until the *US/UNSS Retaliator* returns in about seven months and can be refitted and resupplied. She will not be carrying personnel to Mars this time. Nine months back. Sixteen months, altogether. Then I think that our problems on Mars will finally be settled for good. The planet will be returned to the lifeless state in which we found it."

Promise turned away, abruptly dismissing the man. He'd have rather spoken about this with somebody from DOD. He felt for the cell phone in his jacket pocket. The Secret Service knew all about it; that was one reason for the lavish bonuses they received at Christmastime. For his own protection, somewhat hypocritically, perhaps, he always made a recording of meetings like this.

He waved a casual hand to summon Melanie from her perch. He wished sadly that they could make good his intentions in the garden, but for a number of reasons, including the unseasonable weather, that was impossible today. He liked her best on her knees before him, but even from the back, even from a distance, people would know what that meant. Ah, well. The poor girl was probably cold, like he was. He would warm her up when they got inside.

Billy grinned. "I don't recognize your authority to take my weapons from me, Jack." He held his left hand up, palm outward, anticipating Reubenson's reply as the man took a step forward. "No, I don't recognize *anybody's* authority to do that. We Pallatians have a just and proper way of handling matters like this. An individual is secure in his rights up until the very last moment of the trial in which he's duly found guilty. Then you have enough men handy to subdue him, if he requires it." He shook his head. "I didn't come to Mars for this; neither did my baby sister. As it is, you may hurt me with that popgun you're carrying, but I'd kill you with this .45 Magnum—three times the power of an ordinary .45. And I sure as hell don't want to do that. You're too good a man, Jack Reubenson, too valuable. The settlement needs you."

As Billy talked, two more individuals squeezed in through the flexible airlock, one behind the other. They were Mohammed Khalidov (who Billy appreciated was perfectly capable of doing his own killing given the right reason), and the deceptively pacific Communications Officer, Moose Holder. Billy looked out through the transparent plastic wall of what was the biggest building on Mars (so far). People, many of them armed, were beginning to gather outside. He saw the Deutsches and Julie Segovia. He deeply regretted that, now, he'd probably never get to know her any better. Or, for that matter, the alluring Lieutenant Junior Grade Spring Comity. He felt his right hand hovering over the open-topped holster that had been his father's. He'd taken off the hammer-thong days ago.

Billy said, low and slow, "Gettin' kinda crowded in here, isn't it boys?"

"You're still sayin', are ya," replied Holder. "That this here Rockwell feller shot your little sister twice for no discernable reason?" That word, "discernable," had been a mistake. Holder liked to play the slow-witted rustic, but the man's wife had revealed that he had a Ph.D. in Ethical Philosophy.

"Yes, Moose, until we know more, that's just what I'm saying."

"And that guess wouldn't be very far from wrong," said another voice. Billy watched as the flimsy membrane opened again to admit the figure who had come through the airlock. It was Doctor Bonney, who soon had her helmet under her arm. She set it down on a crate that was serving somebody as a desk, fished around in a pocket of her suit, and presented Billy the results.

"What is this?" Billy asked, holding up the tiny zip-lock bag.

"It's exculpatory evidence, Mr. Ngu, that's what it is," she said. "Show the Expedition Leader. Show your counselor. You're owed an apology. I found it rattling around in your sister's environmental suit. The shooting was a through-and-through, as the crime dramas say, but that damned thing didn't quite make it out of the suit. It's like those Civil War souvenirs they used to sell in gift shops where I come from, and at roadside stands—hell, maybe they still do—two bullets fused together as if they had collided in mid-flight during a battle. Only most experts believe they were created when one bullet hit another on the ground."

"I can see that," Billy responded, "But—"

"But nothing," Doctor Bonney interrupted. "In this particular case it's pretty clear what happened. The nickel-plated, ten-milli-meter, hollow-point bullet smacked right into the back end of the brass-jacketed thirty-two bullet at high velocity and fused with it in that position. Your intuition was absolutely correct. Porter Rockwell shot your sister, twice. The first shot killed her outright. I'd guess he wanted to throw us off. And that's how my official report will read. He was killed while resisting a lawful citizen's arrest. Three twen-ty-seven Federal, ten millimeter automatic, forty-five Winchester Magnum. My god, it's a three-caliber killing!"

Billy turned to face Spring. "Okay, Lieutenant. You heard the woman. I'll be keeping my weapons—and I assume you've seized my sister's pistol. It's been evidence to this point—but now, by all rights, it belongs to her brother."

Spring frowned, first at Billy and then at Reubenson, opening her mouth to speak—but then, thinking better of it, she bent and opened a safe, producing the pistol from it and holding it out to Billy. "Here," she said, slightly huffy. "As if you don't have enough."

"Not me," Billy said, taking the 10mm and checking first the magazine and then the chamber. "But I'll see to it that Brody gets it."

CHAPTER TWENTY-TWO:
HOME ON THE RANGE

"Sailors at sea look for seagulls to tell them they're approaching land," Conchita told Desmondo. "And spacemen see their destination millions of miles away. What do interdimensional travelers like us look for?"

—Conchita y Desmondo
in the Land of Wimpersnits and Oogies

Over the next couple of weeks, a very faint yellow fuzz began to be visible along the horizon of the gently rolling prairie, south of the settlement. It could almost have been the product of wishful thinking.

"If Teal were here," Billy told Julie, "she'd say we're turning Quadling country into the land of the Winkies."

"Is this Oz, again?" the former Marine Lieutenant peered up at him suspiciously.

"Classical reference," he answered. "Just one of many that didn't make it into the movie."

It chafed more individuals than Julie that binoculars were completely useless to those wearing environmental suits, and that they were useless from indoors because they could not overcome the optical distortions of the plastiglass they were trying to build with. Something had to be done about both of those problems. The Ngus had brought several pairs of high-powered glasses with them.

Scouts in the middle of what they hoped someday to call the "macaroni plains," reported a similar phenomenon up north, between the colony and Derbyville. Nobody ever visited the *Zelda Gilroy's* abandoned landing site anymore, but everybody guessed, as the original source of the lichen spores, the organism would be thickest there.

And wherever her balutes had ended up.

Billy and Jack took turns wishing vainly that they had a surveillance satellite in orbit. Somebody very likely did, some obscure agency or nation, maybe India or Malaysia, and they had put the word out. The two men were no less anxious than Mirella was to take pleasure in what her little sister Teal's brief life had bought.

The Old Survivor had finally shown up again, dragging his mighty curved, saw-toothed sword and in his space-suit-of-many-colors, supplied with a fancy brace of special Thompson-Center "Contender" single-shot pistols with ten-inch barrels, in a fancy, felt-lined walnut box. He carried what he called "the dueling pair" in an insulated, air-tight rucksack and said he didn't dare take it out into the Martian environment for fear that the wooden box and perhaps even the pistol grips would freeze-dry and crumble. Everybody wondered where the old man had gotten them, but nobody had asked. "Hated t'miss all the hoo-raw an' excitement," he told them. "These coulda turned out handy, but I was a mite late. Been kinda busy, waterin' an' weedin' m'vegetable garden."

Billy wondered how far a gun like that could knock you—at either end—in the feeble gravity of Mars. He and the machinist Roger Leigh looked down admiringly at the beautifully nested weapons, shiny black, with octagonal barrels and artistic impressions on the receivers, in Reubenson's office. They weren't quite *Code Duello* standard, he knew from his studies of the18th and 19th centuries. They were chambered for .44 Remington Magnum, instead of some muzzle-loading .40 that was traditional, and they had good, big iron sights. He hoped sincerely that there would never be a need for them on this planet again, but he was doubtful and grateful that the old man had thought of him and the other settlers.

Time passed. Over the period that followed, Billy found himself seeking out the company of pretty Julie Segovia more and more, and trying to remain aloof, politely, from Spring Comity. Although he often found her in his dreams, with those strange, haunting eyes of hers. He didn't dare ask himself why that might be. A soft and sultry platinum blonde and a petite, energetic brunette with sparkling dark-blue eyes. He was usually less confused than this. An embarrassment, as his mother used to put it, of riches. The centuries-old ditty "Did You Ever Have to Make Up Your Mind?" kept running through his head, although he doubted he'd be the one doing the deciding. Both young women were extremely easy to look at and each had her own indisputable charms, but if somebody had asked him, he probably would have said, unromantically, that out here on the frontier, he needed a fighter and a survivor in his life more than he needed a wannabe lawyer.

Put as brutally as that, he felt a bit guilty.

Over a period of several weeks, another three large "buildings" had been erected in the gigantic mouth of the lava tube. From a distance, if the observer squinted, it was beginning to look a bit like Mesa Verde, in West America. The settlers now had a little bit of room for offices, for group meals and meetings, and for recreation. Some of them had even improvised a Ping-Pong table. The balls had originally served some purpose in a pneumatic device. Billy continued to worry about the integrity of the plastiglass that the buildings were constructed of and its ability to resist ultraviolet light—he came, in essence, from a plastic-covered world, but it was a very special plastic, the fruit of William Wilde Curringer's genius and labor in the plastics industry, stretching for hundreds of miles high over the asteroid, half an inch thick, self-repairing, and selectively permeable.

Billy considered. The first human beings to arrive on Mars had come as participants in a series of dangerous and massively expensive East American and United Nations political stunts. The second "wave," from Pallas, came to rescue the first. The third—Colonel Atherton-Nye's Marines—came only to inflict pain and punishment and death on the others. (Porter Rockwell's presence was conclusive evidence of that.) Having failed humiliatingly to do so, whoever she had left behind now lived in isolation in Derbyville and had rendered themselves irrelevant.

Billy tried to see the future the way his father always did: not mystically, but with a deep understanding of where the human race had come from and where it might be going. The red planet, he mused—objectively—had relatively little to offer its pioneers that wasn't easily available in vastly greater abundance, and with far less effort, elsewhere—mostly among the asteroids that were his home. There were, of course, certain individuals who might wring out a decent living on Mars supplying daily necessities to others; they were the sort, often unjustly resented, who always profited most from a gold rush or similar event. That was how humanity had ended up with Levis and hundred-dollar eggs. Limited farming could be done under the colony's flimsy transparent plastic structures until there was enough atmosphere to do it the old-fashioned way. The soil was rich in the planet's many volcanic regions, and the light seemed better here than in the Asteroid Belt.

Importing spores, seeds, and cuttings from Pallas and elsewhere—by way of orbiting vessels that could drop them to the planet's surface in heavily protected packages or lower them on cables from what Billy wanted to call "areosynchronous" positions—might become relatively cheap and easy someday, although all that the self-made Martians could pay them back with, at present, was the equivalent of souvenirs and postcards. That was bound to change, sooner or later. Maybe the macaroni plant was the key. Reubenson had a dream of his own about capitalizing on the expertise that was here and making the planet the high-tech capital of the Solar System.

She stopped the car. "Frannie," Melanie asked, urgency in her voice, "how often do you speak with your brother?"

Thinking that she was about to hear some kind of tearful confession of romantic interest, Francine replied with counterfeit innocence and indifference, "Oh, I don't know. Which one? You know I have three."

"Francine!" The distress in Melanie's tone raised a couple of levels. "You do not have three brothers. Don't be deliberately obtuse; this is important! Hale, the one on Mars."

Francine understood then that something definitely peculiar was up. They had driven, almost in silence, at Mel's suggestion, twenty-odd miles into Maryland, ostensibly to go "antiquing" in some of the small towns there which claimed to be three hundred years old. Once well outside the Beltway, they hadn't gone anywhere near a town of any description; Melanie had parked her little yellow convertible here, in the countryside, within sight of a dozen cows or more, as close to a tall, high-tension electrical tower as she could, with the great, gracefully drooping lines directly overhead. "I've had this vehicle swept for bugs," she told Francine, "by a friend of mine in the Secret Service, but you never know. He suggested this tactic and said it was also 'a fairly good way to avoid drones'—apparently, they're allergic to 200,000-volt fields. I don't know if that's true or not."

"But why?" asked Francine, a bit bewildered. "And what the hell does it have to do with my brother?"

Melanie swallowed, hard. "This is all so horrible, I don't want to think about it, let alone talk about it. But I have to. Your brother and all the other people up there need to know. I didn't mean to spy. I mistook the cell phone on Max's nightstand for my own. I heard a couple of recordings Max had made. All Worlds Are Earth is very angry about what the colonists and the Pallatians are doing up there, and the way that the military has failed to bring them into line. Now the government is planning to send the ship back—to eliminate every living thing on Mars! And Max has approved it! Can you tell your brother that, in this Boontling language of yours?"

Francine sat for a dozen frozen heartbeats, hoping that the Secret Service friend of Melanie's was right about the bugs and the drones and the high-tension lines. Anxiously, she watched the sky, expecting violent death to rain down on them at any moment, and didn't say anything, trying to absorb what her best friend had just told her. She didn't think about Marilyn Monroe, she thought about

Cary Grant in *North by Northwest*. The absolute enormity of it—the President getting ready to commit genocide of a peculiar type. Melanie committing treason and personally betraying her powerful lover to tell her to warn her brother—it was all too much.

"Sure, Sweetie," she said at last, exhaling. "I'll tell him, all right. We talk once a week. He's supposed to visit with me tomorrow night. I'll think about wording the message as soon as we get back. What now? You still wanna do some shopping, for appearances?"

Melanie pressed a number of folded West American bills into Francine's hand. "You'll have to take a bus or a cab, Frannie. My bags are packed. They're in the trunk and I'm not going back—although I am going to stop somewhere and buy some trinket or other at an antique store so it shows up on my credit card account. You never know who's watching. I'm headed west from here. My father's coming to pick me up and smuggle me out to West America."

From a discreet distance, and from behind one of the two parked electric vehicles, Julie watched through the transparent wall of the office structure, thoroughly uncertain what she was feeling or supposed to feel.

Inside the structure, she could see Navy Lieutenant Spring Comity in that soft green form-fitting dress of hers, her space suit hanging uselessly on the wall over a desk. She was talking to Billy Ngu. Neither of them seemed particularly unhappy about it.

Julie observed that the Naval Lieutenant had talked him out of his space suit, as well. He was wearing faded jeans and a short-sleeved Western-style shirt, very colorful, and fastened with pearly snaps. Was she about to talk him out of those, as well? They were standing face-to-face—their toes must have been touching—Billy's hands were down at his sides.

Abruptly, Spring rose gracefully to the balls of her feet, threw her arms around Billy's neck, and kissed him on the mouth. His arms went, perhaps reflexively, around her slender waist as their lips molded together. The whole thing didn't last terribly long, but it made something in Julie's chest hurt. They broke, still talking and

smiling, as Billy pointed at his old-fashioned wristwatch and started getting back into his space suit.

He squeezed through the airlock, and as he walked out into the
cave, Julie was there, walking beside him. She plugged her com-
system cable directly into his own so they could talk privately, not
using the radio.

"Well," she asked sarcastically, "did you enjoy that?"

Startled, he replied, "Enjoy what?"

"Kissing Lieutenant Comity. Was it nice? It was certainly allit-
erative. Was she soft and warm? Did she smell good?"

She couldn't read his expression as he said, "I didn't kiss Spring,
Julie. She kissed me! And yes, it was very nice. It's been a damn long
time."

"Then you ought to do it some more," Julie replied bitterly. "A lot
more. Give her a good, solid checking-out. See if you might want to
keep her around handy for a while! She sure as hell has a lot more
to offer than I do!"

He stopped, turning around to face her. "Wait a minute! Is that
what all this is about?" Suddenly, Billy knew his heart. He put his
gloved hands on Julie's space-suited shoulders. "This goddamned
planet is sure hard on romance! I couldn't kiss you now to save my
life. Look, Lieutenant Julie C. Segovia, we haven't talked about this,
but do you honestly imagine that I'd choose some soft office-worker,
and a junior lawyer at that, over the world's tiniest Amazon?"

Julie blinked. Something inside her was about to break. She
didn't know whether to laugh or cry. She felt like doing both.

"Don't cry, Lieutenant." he advised her, holding her as closely as
he could. "It's a mess in a space suit."

Julie never learned exactly how or when Billy had arranged to bor-
row private quarters for them at this time of day. She didn't really
want to know. As they squeezed through the miniature airlock, he
had flipped down a "DO NOT DISTURB" tab, and suddenly, they
had found themselves alone together in a private space for the first
time since they'd met. Together, they fumbled their helmets off, and

this time, he took her in his arms and kissed her, deeply and ardently. It had to be that way, of course. She didn't know how. She didn't know that people kissing really did that with their tongues, although she'd read about it. It began to set her whole being on fire.

He had her out of her space suit in seconds, she didn't know how. Later, he would tell her that it was "motivation." It sounded to her like the same kind of fire. His own suit was discarded just as quickly. They lay, like a couple of discarded lobster shells on the floor at the back of the BEAM cylinder. What they wore beneath their suits took even less time and soon their naked legs entwined, and their warm flesh touched. The feeling of his hands all over her was like electric current running under her skin. He was big and broad, tanned and heavily muscled. He smelled good to her. She was small and pale and very slender and worried about how she smelled. They began to enjoy each other.

"You'll have to lead, Billy," she admitted to him shyly. "You see, I was raised by my sister, a strict Catholic disciplinarian—at least where I was concerned. I hope this doesn't spoil things too much. You're my first. I'm embarrassed to tell you that I'm a virgin."

A pause, then: "I'm not embarrassed to hear it. Don't worry, I'll be gentle."

She thumped him on the chest with the heel of her hand. "Don't you dare!"

A bit of awkward shifting and they were locked together, his shirttails grazing the bare skin beneath her hiked-up shirt. She seemed endearingly small to him. He was as gentle as he could bear to be with her, yet firm as he had to be, driven by a certain insistence. She never complained of pain or anything else, but began to make strange, wonderful, magical things happen between them, things he'd never known were possible.

"What? Julie, how did you …?"

Her eyes were suddenly downcast, unwilling to meet his, dark lashes astonishingly long on her cheeks. "My sister was a hooker, Billy," she murmured. "A professional girl. When she thought I was asleep, she chatted on the phone with the others. I paid attention."

Her skin tasted impossibly sweet to him. He buried his face in her fragrant hair and lay there for a long time. Feeling himself grow ready again, he caught her eyes and held them. He slowly unbuttoned her Marine uniform blouse to discover modest, shapely breasts. Set in her nipples …

"Nipple rings!" Billy exclaimed suddenly, delighted. "Tiny silver nipple rings!" Playfully, he flipped one of them up and down.

She shivered a little and grinned; he could hear it in her voice. "I thought you'd like those," Julie told him. "Evidence of my wasted youth in Newark. My sister wasn't exactly happy when I got them; I was fourteen. But my thinking was, if I wasn't going to be very big that way, I might as well be decorative. I haven't worn them since I enlisted in the Corps, but I thought you might enjoy them."

He toyed with the tiny shining circlets, flipping them with his fingers, gingerly pulling at them and twisting them a little. "You thought right, Julie, they're very pretty. Thank you. You thought this would happen, then?" He leaned over her and felt them click, one by one, against his teeth.

"I'd hoped …" She settled in under his chest. She sighed and moaned and started to weep. "Oh, Billy, I never thought anyone would ever want to do that."

Before he realized what she was doing, she slid down below his waist. "Here's something else I learned eavesdropping on my sister and her friends—I'll bet you'll like it, too."

When they had finished, he pulled her up, kissed her fervently, and crushed her to his chest, happier than he could remember ever being. He turned slightly, enveloping her in one arm, laid his palm over her throbbing breast, and buried his face between her neck and shoulder. They fell asleep in one another's arms.

CHAPTER TWENTY-THREE: MARS IN BLOOM

"Sometimes you can't go home," Conchita told Desmondo. "Sometimes you just have to build a home
where you are."

—Conchita y Desmondo
in the Land of Wimpersnits and Oogies

When Billy and Julie reluctantly returned to reality, laughing and contented, they got dressed, suited up (two
very different things, according to the Lone Survivor),
squeezed themselves out of the tubular habitat, and in through the
plastic lock of the office structure. There, they could see a famil-
iar-looking tall, blonde, young officer in a Marine Corps space suit,
his helmet tucked complicatedly under his arm, speaking earnestly
with Jack Reubenson and Spring Comity. The expressions on their
faces were grim.

Incongruously, Julie wondered, a bit self-consciously, if people
could look at her and know what had just happened between her
and Billy. Could they tell, she asked herself a question usually asked
by sixteen-year-olds back home, just by the way she walked?

The young officer turned to address Billy and Julie as they
entered from the makeshift lock. "Hello there, Lieutenant Segovia.

Very nice to see you again. And that's Mr. William Wilde Curringer Ngu with you, if I recall correctly. You may not remember me: I'm Captain Hale Carmody, United States Space Force."

"How could I possibly forget," Billy answered Hale with an enormous grin, "the fellow who very kindly refused a direct order to shoot me? Hello yourself and welcome to the civilian world, Captain."

Carmody blinked. "Just visiting, I'm afraid. No, I am not defecting, folks, or deserting. I was just telling Jack and Spring, here, that Colonel Atherton-Nye's successors thought it might be courteous and neighborly to let you all know that the *US/UNSS Retaliator* is going to be refitted as soon as she makes Earth orbit, turned around, and prepped to return to Mars just as fast as they can manage it. Once she starts back, she'll be here in 272 days. Only this time, her orders are to carpet-bomb every living thing on the surface of this planet out of existence. Including what's left of a bedraggled company of United States Marines. 'Collateral damage,' they'll call it."

"Or 'decontamination,'" said Spring.

Somebody in the little office whistled. Jack Reubenson shook his head ruefully. "I've heard they're claiming that we're turning Mars into West America," he told them.

"Or maybe Pallas," Billy suggested, evoking more than one laugh.

Julie surprised herself. The news didn't make her fearful, it just made her angry. Billy, too, apparently. "How do you come to know all this?" he asked the Space Force captain.

Carmody spread his hands in a gesture of helplessness. "I'm afraid I can't tell you that, sir. Lives are involved back home. Let's just say that I have it from the very top of the food chain. The orders came from Maxwell Promise, the President of the United States, himself."

"East United States." Billy corrected the man automatically. He thought back to Promise's "secret" banquet speech to the power elite that he and his family had seen and listened to at home on Pallas. "It makes a kind of demented sense." He nodded. "So what exactly do our fellow carpet-bombees-to-be, successors to the late esteemed Colonel Atherton-Nye, intend to do about it?" Billy had a suspicion that Carmody saw himself as one of those successors.

Carmody shook his head. "I have absolutely no idea, sir. I was just ordered to bring you people the news. I thought I'd better get moving before they changed their minds. That's a long hike for a Space Force officer—we're used to riding. Nice to see Spring again, though, and the others who've come over."

"To the Dark Side?" Julie suggested. "You make us sound like vampires."

Carmody reddened. "No offense intend—wait a minute, you're joshing me, Segovia, aren't you?"

She laughed. "That's right, Carmody, I am."

Her Pallatian companion patted Hale on the shoulder. "And I'm not a 'sir,' Captain. I'm a 'Billy.' As the next best thing to the Pallatian Ambassador to Mars here, the first thing I'm going to do— after arranging a buggy ride back for you—is let my people back home, and everybody else on the Solarnet, know what's happening. Maybe we can shame that rat bastard Promise out of this. Any idea when they plan to start?"

Hale shook his head again, slowly, which Julie thought looked funny, sticking out of the collar ring of a space suit. On Mars, from time to time, everybody looked like Earthworm Jim, a classical childhood favorite of hers. "I've told you everything I know ... er, Billy."

Billy grinned. "No, you haven't, Hale, but I understand."

Harmon Wu crossed what everybody was stylishly calling the "frontier," these days, between West America (a name its inhabitants liked very much and were proud of) and East America (not so much) in a big, handsome, white, rented Kenworth semi-tractor trailer truck he'd driven a long way today. At this particular moment, the trailer was completely empty, and had been inspected almost microscopically by the East American security guards at the border. He'd understood that it wasn't so much that they wanted to stop smuggling, as that, if there were any action like that afoot, they wanted their piece of it.

Freshly painted on the outside of the trailer, on both sides, in huge, fanciful faux-oriental characters, were the words, "Happy Dragon Cookie Fortune Company," along with a brightly colorful cartoon of a Chinese dragon. Nobody ever seemed to notice that he wasn't offering to trade in fortune cookies, but in cookie *fortunes*, a purely editorial undertaking. Harmon was a philosophy professor at the University of Wyoming, a rare scholar in the 20th century works of the founder of General Semantics, Alfred Korzybski.

He had previously arranged to meet his beloved only child Melanie—at home, he, she, and her mother had all spoken an obscure regional dialect of Cantonese, safe to use over the telephone—outside the tiny midwestern farming village of Gifford, in northeastern Illinois, and when he got there, she was already waiting for him under a tall, thick, stand of trees next to the modest frame offices of "Frudent & Prugal, Certified Public Accountants." The office was closed, and the leaves were mostly fallen. Climbing down from his tall cab, he spread his arms wide just in time to catch his daughter who had thrown herself at him, streaming both laughter and tears.

He patted and stroked Melanie's shiny hair, exclaiming, "My little girl! My little girl!" The cold, humid northern Illinois autumn wind blew across the recently harvested cornstalks, biting through what they wore and chilling them both to the bone. Snow, he could sense, wasn't very far behind that wind. Was there anything more bleak than nighttime snow within the borders of a totalitarian country?

Quickly, he raised the trailer's big rear door, opening up the back of the truck, and with his daughter's assistance—he made her wear work gloves—slid out and set a long, sturdy plywood ramp in place. Only a bit uncertainly, the girl drove her little yellow sports car up into the trailer, set the brakes, crawled out over the back (good thing it was a convertible, she thought), and watched as her father anchored the sporty little vehicle down with cables. Then he drove the truck forward a yard and let the ramp fall to the ground with a dusty thump. Together, they flipped it off the pavement to the side of the road. Somebody in the providential little farming community would surely find a practical use for it. They pulled down the door, locked it, and climbed up into the warm cab. Each put on a set of well-worn coveralls and baseball caps and headed for the freedom of West America.

They drove all night across the East American state of Illinois, expecting a roadblock or a drone attack every moment. Maybe, Melanie thought, just maybe, we aren't important enough to pursue. But she rather doubted it. She was—or had been—the President's mistress, after all, and she had betrayed the man, and broken security to save lives. In the United States of East America, (they hated it when you called it that) that was not an advisable career choice.

Harmon could see clearly that his daughter was deeply troubled. Self-revelation was not her long suit. Attempting to take her mind off her worries, he played with the vehicle's audio-visual system, discovering nothing but what he considered moronic talk shows, blatantly falsified news reports—he was pleasantly surprised that he and his fugitive daughter were not a featured item—trivial sports that neither of them gave a damn about, and, inevitably, the dull, gray-brown, saw-toothed roar of powerful jamming stations, charged with keeping minds like theirs "safe" from West American or other foreign "propaganda."

At long last, he twisted the knob to OFF and remarked, disgustedly, "Nothing on tonight but babble-bimbos and bobble-heads!" She laughed, feebly, and he knew that he had done his fatherly best for the moment.

A few miles further on, they arrived at the clearly marked "national" border, otherwise known as "The Webb Line—Where the Prairie Meets the Trees," along a little-used back-county road, where he had already prepared the way in advance. He stopped the semi at a border-post, where a bright-colored barrier had been swung down in their path. A sleepy, overweight, poorly shaven guard in a rumpled and dirty uniform, hopped up onto the giant Kenworth's running board, smelling badly of sweat and cheap alcohol. "Professor Wu! How the hell are you doing, tonight, boss? Who's that, there in the cab with you? Just two Japanese fellas out for a nice midnight drive, is that it?"

It sounded obscene, somehow, to Melanie. Trying absurdly to look masculine, she looked up from under her ballcap, into which she'd stuffed her hair. She had also smudged her face with motor oil and road grime.

"That's just my assistant, Song Tay," her father told him. "He's Korean, actually. Here are our travel and import-export papers." Fastened to the clipboard was a crisp new $100 West American bank note, a gold certificate. She knew that, in the left-hand door pocket, under a dirty rag, her father kept a deadly and imposing eight-shot .357 Magnum revolver, just in case the bribe failed to work.

"That's fine, Professor Wu," the fat guard said, handing back the documents—minus Harmon's hundred dollars. "Times must be pretty bad over there if they've got college professors out driving trucks, eh?"

Melanie didn't know if the man was joking or not. She also didn't know the current exchange rate, but the bill was worth at least a thousand East American dollars.

"Your papers are in order, Professor. You and Mr. Song have yourselves a nice little evening."

When they had rolled a dozen yards or so, Harmon told his daughter, "It never surprises me at all that they're for sale, but that they're so *cheap!*"

She laughed again. His daughter would be all right, he knew.

The barrier was raised, and Harmon's mighty truck rolled across the border. Twenty, thirty, fifty yards; they were now inside the other half of the formerly United States of America. Just as the tension between their shoulder blades began to ease, the night abruptly came alive with searchlights, spotting lasers, and flares. Loud alarm bells and sirens filled the air. Melanie and her father were somehow aware, in that moment, that a swarm of two dozen deadly armed drones had crossed the border behind them. The girl had a horrible vision—purely her imagination—of Max himself, standing behind the shoulder of a drone operator, personally directing the attack on her and her father. She'd seen him angry more than once. They could not know that, further back, two cruise missiles blasted toward them through the air.

191

As the truck trundled onward, amidst the noise and glare, over the racket, Harmon hollered. "Don't worry about your car! The box is lined with sixteen-layer Newlar!" Harmon sawed the wheel back and forth, trying his poor best to drive evasively. He need not have bothered. Suddenly, on either side of the road, the ground rumbled and erupted, dirt spilling off of metal like water, as half a dozen great, dark structures levered themselves upward, into the night.

They were radar-guided computerized eight-gauge electric Gatling guns, six of them, capable of firing ten thousand rounds a minute apiece. each round launching hundreds of tiny steel needles—flechettes—instead of lead shot, at six thousand feet per second. As the drones pursuing Harmon and Melanie encountered what amounted to a wall of high-speed projectiles from the Gatlings, they were shredded. One cruise missile exploded, making the truck rock, even brighter and noisier than the alarms that threatened to render thinking impossible, and the other missile fell to the ground, inert, plowing up a long furrow.

"Now those," Harmon told his daughter with a grin, "are some border defenses you can believe in." They drove a mile further. "Welcome," he gleefully added, "to the United States of (West) America!"

The other cruise missile exploded harmlessly.

CHAPTER TWENTY-FOUR: KING TOM

"Sometimes I think the reason that space aliens lie low and won't talk to us is that our Solar System is under quarantine," Conchita said to Desmondo. "There must be big signs floating in space all around us saying, 'Look out—these creatures suffer a disease called Authority.'"

—*Conchita y Desmondo*
in the Land of Wimpersnits and Oogies

Billy stirred water into the mixture of sand and finely ground rubble, hoping it would be absorbed before it boiled off. It also contained calcium from a local geological vein that he and Julie had laboriously burned into calcium oxide, or lime, far back in the lava tube—until they'd found more as "xenoliths" in billion-year-old volcanic ejecta. It was not biological in origin; they'd inspected it carefully, but in vain, for microfossils. It was still necessary to keep the big bucketlike container covered as he stirred it in an attempt to keep the water from evaporating before he could use it on the wall he was constructing.

"Here's another rock that we can use as a brick!" Julie puffed, lugging a large russet stone to the spot where Billy was working.

They weren't the only ones laboring to seal off the mammoth entrance to the lava tube that the colonists had settled in. A dozen couples and assorted individuals were working at it. They were all looking forward greatly to establishing a "shirtsleeve" environment they could take their space suits off in, free of the radiation and micrometeorites that inflicted themselves on the unprotected surface of the planet. Concrete was exactly the right material for the job, but it was difficult to manufacture and handle on an almost airless world.

They planned to close the "skylight" off with plastiglass or something like it. The radiation didn't matter as much back there.

Billy looked up at the slender young female who had rapidly become more important to him than anything else he had ever treasured in his life. "Should you really be lifting something like that—"

"—in my 'delicate condition,' you mean?" Julie finished the thought for him. "Oh, poop, Billy, this thing might weigh a hundred pounds on Earth; it only weighs about thirty pounds here. What would it weigh on Pallas? Ounces? Besides, I'm less than six weeks along. Pregnancy is not a disease, Billy. I'm not sick. I won't be an invalid, especially not for this. I feel like dancing!"

She started to show him but thought better of it.

Together, they set the stone in its place on a thick bed of home-made concrete mortar and smoothed the soft material so it would become an airtight barrier. That one had finished the first tier. They were working on the inside of what would be the wall, behind layers of sheet plastic and flexible metal to protect them and the concrete from radiation and other hazards.

"And what does your sister say?" He had yet to meet the formidable Millicente, even over the radio. He thought Julie might be avoiding it.

"Believe me, you don't want to know." Millicente was happy enough for Julie, but she had wanted to hear when Billy was going to make her "an honest woman"—an astonishing concern, the younger sister thought, considering Millicente's (now) former profession. In the absence of that lifestyle, she was rapidly becoming what Julie thought of as a typical middle-aged, middle-class Catholic mother-type. If not a self-made nun. It was a damned good thing that she had Lafcadio (who had become a good friend) to jar her out of it now and again.

On the other hand, Julie thought, look at me, a "serenely independent" warrior woman and an (East) United States Marine lieutenant. Now here she was, deeply in love with this young man beside her, whom she couldn't imagine being without, ever again. And she was pregnant with his child. Pioneers don't have a lot of use for birth control, and none had been sent with either group. She had no idea what he wanted to do about it—if anything. People still got married on anarchistic Pallas, didn't they? She reminded herself to have a long talk with Mirella and find out. Neither she nor anybody else knew yet what was happening.

Billy unplugged the electrical lead from his helmet microphone to his suit transmitter and plugged it into an auxiliary jack at the base of Julie's helmet. What a Freudian might have made of that, he never considered. "I hope we haven't shared our private business with the whole world." It was literally possible. "Although I personally want to shout it from the housetops—or the Bigelow BEAM tops. But you're the boss in this respect. I do have a question for you—although this damn lead isn't long enough for me to kneel—how would you like to be married by a king?"

She felt a strange electrical sensation in her chest. She had actually thought—even recently—that this was never going to happen to her. "A king? I didn't know you were a king, Billy. The king of Pallas? What about your father?"

"I'm being completely serious, Julia Conchita Segovia. I, William Wilde Curringer Ngu, want you to marry me. Also, I want to marry you, in a public ceremony officiated over by the fellow who wants to be the King of Mars. Please tell me what you think—what you want."

But Julie couldn't tell him. She was too busy trying hard not to cry in a space helmet.

Julie was aware that, as the Martians began to settle into their new lives, there had been the inevitable talk of holding a "planet-wide"

convention—"tunnel-wide," more likely—and forming some kind of government. She had never had much use for governments and had avoided them whenever she could.

"But you Pallatians don't really believe in all that, do you?" She was having dinner with Billy and his siblings in the Bigelow habitat that Mirella shared with Brody. The blushing couple had just told them their happy news, that they were going to have a baby—possibly the first to be born on Mars—and that they wanted to get married, "properly." Mirella was absolutely delighted: "Mother will be so happy!" At least partly because she missed her beloved little sister Teal, she'd come to adore Julie, and had informally adopted her. Now she would have a little niece or nephew to spoil! Even Brody, who might have been expected to harbor a crush on Julie, shared their enthusiasm; he was going to be an uncle!

He tried it out quietly when he thought nobody was paying attention: "Uncle Brody. Unk."

Perhaps as a consequence of all this election-talk, many Martians had started receiving periodic door-to-door visits at their habitats and their places of work from an odd individual who informed them that he wanted to be known henceforward as "King Tom," and who likened his recent arrival on Mars to Santa Claus coming down the chimney.

The man was not particularly young, but he had a broad, open, youthful, somewhat florid face, and a head of close-cropped gray-blond hair. People tended to like and trust him immediately; he had that kind of personality—although some of them reserved natural suspicions. He also carried a weapon of unfamiliar make and appearance, slung low on one thigh in a genuine leather holster, specially treated. He explained it was a .40 caliber replica "Dardick" and used triangular plastic cartridges.

King Tom, she understood, was originally from Earth, at least he'd said as much, by way of Pallas. Nobody had any idea how he had gotten down to the Martian surface (or what his last name was, for that matter), possibly by parachute, given his Santa Claus remark. He made a simple proposition to every individual he encountered: "Hire me to be the Monarch of Mars. Call me King Tom. No, don't worry, I won't start a government of any kind. I'll sign a contract with you to that effect and post a big, fat bond. In fact, my *noblesse oblige* will be *not* to rule. It will be my job to act as a political zero, a placeholder. My presence will then fill any potential power vacuum that might develop, *preventing* the formation of a traditional kind of government, and preserving your freedom."

Pallatians were apparently born cynical about government, Julie thought as she listened to the three of them debate this King Tom fellow. They were cynical about political power and uniforms and badges and guns in the hands of violent thugs licensed to kill by shady politicians and bureaucrats. And to think she was about to become a Pallatian, herself, by marriage!

Instead, King Tom promised them, "I'll found a company—not a corporation, mind you—to provide whatever physical security you can't provide for yourselves, under rules that you specifically agree to. Anybody can opt out of it at any time. I'll help you create a commercial court system to adjudicate disputes, under which traditionally "criminal" offenses, even murder, will be treated in exactly the same fashion as civil matters. There's precedent for that from Pallas. And should the planet require protection from some outside threat—like the one that's on its way right now—I'll help organize its defense, if you'll let me. My contract with you will terminate when I die, and if you don't like how I did my job, then don't rehire my successor."

They resolved nothing that evening and their conversation drifted on to other topics. The fact that there was a flying battleship (actually, a passenger vessel converted to freighter—carrying a cargo of high explosives in its belly) on its way from their home planet to kill them all changed things less for the Martian colonists than might have been expected.

At least it wasn't nukes, their sources told them, the bad publicity would have been unsurvivable for Maxwell Promise and his statist minions. The delivery system was the same vessel—the only such vessel East America possessed—the colonists and Marines had all traveled aboard to get to this planet—except for the Pallatians, of course, and probably King Tom.

The settlers in the titanic lava tube were far too busy simply living their lives. Julie's wasn't the only pregnancy now among the colonists—Beliita Khalidov was beginning to look a bit thick

197

around the waist, to her obvious delight (and relief). Mohammed was whistling everywhere he went. They had all become accustomed to an environment in which, at every moment, *everything* was trying to kill them. Moose Holder's Helmet Radio Network even began a darkly comical countdown of days before the *US/UNSS Retaliator* arrived. It might have been wrong by as much as six months, depending on how long the refit in Earth orbit took.

The legendary stoic Martian character had begun to be forged.

For the East American Marines in Derbyville, *everything* changed as, despite themselves, they began to question their loyalty to a government back on Earth, in Washington. D.C., in East America—a government that had ordered them here to Mars and was now preparing to carpet-bomb them out of existence. Typically, it never occurred to them to question the Corps itself.

Colonel Atherton-Nye, it was said, had stood tall and proud, determined to die for her country. The young men and women who had escaped her grasp said she had grown a little crazier every day.

Billy and Julie were continuing with their plans for the future. Julie had introduced Billy, and spoken with her sister, with Lafcadio Guzman, and had even sent a message to her old Drill Sergeant in Florida. She hadn't heard back from him and didn't really expect to. Theirs would be the first wedding—that they knew of—to take place on the red planet.

"I don't know, Julie," Holly Archuleta told her as she did her best to pin up Julie's wedding dress. Billy had fabricated the pins from fine steel wire. Holly knelt at Julie's feet, spare pins held in her lips, working on the hem of the skirt. It was an extremely simple pattern. The kindly Deutsches had contributed the fabric, an extremely light canvas they'd called "duck." Nobody they were aware of had any idea how to make a wedding dress. Instead, they were following instructions they'd found on the Solarnet. "I don't know, Julie," she said when she could talk. "If I were part of one of the first six Expeditions, and I knew I was going to die, I just might accept a proposal so I wouldn't have to die single and alone."

"There's no way to tell," Julie answered "from a body in a grave, if it was married and when. Besides, we all die alone."

A while ago Jack and Billy had gone out hunting for the final sites of previous expeditions looking for whatever equipment and material the present colonists could make use of. "And a punch on the nose," Moose Holder had pronounced over his network, "to anybody calls it 'grave-robbin.'"

What they'd found had amazed them. At each of the five sites they'd managed to discover, in addition to two vehicles and other useful things, they found rows of tidy graves—which they did not disturb—with neatly written markers. They could only assume that this had been done by the Old Survivor.

CHAPTER TWENTY-FIVE:
LIFE ON MARS

"Isn't it strange, Desmondo," Conchita asked her little cousin, "how, the closer you get to home, the further away it seems to be?"

—*Conchita y Desmond*
in the Land of Wimpersnits and Oogies

Moose Holder reported to the listening colonists one evening that the newly ubiquitous macaroni plant had recently been photographed from orbit atop Mount Olympus by a Brazilian satellite and glimpsed by the Chinese down in the depths of Valles Marineris, Mars' Grand Canyon, more than ten miles below the average surface of the world. It was present and flourishing even in the deepest, coldest places on the planet, like the Hellas Basin near the South Pole, where, it had been theorized, a giant asteroid had struck this world a couple of billion years ago or more, nearly cracking the red planet in half, and stopping the world's "clock"—its spinning iron core—killing its protective magnetic field. If that literally world-shattering disaster hadn't happened, the colorful communications officer speculated, Mars would still have an atmosphere and be like another Earth today, perhaps a fabulous vacation world for the very rich.

Macaroni plant had begun to be processed variously by what threatened to become an ambitious cottage industry, producing food (the new little chickens and pigs loved it), fuel, lubricants, and plastics. Water could be extracted from it, as well. At the same time, mining water directly from the multi-billion-year-old permafrost, employing Pallatian catalytic fusion, or even primitive solar power, promised to become a career in itself.

Environmental hysterics back on Earth were going crazy as the red planet gradually began to turn Orange on its way to Yellow, their fascistic leaders foaming electronically at the mouth, telling all their usual tall tales of imminent disaster and death. But, aside from posting their more amusingly totalitarian pronouncements online— Solarwide, with appropriate commentary—and on old-fashioned bulletin boards scattered around the giant lava tube, the Martians largely ignored their gibberings and rantings. What could anybody do? The craziest of all, Maxwell Promise's Presidential order to have them all exterminated, was already more than enough.

What blind ambition it represented, Holder opined. "Even Adolf Hitler, Mao Tse Tung, Pol Pot, Josef Stalin, and the Ortega brothers combined didn't aspire to wipe out a whole damned planet!"

Meanwhile, he informed his tiny audience, "Timothy Albert Strahan, the founder an' head of All Worlds Are Earth has announced grandly that he will be aboard the *US/UNSS Retaliator* when it returns t'Mars, t'personally oversee the extermination of every single invasive species—meaning macaroni plant and us human bein's—on the planet." The man's almost daily propaganda broadcasts from Earth inadvertently informed the colonists of what stage preparations for their demise were in—the ship had finally gotten back to Earth and was being refitted—and how much time they had left to prepare their defenses.

Three gleaming skeletal electric vehicles dashed across the alien desert at three times the velocity they'd been designed to deliver by their East American/United Nations space agency developers. Brody Ngu had "tweaked" them all after overhauling both of the cars—from the doomed Fourth Expedition, it was believed—that his elder brother and Jack Reubenson had brought back—with considerable difficulty—from their recent explorations, and returning them to service.

Sand and dust flew up in sporty cockscombs from the four powered wheels of each machine, but these plumes didn't remain aloft for long in the near vacuum. The colonists were accumulating quite a fleet—and there were ten more vehicles to be found and salvaged out there among the abandoned possessions of the six other expeditions; sooner or later Mars would need its first parking lot—which ought to drive the Earthside snowflakes even buggier, Billy thought with an inward grin. Their fourth machine—essentially identical to the pair they'd brought to Mars with them—they'd left back at their own settlement just in case.

With Brody, Jack, and Billy, respectively, behind the wheel of each electric car—Julie and Mirella were both highly disgruntled that they'd been left behind—they were racing to be in place before the next parachuted cargo touched down on the surface. They could easily see the brilliant, eye-distressing, fluorescent safety orange and lime green stripes of the canopy above it. The carrying racks they'd improvised on their vehicles were already filled with bungeed-down "Care Packages" that had been dropped to them from orbit today by the Ngu brothers' father Emerson, Fritz Marshall, and others. They were going to have to think about some kind of trailers—perhaps an unexpected use for bicycle wheels.

"There it goes, turn left!" Jack shouted into his helmet mike as the newest delivery encountered an unexpectedly strong "gust" that wouldn't have stirred a flag on a flagpole back on Earth. The solution to getting goods down to the surface from orbit had turned out to be serial tiers of gigantic parachutes, each set larger than the last, as the payload fell lower and slower. The acres of parachute fabric didn't go unappreciated, either, having found a hundred uses in the colony. The vehicles jerked left, then right again, as the package nearly fell on Brody. Perhaps, his brother reflected only half humorously, the universe *was* out to get him.

Sometimes the final stage was a Vectran "bouncy ball" that absorbed the last landing energy and protected the lander's contents. There were new contributors now, as well. Merchants and manufacturers, mostly Pallatian, were eager to exchange whatever they delivered to the Martian colonists—food, equipment, even the latest style in clothing—for video endorsements from the heroic pioneers they could broadcast all over the Solar System. He'd seen a Pallatian brand of pocketknife advertised "As used on Mars, by Martians!" Lunar, as well as West American, concerns wanted in, too, but there was no time at present, with the *US/UNSS Retaliator* on the way.

The colonists' almost universal popularity, System-wide, must have annoyed the hell out of Maxwell Promise and his allies, Billy thought with amusement. They were sort of a combination of American Wild West and Australian Outback. As the brick-and-mortar wall went up at the great lava tube, closing off their spacious habitat so it could become a pressurized, shirt-sleeve environment, they found themselves growing "wealthy," compared with the way they'd started, and even saw something resembling comfort looming before them.

"How the funny, furry, flaming hell are we ever going to get this damned thing home?" Jack complained, watching Brody untangle himself from the colorful canopy and shrouds. "It must be a hundred feet long!" The package itself had just missed Brody by inches and was lying on the ground beside his vehicle.

"That's *exactly* how long it is," said Billy, "under all that protective packaging. We'll just put an end up on each of two cars—one in the middle if we need it—and head back nice and slow. Brody says this may be the most important delivery we've ever received."

"What the hell is it?" the expedition leader demanded, without extra adjectives, as they placed their cars correctly, levered the cargo up onto them—the Martian gravity made that easier than they'd expected—tied them down, and slaved their controls to Brody's.

Brody said, "It's a big, plastiglass tube from Curringer Industries, in solar orbit near Pallas. I found it in one of their online catalogs. It's two inches thick, a hundred feet long and a foot in inside diameter. The latest thing in silicopolymers: highly shock and heat resistant."

"What?" was all that Jack could manage. He could see plainly that Billy was enjoying this.

The younger Ngu told him, "Think of it as a giant peashooter."

"What's it for?" Jack asked.

"Shooting giant peas."

The first wedding ceremony known to have been held on Mars officially began when maid-of-honor Holly Archuleta, being very careful not to get her best clothing dirty, ceremonially cemented the final "brick" into the wall, closing off the settlement from the deadly solar and cosmic radiation of the exterior. Everybody cheered. She'd won a drawing for that honor. The space that she had sealed off wouldn't be fully pressurized and ready for use—such as the ritual going on today—for at least two weeks, but they could dream about the future. That was what this was all about, after all, the future.

The ceremony would take place outside, under a big canopy made from a salvaged atmospheric entry "balute." Nobody knew if that afforded them any real protection—typically, the expedition had been sent into the radiation hell of Mars without any reliable means of detecting it—but it made them feel better.

"We are gathered here today," pronounced King Tom in his pleasant voice, Billy and Julie standing before him, "to witness the formal joining of this man, William Wilde Curringer Ngu of Curringer City, Pallas, and this woman, Julia"—he pronounced it correctly—"Conchita Segovia of Newark, New Jersey, East America, Earth, in matrimony, which is a most honorable estate among human beings, stretching right back to the very dawn of our species, and therefore never to be entered into lightly or unadvisedly, but respectfully, discreetly, and solemnly. It is into this esteemed domain that these two individuals present now come to be joined in the sight of their relatives and friends here and across the entire Solar System. If any person can show just cause why they may not be joined together, then let him or her speak now or forever keep their trap shut."

Gentle laughter filled the frequencies they all shared.

Even though her veil had to be draped over her helmet, the bride was more than beautiful in her homemade wedding dress, blushing and beaming and gratifyingly pregnant—which was exactly how it ought to be for a pioneer bride, in Billy's opinion. Her dress, which everyone agreed was lovely, had to be worn over her environmental suit. Poor Holly had been compelled to let it out twice in the past few days. In a couple of generations, Julie thought, museums might want it; she would make sure before then that it was retailored to more human proportions.

Julie still didn't show her "delicate condition" very much, unlike their other matron of honor, Beliita Khalidov, who had begun her pregnancy at about the same time as Julie but was already as round as a bowling ball. Individual differences, Julie figured. King Tom had a brand-new Stetson he'd acquired somewhere waiting for him once the party moved back indoors—Julie thought it beat the hell out of a crown—and a formal black pistol belt for his weird weapon, which he was wearing now.

Julie may have been the first woman anywhere to be married with a sixteen-inch Bowie knife on her hip. She had fought too hard to keep it, and it was now a part of her. Billy was similarly accoutered with his father's .45 Magnum automatic and his big kukri. She would not promise to obey him, but to love him faithfully (passionately was their own business) and to stand by him through thick and thin until they were parted by death. If she had to die, she wanted it to be in his arms—a long, long time from now. Their ceremony was being beamed to Pallas and rebroadcast to Earth where it was probably being jammed. Nevertheless, Julie hoped her sister could see her transformed magically into "an honest woman." And Lafcadio, and maybe even old Sergeant Spanner. They were all the family she had.

"And now," proclaimed the king, "by the authority vested in me— by you folks—I hereby pronounce them husband and wife. You may embrace, but the kiss is gonna have to wait 'til later."

On Pallas, Billy's mother Rosalie couldn't weep at the wedding, so she wept over the Solarnet, instead. If Billy was embarrassed, he concealed it well.

Amber Archuleta, Holly's sister, also caught the bride's bouquet of colorful hand-made artificial flowers, just as Julie had intended. The bride and groom now asked each other with their eyes, did Brody look a little sheepish and embarrassed when that happened? Were he and Amber next? They were vaguely aware that Mirella had been discreetly seeing Hale Carmody now that nearly everyone had abandoned Derbyville. Billy thought the Space Force Academy graduate would have gone for Spring Comity, the only thing resembling a lawyer on Mars. But he admired the fellow's taste. His sister was the best people there were.

Going back inside, everybody nervously checked the suit dosimeters Fritz Marshall had sent them. The "reception" was being "catered," among others, by several colonists who'd been experimenting to make the expedition's rations more palatable, and there were even a few selections featuring macaroni plant. Jack Reubenson and his fellow bootleggers had printed shiny new adhesive labels for their spirits, sardonically reading "Bicycle Booze—Fine Potato Whiskey".

Mohammed wouldn't let them call it "vodka." The Russians among the expeditionaries agreed after one taste. "This is *not* vodka!"

Jack objected, "What do you care? You can't even drink it anyway—you're a Muslim." He had spent the morning planting oak saplings in the greenhouse to provide future barrels for aging.

"I am not a Muslim," Mohammed told him. "But I am a Chechen."

Colonel Atherton-Nye was now remembered respectfully by fewer and fewer "retainers." Billy cynically wondered what she had paid them. There had been a pool, he knew, going on among the colonists concerning when she would take that big Webley six-shooter of hers into another room and "do the right thing." Typically, she had spoiled it by dying unexpectedly of natural causes. He had no way of knowing that there was a similar pool going on in the White House.

Better to rule in Derbyville, she must have reasoned, than to serve anywhere else.

CHAPTER TWENTY-SIX:
THE UNFRIENDLY SKIES

"I don't know, Desmondo," Conchita said to her little
cousin. "What if this isn't a *real* portal back home?
On the other hand, what if it is? Is this what they
mean by 'analysis paralysis'?"

—*Conchita y Desmondo*
in the Land of Wimpersnits and Oogies

B illy had a plan—actually, it had been Brody's plan to begin
with. Like many another young man, Billy's brother was an
avid student of the history of war. He possessed dozens of
model airplanes, historic surface vessels, submarines, and spaceships,
all hanging on fine monofilament fishing line from his bedroom
ceiling back home. During World War One (he had explained to
Billy, then to Jack, then to some of the others) Germany, the Kaiser's
side, had produced a pair of massive super-weapons they called "the
Paris Guns" but everybody else came to call "Big Bertha." Manufactured by the infamous Krupp works, they had been cobbled together
by thrusting a big artillery barrel through the stubbed-off breech of
an even larger cannon. Mounted on railway cars inside Germany,
they proved capable of shelling targets seventy-five miles away in
France.

"That's not very far away," Mohammed objected. They were in the Bigelow BEAM quarters Julie and Billy now shared as newly-weds. Julie was at the back of the cylinder, trying to get some mid-day sleep as Dr. Bonney had suggested.

Brody replied, "It sure was in 1918."

The Germans had accomplished this historic feat of artillery, Brody explained, by shooting projectiles twenty-six miles up into the stratosphere. "They had physicists and even meteorologists helping them to aim the guns, even taking the planet's rotation into account—eleven hundred miles an hour—and enjoying the ballistic advantages of much thinner air—almost as thin as it is here."

He'd shown them all a simple diagram on his tablet. "Each of the guns had a truss—that's a steel cable running from the breech to the muzzle over a post—to keep it from drooping as it heated up. The shells had to be fired in a particular order, as each wore the barrel and chamber measurably." Some of the German shots had fallen on a crowded church in the neighboring capital, he told them, killing dozens of people. In a panic, Parisians thought they were being bombed by a dirigible flying so high they couldn't see it.

Physicist Mohammed Khalidov agreed with the young man's reasoning and math immediately. Beliita, the genuine mathematician of the pair, struggled up from the cot she'd also been napping on and waddled over to contribute her scientific stamp of approval. Instead of a 234-pound steel shell loaded with TNT like the Germans used in 1918, Brody recommended a much lighter fiberglass projectile with special contents that could achieve orbital altitude—if not velocity. Jules Verne to the contrary notwithstanding, they would not be launching a satellite with a cannon (although it was theoretically possible, he argued). The question had been, where to get the gun barrel. It had to be long and straight and rifled—cut inside with spiraled grooves from breech to muzzle—to get the job done properly.

Time, meanwhile, was marching on. The refit of the *US/UNSS Retaliator* relentlessly continued. Moose Holder's helmet radio broadcasts did as well (he had covered the wedding in his customary colorful manner), and last night he had told his audience that the East American government had just announced the eminent domain seizure of all intellectual property under the Supreme Court's newly forged "higher use" doctrine. The copyright and patent offices had been shut down. At the same time, gene-sorting scandals were ruining individual East American politicians. From the safety of France, somebody named Gladiola Pivnik had accused President Promise of sorting her genes, as it were. Here at home (on Mars), the Deutsches had just produced a practical substitute for leather, made from the macaroni plant.

One of the original East American colonists, an electrical engineer named Steven Heller, began working with his opposite number among the former Marines, a technician everybody called "the Wizard," named Charlie Jackson, to solve the rifling problem. The practical objective was simply to put a stabilizing spin on the projectile. It didn't matter how it got there. Because of those two, Brody had obtained the huge plastic tube. Now it was up to the women (as usual, they each said), principally Julie, Beliita, and Holly, to make their idea work.

Sufficient room had been cleared for the giant plastic tube down the middle of the huge cave, the would-be cannon manufacturers propping it up to waist height on crates and boxes from the orbital deliveries which kept arriving. When businessmen on Pallas had noticed that Emerson Ngu and Fritz Marshall kept shipping supplies by automated spacecraft to Mars, where it was landed by parachute or bouncy ball, they started doing the same, partially out of a well-publicized charitable impulse, but also in the hope of gaining some unknown future profit.

Using ordinary soft-leaded pencils, Brody, Jackson, and Heller laid out a careful pattern on the tube itself. Using ordinary duct tape, Julie fastened the end of a big spool of plastic-coated copper wire to one end of the tube and began winding it around and around to create a copper coil in the pattern specified. It was a difficult, awkward job, working around a foot-diameter cylinder, especially for a young woman who was getting a little more rotund in front every day.

The other two women, Beliita and Holly, did the same a few feet further down the tube. The ends of the resulting coils, Brody explained, would be soldered together in series. When she heard what was going on, Mirella came out to join them, with Spring Comity. "Women's work!" she proclaimed, looking for the reaction it would provoke.

"Grrrrr!" replied her new sister-in-law agreeably.

A foot at a time, they labored to cover the outside of the tube in copper coils, applied in a particular, peculiar pattern.

The atmosphere inside the cave was still too thin to do anybody any good, A shriek interrupted their efforts, as Holly discovered she had punctured a glove and was now leaking both air and blood. Julie grabbed her hand and squeezed it off. Beliita applied duct tape.

"Don't worry, Holly," Julie told her. "We've got a few spare gloves around and we'll get the doctor to look at that puncture."

"Why the hell bother?" the injured girl demanded tearfully. "So I can go on helping to knit this horrible weapon, whatever it is, with you? Tell me, Mirella, is this what we all came to a new world for? What is it about human evolution that makes it so goddamned easy for some clever individuals to murder others?"

Mirella was shocked and speechless.

"Asks the ex-Marine," Julie replied blandly.

"Says the poverty-stricken Mississippi teenager who was arrested driving drunk—exactly once—and pressed into joining the Corps by a rich Anglo judge and her own goddamned court-appointed white lawyer!" She made it clear some of the things those two "officers of the court" had threatened to do to "persuade" her to join the Marines. She'd learned later that they were paid a bounty for each new "recruit." "You see, their system forced me into killing people! Human beings are nothing but killer apes—natural rapists and murderers!"

Julie wanted to ask Holly exactly how many people she had personally raped and killed so far but recalled the way she'd saved Billy's life—for which Julie was very, very grateful—and refrained.

Mirella took the young woman by both shoulders and looked her straight in the face, speaking very calmly and deliberately. "Holly,

I don't ever want to hear you spouting crap like that again! It isn't humanity that's violent or warlike by nature! It isn't white people or men! It isn't even Americans, East or West! Only *governments* start wars! Only *governments* slaughter innocent individuals in the tens of millions! The only thing you can blame most people for is that they tolerate it instead of stamping them out forever as we have on Pallas!"

Julie added, "So we're apes. So what? We had to come from somewhere, didn't we? And it's absolutely unmistakable with men." She could hear her sister's voice in her head. "It's true that what a man first notices about a woman is her 'beauty.' He may not realize it, but what he's looking for in a woman is reproductive health. But it would be unjust to say it's shallow of him, or that he's only built that way. Believe me, you wouldn't want to live in the world that would result if he were not. If she's extraordinarily lucky, he notices the character that lies beneath her beauty some time after that. And on occasions that I'm surprised aren't a great deal rarer, her character will sustain their relationship for decades after her beauty has departed—although he will never cease seeing it, altogether, whenever he looks at her."

Holly sniffed back tears, "What about Gaia's Guardians? What about the Jihad?"

Beliita observed, "I would call those governments of some kind. At least they couldn't do their dirty work without some government, somewhere, running interference for them."

"And those governments are coming to kill us, Holly!" Julie told her. "We have no choice but to fight back the best way we can!" Are we so damned comfortable now, that we've forgotten all of the ugliness and oppression that we left behind? Beliita and I are making this thing, whatever the hell it is," she added, "so our babies might get half a chance to live and grow up! That's the exact opposite of murder. If you don't want to help us, even for the sake of some baby you might have someday, then go the hell away!"

Mirella took Holly by an arm. "We'll go see the doctor and get that thumb patched up before you get an infection. Then we'll see, all right?"

Holly nodded submissively, disastrously close to the calamity that was tears in a space helmet. The two departed. Julie and

Beliita went on following Brody and Jackson and Heller's penciled instructions.

When Mirella and Holly had departed, Julie found herself working, shoulder to shoulder, with the pretty young Chechen woman, who plugged an audio lead into Julie's helmet. "Excuse my forwardness, Julie, please," she said, "I'm not yet quite accustomed to speaking freely in public. I just wanted to say to you that you are right. Some of us—like Mohammed and me—are absolutely determined to produce big pioneer families, to put it bluntly."

Historically, Julie knew, such families became the backbone of pioneer cultures socially and economically. The ex-Marine grinned, nodded, and squeezed Beliita's arm.

"Mohammed is a particle physicist," the Chechen woman continued, "I am a mathematician, but we don't really give a cricket what we have to do for a living—scrub floors, clean toilets, sanitize space suits—as long as we may remain free of the endless mortal struggle and oppression that drove us away from our homeland on Earth to begin with."

"Just look at me," Julie answered her, "I was a United States Marine. Now I'm going to be a Martian mommy." They both laughed.

"If I have a little girl," Beliita mused, "then I shall call her Jasmeen after my baby sister whom I loved until she was murdered by Russian thugs. If I have a little boy, Mohammed will name him Fiodr after his favorite professor in Paris. Then we will both try very hard to find some other names!" They laughed again.

"And I have an idea or two for some nice, subversive childrens' stories I can write for little Jasmeen or little Fiodr—or my own children, for that matter!" Julie pointed out with a twinkle in her eye—or was that the reflection of her suit helmet? "I'm thinking that President Promise and his cronies won't like them at all!" She didn't tell Beliita that, if she could—if her baby came before the Chechen woman's, and Billy agreed—she would name him Adam, the first human being to be born on Mars.

Julie showed Beliita what her father-in-law on Pallas had sent her as a wedding present, extracting it carefully from the stiff new synthetic space-proof leather holster that had arrived with it. Emerson had sent his prospective daughter-in-law—and most likely the mother of his first grandchild—one of the twenty-shot stainless steel Ngu Departure 10mm pistols he had invented so long ago. This latest model, customized with a six-inch barrel that tipped up to be loaded, had a portrait of her, from a photographic profile he had obtained somehow—probably from Billy—beautifully engraved in its silvery receiver.

She reholstered the heavy gun.

Almost at that moment, a greatly humbled Holly returned with Mirella, showing a suit glove that no longer matched her own environmental suit in color. "I'm okay, now, I think," Holly told them, her eyes downcast. "They said they're gonna fix my glove. And I'm very, very sorry, Julie, Beliita. I don't know what got into me. Must be all the hormones flying around. I realized while I was sitting in there in the doctor's space, that I'm gonna know you guys for the rest of my life. And that you're right, Julie, about this thing we're making. I want to do it for the sake of a baby I might have someday."

She blushed.

CHAPTER TWENTY-SEVEN: RODS OF GOD

"A wise man once told me, Desmondo, that 'To know what you know, and to know what you don't know, is to know.'"

—*Conchita y Desmondo*
in the Land of Wimpersnits and Oogies

"It has finally occurred t'me that our little settlement in this here giant lava tube which I guess we ain't never somehow thought of as permanent—we've never given it a name!" Moose Holder was holding forth on one of his nightly broadcasts on his Helmet Radio Network.

"If we're all drillin' so ambitiously for water," he suggested to his listeners, "then how about Orson Wells? Wait a minute, wait a minute, is that pitchforks an' torches I see pilin' up on my doorstep? We live underground—we could always call this place the Edgar Rice Burrows."

After the nearly unanimous chorus of boos died down, Moose discovered that over half of them couldn't seem to pronounce the name "Heinlein," famous author of *Red Planet* and *Stranger in a Strange Land*, which had a human protagonist, born and raised on Mars.

At long last, Mirella and Hale showed up at Moose's quarters. He had moved on and they interrupted him in mid-discourse. "... but Lilith was too much fun, y'see? So God replaced her with Eve, and Man has been tryin' t'turn Eve back into Lilith ever since then ..."

"We have a suggestion to make," the Pallatian scientist told the communications officer and his audience. "Since we colonists seem to be writing the real *Martian Chronicles* right now, ourselves, then how about Bradbury?"

"Whaddya think, Pat?" Holder asked his wife. She smiled and nodded.

New whiskey labels appeared the next morning: BRAD-BURY'S BICYCLE BOOZE.

King Tom, Moose informed them, had brought two more electric cars back to Bradbury, and claimed one of them for himself, so that he might become history's first "circuit king." Nobody objected. For some reason nobody understood, the Monarch of Mars had put big signs on either side of his car: HAPPY DRAGON COOKIE FORTUNE COMPANY. He had been a graduate student of a certain Wyoming professor of General Semantics.

Meanwhile, in Earth news, Moose announced to his listeners that the latest Broadway sensation The Civil War, the musical had just opened. The big hit tune, so far, was "Frankly, My Dear." He also said that the East American government, its "phony scientists an' media whores," were furious "because the West Americans have been killin' off tornados usin' lasers from orbit before they can damage anyone or anything. They call it the Bova Process. Them Eco-easties're callin' it 'an abomination of arrogance'!"

Brody had constructed a primitive lathe, he explained to Amber Archuleta, and was using it to finish some peculiar objects he had cast—in molds he'd made of Martian clay—of resin and glass fiber. "Here, put this filter over your suit intake so you won't breathe in dust from the lathe."

He was working under almost natural light. The colony's experimenters had learned to cut and weld the Bigelow habitats to serve their various purposes. The giant tube's "skylight," location of the fateful Battle of the Rubble Pile, had been closed with material salvaged from a damaged Bigelow bottle, and surrounded by aluminized mylar reflectors, producing a bright, translucent window over the historic site and the graves of the fallen—including that of his twin sister Teal. Everything became much easier, the more air pressure there was in the enormous lava tube. Right now it was about the same as the summit of Mount Everest—not quite breathable yet.

There were six of these strange objects that Brody was making, altogether. They were translucent amber in color, a perfect foot in diameter, about three feet long, pointed at one end and tapered at the other in what was called ballistically a "boat tail" form. A neat copper coil of unusual design, provided by Jackson and Heller, was embedded in the surface of the resin. The pointed end unscrewed on carefully crafted threads. All in all, the objects looked like giant plastic rifle bullets, and they were about to change the course of history.

Julie's speculation concerning Mirella and Hale Carmody may have been correct, but it was unconfirmed by anything that anybody heard or saw them do. The pair were too discreet, and the immense amount of room and clutter and quiet in the gigantic Bradbury lava tube permitted it. There came a time, however, when they began making romantic plans, and the first person they decided to tell was Hale's sister Francine. Hale didn't have any other family he could tell.

As the Martians gained more and more prominence on the Solarnet, the East American jamming was now more or less constant—technical failures were frequent but unpredictable; apparently it was harder and harder to find competent help in the failing socialist country—but Hale was eventually able to contact Melanie Wu in West America—in Laramie, Wyoming, specifically— where he remembered that her father Harmon Wu was a university professor of what he termed, perhaps somewhat misleadingly,

History and Moral Philosophy. Melanie congratulated the couple and promised to try to contact Hale's sister.

Mirella wondered how she was going to tell her parents that she wanted to marry an (East) United States Space Force Officer. He laughed and told her he was with the Martian Space Force now. But he wondered how he was going to tell his sister he wanted to marry one of the notorious Ngus of Pallas.

Over the next few days, a strange presence began to manifest itself on the macaroni plain a mile or so south of the great tunnel mouth. It began as a reddish concrete platform, built on a foundation of long steel rods driven deep into the ground, the whole thing carefully leveled and smoothed off. Then came a steel base atop the brick, made up of bits and pieces carefully welded together solidly to form a kind of cradle the size of a truck trailer.

Into this cradle-shape, the hundred-foot tube was laid, covered in cheerfully multicolored copper wire, anchored down, and ready to be hooked up to a suitable power source. Roger Leigh added a reinforced breech he'd created from a block of solid steel he'd acquired somehow, equipped with a swinging breechblock or door. Nearby, a telescope was connected to a computer, crosshairs superimposed on its screen, brighter in the Martian outdoors than it would have seemed on Earth. The computer could be used to raise or lower the tube, to slew it from one side to another a few degrees, and to time and fire the weapon.

As the work went on, Brody brought his fiberglass creations out in one of the electric rovers. Jack had built him a trailer on four bicycle wheels. The cargo looked like a giant six-pack of some kind of drink. A second automobile followed, with Roger Leigh at the wheel, carrying a pile of odd, heavy cloth bags. At the platform, they unloaded three of the fiberglass containers and, holding them one at a time between his knees, Brody unscrewed their ends. Amber, Heller, and Jackson formed a sort of fire brigade to get the heavy bundles up onto the platform where Roger cut them open and Brody poured their contents—ten thousand BBs per bag—into the tapered cylinders.

When they were half filled, he slid a fist-sized object inside, held in the center by a springy wire frame. He then poured more BBs in, burying the object, finished filling up the container, and screwed the end back on.

With practically the whole colony watching and increasingly curious, Brody swung the steel door open at the back of the tube. Into its foot-diameter opening, and with the help of Roger and Heller and Jackson, he levered one of the now very heavy fiberglass containers he'd filled, but not before Amber slathered it with thick silicone lubricant. He pushed it in to a predetermined depth, then inserted three fat packages of some granular substance, poked a hole in the last bag and inserted an ordinary blasting cap affixed with a short antenna.

He closed the steel door in the breech that enveloped the last yard of tube and retreated.

"Everybody stay clear!" He hurried past a line in the dirt that circled the big contraption at a hundred yards and spoke again, "Jack, Billy, do you hear me?"

"Loud and clear! Julie's here, too!" They were at a predetermined site a hundred miles away, their car carrying extra batteries.

"Okay," Brody told him. "Here comes Test One!"

He watched Beliita's fingers play over the computer keyboard and a screen-filling digital clock-face appeared, counting off the seconds. The explosive suspended in the center of the shell would be triggered at the same time as the ignition but delayed by a timer until just before impact.

For the first time Brody noticed that his elder sister had strapped Teal's pistol belt across her own and now carried both weapons on her hips like a 19th century gunfighter. He missed his twin with an ache that would never die, but he was grateful she had a kind of presence here today.

"Five, four, three, two, one!" They actually heard the giant gun go off, thanks to expanding gasses from the muzzle. The coils wrapped around the tube and the induction-fed coil around the projectile turned the weapon into a giant electric motor and gave the projectile a stabilizing spin. Then they waited. Three and a half minutes later, he heard Julie shout, "Touchdown! Mars gets a brand-new crater!"

"Did the center charge go off?" Brody wanted to know.

"Spectacularly!" his sister-in-law told him. "Kind of spoiled the crater, though."

Brody didn't take time to celebrate. He and the Khalidovs had determined the night before what the second test target would be. Now, he fidgeted as Beliita entered the numbers while Brody's artillery team checked the gun (they could call it that now), swabbed the barrel, and reloaded it with another shell and three bags of coarse smokeless powder.

"Stand by for Test Two!" Brody made careful control entries into the base of the telescope; it swung by itself, and a peculiar object appeared against the sky on the computer screen. It was a satellite that the Chinese People's Republic had placed in orbit around Mars. It had even photographed the macaroni plant growing deep inside Valles Marineris. But it had recently been observed at close range by a Pallatian orbiter—carrying two dozen or more ten-foot tungsten "Rods of God," each of them six or seven inches in diameter, that could be individually deorbited, enter the atmosphere without burning up, and penetrate and destroy any target on—or under—the ground, a clear threat to the sub-arean settlers of Bradbury.

Beliita's fingers flew across the keyboard. The computer would handle the actual aiming and timing, sending orders to the gun, but Brody shouted, "Fire" anyway, just because he wanted to. The gun roared, and they waited.

In minutes, the projectile had achieved orbital *altitude*—but not orbital velocity. The projectile's central charge detonated. A million BBs spread in the Chinese satellite's path, effectively stationary relative to the Chinese object's multi-thousands of miles per hour velocity. It was like hitting a solid wall of iron. The thing on the screen disintegrated. The rods would remain harmlessly in orbit to be tracked and avoided by future traffic. "I guess the People's Republic won't be dropping tungsten rods on anybody real soon!" said Brody.

Mars was now armed and dangerous.

CHAPTER TWENTY-EIGHT: WAR OF THE WORLDS

"The greatest mystery of physics," Conchita told Desmondo, "is the way that time flies when you're having fun."

—Conchita y Desmondo
in the Land of Wimpersnits and Oogies

Timothy Albert Strahan leaned forward in his acceleration chair, eager to see the face of Mars "up close" for the first time, from thousands, instead of millions of miles away. He had insisted that this special seat be installed at the back of the control deck for an excellent reason. This was his mission. He had a great deal of unfinished business to resolve on this world, a lot of scores to settle, and he wanted to make damn sure it was done right.

The cockpit looked exactly to him like that of a giant transcontinental airliner: two men up in front, piloting the spacecraft, another behind and to his right, doubling as flight engineer and, ultimately, bombardier. Of course, they would all have to be quietly disposed of, once they'd returned him safely to Earth.

The ochre surface he'd unconsciously expected on his way here no longer existed. What he saw below him was a mostly orange landscape with occasional big swatches of yellow. Major features—the Grand

Canyon to end grand canyons, and the three great volcanoes were still easily visible. To his eye, the planet looked diseased. It was said that a man couldn't live down there yet without a space suit. He was determined to make sure such a thing never happened. Altering the nature of an entire world was an obscenity beyond imagining.

Below him, he knew, there were misfits, recalcitrants, refuseniks, social failures, constitutionalists, outright traitors, and enemy agents from evil outlaw polities like West America, and that asteroid infestation Pallas. They were all dedicated to benefitting themselves and their unsanctioned progeny, and to selfishly retarding socio-economic progress and moral evolution. They were also heavily armed, thanks to the Pallatians, and could never have been brought under control by military forces with a fifty-million-mile supply line.

On Earth, whenever an invasive species threatened to take over a territory, it was burned, so that the land could return to the state of nature. On Mars, the state of nature had been lifeless rock, which was what would be left after the *US/UNSS Retaliator* had finished its work. Investigators a thousand years hence might look at bone fragments found down there and wonder.

Let them wonder.

Brody sat, nearly dozing at his firing station computer, holding hands with Amber, which was the best they could do in their space suits, when the orbital alarm sounded. Sure enough, it was the *US/UNSS Retaliator*, an object the size of an aircraft carrier, just entering orbit high above the surface of the planet. He had no idea whatever how many preliminary passes they would make before spewing indiscriminate death and destruction on the world below.

He'd discussed this the previous night with Beliita and Mohammed. his brother and sister, and the others. They would fire as quickly as they could. A shell had already been prepared and loaded. Roger and his crew now loaded the powder and cleared out. The Earth ship arose on Brody's computer screen. He gave the order, "Fire!" then waited, somewhat anticlimactically, until the computer agreed with him.

The gun finally barked a third time and a shell rose high above the surface of Mars, straight into the path of those who had proven their murderous intent simply by being there. Looking at another screen, attached to the telescope, Mohammed observed, "The spreader charge has fired."

Aboard the *US/UNSS Retaliator*, the "flight engineer" sat ready to launch the first thousand giant bombs. The administration had pusillanimously refused to let Strahan use nukes, as if the harm they did would linger to hurt anyone still living. The bombs they had would decelerate in a kind of heat-shielded "tray" or container, then break apart and scatter to drop on the surface of the planet below. The man looked over his shoulder as if asking Strahan to give him the order.

Strahan opened his mouth to speak, then noticed, through the pilots' windscreen, a tiny bright explosion miles ahead.

"What the hell does that mean?" he demanded.

The co-pilot turned to look at him with a grimly neutral expression on his face. "It means we're fucked."

Just then a small object penetrated the windscreen and made a tiny hole in the back of the co-pilot's head. The exit wound was the size of two fists and practically obliterated the man's face. The pilot was killed by a half-dozen torso hits, and the flight engineer lost his head altogether. The vacuum building around him sucked a final, agonized scream out of Strahan that nobody heard. He lived just long enough to sense the warship disintegrating all around him.

Then a small fragment, white-hot from its passage through the ruined warship, ignited one of the bombs, which exploded deep in the bowels of the craft, igniting many more. *US/UNSS Retaliator* expended its fury on itself and empty space, and All Worlds Are Earth died with it.

Down on the surface, nobody cheered. They had lived too close to death to wish it on anybody else, no matter how much they might have deserved it. What amounted, at this distance, to the orbital fireworks display lasted for two hours as fragments of the battleship consumed themselves. Brody watched every minute of it with Amber pressing close beside him.

The crowd began to break up and quietly leave. Hale and Mirella went inside and disappeared, as was becoming usual with them. Brody and Amber still lingered outside. With Billy's siblings each staying with their respective companions, he and Julie had the Bigelow habitat to themselves. They went inside and shed their helmets and armor. Billy picked Julie up, laid her down tenderly on a cot, lay down beside her and they were flesh again, free to contemplate the future in one another's arms.

EPILOGUE:
DESERT FLURRY

"Home again!" Conchita exclaimed. "And out from
under the thumb. I wonder how long it will take us
to forget to appreciate it."

—Conchita y Desmondo
in the Land of Wimpersnits and Oogies

"And that," Big Mike said, "is how Martian civilization was
born, and the central part that the creator of Conchita
and Desmondo played in it."

Jerry asked, "Did she have her baby okay?"

"She and Billy had five children altogether," Mike told him.
"Three of which survived past birth. That's the way it is on frontier
worlds sometimes. Those that lived were sons: Lindsay and Arleigh,
and they named the first one Adam. He's Chief Engineer of the
Ceres Terraformation project."

"How about Beliita?"

Mike strained to remember. "Fiodr was her first; he eventually
moved to Pallas. She and Mohammed had ten children. The last
one is named Jasmeen. I don't know about Hale and Mirella—they
went off with Emerson and Rosalie, and Drake and Amy, aboard
the *Fifth Force*. Brody and Amber were eventually married, but it

didn't last. It happens. You know we finally built a baseball stadium in Coprates and named it after the Old Survivor.

As their truck-train neared its destination, Butler and Bonnet tried to raise the Virginia Dale terminal by radio, but the terminal wouldn't answer. Butler began preparing for the worst.

Something called the "Mass Movement" had arisen with the demise of All Worlds Are Earth and Gaia's Guardians. The fraudulent environmental claim now being made was that importing materials from the rest of the Solar System would add to the mass of the world's crust, eventually causing it to slow, with respect to the planet's fluid core, and buckle disastrously amid an apocalyptic storm of earthquakes and volcanoes that would end all life on Earth. A militant splinter group, the Mass Movement's muscle, called itself "Null Delta Em," for "no change in mass."

Big Mike reminded his young apprentice that the members of Null Delta Em, no matter how contemptible they may have been, had an absolute right to free speech, an ancient West American value that many of the first Martians had fought for and died to protect. "On no account, Jerry," he told Bonnet, "must you employ deadly force or the threat of force just to prevent these environmentalist wackos from expressing their distorted point of view."

However, unlike anywhere on Earth (even West America), on Mars (and in the Asteroid Belt, as well), property was afforded the same protection as life, because somebody gave up significant portions of his or her life to discover, create, or acquire it. Should the Null Delta Emmers attempt to destroy anything that people on Mars had worked so hard and suffered so much to build, they could, said the truck driver—and should—be shot down like dogs.

The two arrived to find an almost comical scene. About half of the Mass Movement demonstrators were surrounded by a circle of inward-pointing tractors. Drivers standing up in the doors were pointing weapons at them.

On the ground, around the shattered remains of one of several fuel pumps, the demonstrators had abandoned dozens of clear plastic shields, large clubs, gas masks, and riot helmets. No police were present; there were no police on Mars.

Instead, Queen Erica, daughter and successor to King Tom, was there among them—hearing of the riot, she had rushed over from the settlement at New Waco—explaining that they had damaged a B2P pump, and that they would have to pay for it right away, since otherwise, they could be shot.

The demonstrators had a hard time believing something they could have learned from tourist brochures, that every Martian from about the age of six was armed, that there were no non-lethal munitions on Mars that their shields, masks, and helmets might have protected them from, and that if they were killed destroying property, the person or persons who killed them would not be prosecuted, but celebrated.

The would-be rioters hastily searched their pockets.

"Some people," she told the truckers surrounding her, "have a black belt in stupidity."

Having declined to fight a duel with the owner of Virginia Dale (and the B2P pump), the self-declared leader of the protestors was now being kept busy washing dishes in the station restaurant to work his debt off, after which he would spend the night "slopping the hogs"—carefully separating garbage and feeding it into the station's hungry B2P convertors.

It was the last environmentalist demonstration in Martian history.

Printed in the USA
CPSIA information can be obtained
at www.ICGtesting.com
JSHW081757161123
52249JS00001B/1